William C. Martyn

John B. Gough - the Apostle of Cold Water

William C. Martyn

John B. Gough - the Apostle of Cold Water

ISBN/EAN: 9783337400101

Printed in Europe, USA, Canada, Australia, Japan

Cover: Foto ©Andreas Hilbeck / pixelio.de

More available books at **www.hansebooks.com**

JOHN B. GOUGH

The Apostle of Cold Water

BY

CARLOS MARTYN

Editor of "American Reformers," and Author of
"Wendell Phillips: the Agitator," etc., etc.

PRINTED IN THE UNITED STATES.

New York
FUNK & WAGNALLS COMPANY
LONDON AND TORONTO
1893

To

My Wife,

Mercedes Ferrer Martyn,

This Book,

Encouraged by her Counsels,
and Pruned by her Criticisms,

Is

Lovingly and Gratefully

Dedicated.

CONTENTS.

PART III.

THE INFERNO.

PART IV.

RECOVERY AND RELAPSE.

PART V.

IN THE ARENA.

PART VI.

THE FIRST VISIT TO GREAT BRITAIN.

PART VII.

AT WORK IN AMERICA.

PART VIII.

THE SECOND BRITISH TOUR.

PART IX.

RENEWED USEFULNESS AT HOME.

PART X.

THE THIRD ENGLISH VISIT.

PART XI.

THE HOARY HEAD.

PREFACE.

THIS is an old story retold. Mr. Gough has written and spoken so voluminously and charmingly of his life, and his career was run so continuously under the public eye that it is well nigh impossible to jot down new facts. Nor is there need of it. His experiences are so full of moral warning in his fall, and of moral inspiration in his recovery, that they will be profitably rehearsed for generations. All that any individual. biographer can hope to do is to group the ascertained facts in a new setting. In the performance of this task the writer has made free use of the existing material, and here confesses his special indebtedness to Mr. Gough's own records. When other and related topics have called for treatment, other and related books have been used.

Although of English birth, we have appropriated Mr. Gough as an American reformer. He was an American citizen. His home was here. He voted here. His public career began and ended here. And his Americanism was of the most pronounced and lofty type.

John B. Gough was a man of the people—an inspired mechanic. He began life at the freezing point of the human thermometer. At the age of eighteen he fell below zero. Seven or eight years later he rose to summer heat, and produced the flowers and fruits of summer. He maintained this heat and fertility through forty-three years, and died at sixty-nine degrees Fahrenheit. Such a life is instructive in all its phases. It carries inspiration to the poor and miserable and blind and naked.

Mr. Gough's career as a reformer was based upon his personal experience. In pleading with men and for men he obeyed Sir Philip Sydney's recipe for poetry, "Look into thine own heart, and write." His utterances were realistic because he had realized them. He touched others to smiles or tears, because he was familiar with the grotesqueness of the evil against which he inveighed, with the maudlin laughter, and the *delirium tremens* of the drunkard.

To this fundamental knowledge of his theme he joined rare powers of speech. 'Tis difficult to classify him as a public speaker. He was *sui generis*. God made him, and broke the die. He was a whole variety troupe in one little form. In the course of an address he enacted a dozen parts, with such fidelity that the last seemed the best. He told a story now in the Irish brogue, now in broken German, now in the Yorkshire dialect, and the hall was convulsed with laughter. He made an appeal, and the people were intensely stirred. His voice sank into pathos, and the storm broke in a rain of tears. He turned upon an interrupter, and his repartee blazed and burned like a flash of powder. He had that wonderful power which we call magnetism. He used the language of the people. He spoke all over, eyes as well as hands, face as well as lips, even his coat-tails. And his earnestness made him the unconscious hero

of his own cause. Mr. Gough on the platform was
an histrionic exhibition of a superlative type.

His voice was not particularly sweet, but it possessed incredible power, and ran the gamut of thought
and feeling,

> " From grave to gay, from lively to severe."

In listening to him one recalled Bulwer's description
of O'Connell's voice:

> " Beneath his feet the human ocean lay
> And wave on wave rolled into space away.
> Methought no clarion could have sent its sound
> Even 'to the center of the hosts around ;
> And, as I thought, rose the sonorous swell,
> As from some church-tower swings the silvery bell.
> Aloft and clear, from airy tide to tide
> It glided, easy as a bird may glide.
> Even to the verge of that vast audience sent,
> It played with each wild passion as it went:
> Now stirred the uproar, now the murmur stilled,
> And sobs and laughter answered as it willed."

Is it any wonder, after all, that such a man, thus
variously gifted, and with something to say worth
hearing, should have held audiences breathless on
both sides of the Atlantic for nearly half a century,
with no diminution of his power whether to draw or
to inspire?

But Mr. Gough had other strengths besides his
gifts. "There is no eloquence," said Emerson, "without a man behind it." He put an honest character
behind his words. You believed in the man. It was
not a mere exhibition that he gave. In the midst of
his wildest utterances he maintained his balance. A

robust common sense was always dominant. And
there was a high moral purpose that dignified his very
mimicry.

As a temperance leader Mr. Gough has not been
and will not be outgrown. He grasped the reform he
advocated as Atlas did the globe. And he put it upon
the indestructible basis of moral suasion, personal
piety, and prohibitive law.

Have we gotten, can we get, beyond his ideal?

Two women were this reformer's guardian angels.
First, his mother; when he lost her he lost himself.
Next, Mary Gough; when he found her he found
himself.

'Tis the purpose of the following pages to show how
God made him; how drink unmade him; and how
sobriety and a moral motive remade him.

CARLOS MARTYN.

CHICAGO, 1893.

PART I.

Sandgate by the Sea

The influences that go into us in boyhood
fashion the experiences that we go into in
manhood.

—CARLOS MARTYN.

I.

BESIDE THE CRADLE.

JANE GOUGH presented her husband John with a
bouncing boy on the 22d of August, in the year of
our Lord, 1817. In the hour of birth the mother
cried, and the babe cried; the first, in pain, the second,
to start his lungs (so the doctors said), ever after
in good working order. In the death-hour, nearly
seventy years later, these early weepers were hushed,
and the world did the crying. Birth—death! and
between the two the unconsciousness of infancy, the
carelessness of boyhood, the recklessness of youth,
the sunlight and shadow of manhood—in one word,
life!

These parents lived at Sandgate, in the county of
Kent, England. The father was a common soldier,
who had served through the Napoleonic wars, first in
the Fortieth and then in the Fifty-second Regiments
of Light Infantry. He entered the King's service in
1798, and was discharged in 1823, with a pension of
twenty pounds a year, and a medal with six clasps,
commemorative of his bravery at Corunna, Talavera,
Salamanca, Badajos, Pombal, and Busaco, in the
Peninsula War. Unfortunately, being a soldier, he
was unfitted for any other calling, and after his dis-
charge, he found it hard to secure employment.

2

That medal was good to look at, but it was harder than "hard tack" to bite. And $100 (the value of the pension) was a small sum with which to bridge the chasm of food and clothes and shelter for a twelvemonth.

Happily, the mother was a breadwinner, too, in a small way. For twenty years she taught the village school. The length of her service shows that she did it well. Mrs. Gough was well educated, considering her position in life, had a kind heart, possessed a gentle, affectionate disposition, and was withal an excellent disciplinarian. She won the hearts and commanded the wills of her pupils and of her children.

John and Jane Gough were a devout couple; he a Methodist, she a Baptist; though in the absence of a church of her own denomination in Sandgate, she habitually worshiped with her husband. She had lived in London, and while there united with Surrey Chapel, made famous by the ministry of Rowland Hill, and kept so by that of Newman Hall. It was that metropolitan experience, no doubt, which helped to win her the position of schoolmistress, for one who had been to "Lunnon" was stared at in those days; but an attendance at Surrey Chapel must have been a sorry preparation for the rude conventicle in Sandgate. However it may be, she never murmured, and, after the manner of her sex, put up with self-denial so that it was changed to coronation.

This worthy couple decided to name their babe after the father, *John*. In order to avoid a junior, Bartholomew was added. So John B. started with an honest name and a stout pair of lungs. Until

seven years of age, his mother taught him at home.
Then he trudged off to the neighboring and larger
town of Folkestone, a mile and a half away, to a
"seminary," where presently he became a teacher
himself, if you please (this child), and, as he says,
"initiated two classes into the mysteries of learning—
one of them into the art of spelling words of two
syllables, and the other into the knowledge of the
Rule of Three." When ten years old he left school—
his education finished! Or rather, he went out into
that greatest of schools, the world, whose teacher is
experience, whose text-books are hard knocks, and
whose terms come high.

As young Gough developed certain traits of the
future man began to show themselves. Earliest of
all, perhaps, his power of imitation. He had a sister,
his junior by two years, and his constant playmate.
She was a master-hand at dressing rag dolls. These
he would often borrow, seat in stiff and starched pro-
priety in front of a chair which he used for a pulpit,
and then, with Bible and hymn-book on the seat, proceed to exhort his dumb auditors—about as effectually
as his clerical patterns sometimes do theirs of flesh
and blood! When church was out, he would imagine
it was Monday, and so pass to a Punch-and-Judy
show. Standing in a bottomless chair, appropriately
concealed himself, and reproducing the peculiar tones
and antics of Punch and Judy, he both amused himself and entertained the wandering rustics who gathered to see and hear. Thus, as Joseph Cook
remarks, among his earliest playthings were a pulpit
and a Punch-and-Judy box. They were among his
last.

Side by side with this mimetic gift, and as its vehicle John exhibited rare vocal powers. Ventriloquism was natural to him. He read superbly—was the show-reader of the town. And he earned many a sixpence in that way, and in recitations in the taproom of the village.

These were innate characteristics. They implied quick powers of observation, a sensitive, impressionable nature, and the ability (which Gough had preeminently) to translate feeling into exact expression.

II.

EARLY SCENES AND INCIDENTS.

SANDGATE was then, as it is now, a watering-place. People who desired to get away from " the madding crowd," or who wished to inhale the tonic salt breezes, or to sport in the breakers, but whose tastes were quiet, or whose purses were slender, found there what they wanted. The houses were strung along a single street, back of which were hills which were gemmed here, there, and yonder, with more pretentious mansions and grounds of the gentry.

It was an historic neighborhood. Here stood the Castle of Sandgate, built by Henry VIII. in 1539, which had been honored by the presence of Queen Elizabeth half a century later. Near by were a dozen other castles, half ruinous, each with its legend. And not far away were Dover, with its cliffs, and Canterbury, with its magnificent cathedral, and Folkestone, in whose High street stood the house where Harvey (who discovered the circulation of the blood) was born ; while away there across the straits loomed France, in plain sight on a fair day. Jane Gough before her marriage came hither to teach school. John Gough was stationed near by with his regiment. Here, therefore, they met, married, and settled. It was a happy selection of a residence for

young John. He reveled in the diversified scenery
and associations of the place, and found

" .   .   . tongues in trees, books in the running brooks,
Sermons in stones, and good in everything."

He haunted the Castle of Sandgate, whose keeper
became his close friend. Speaking of it long afterwards, he says: "As I acquired some knowledge of
Bluff King Hal, I would wander through the court-
yards, the turrets, and the battlements, and build
castles in the air, and, in fancy, people the place with
its old inhabitants, and see plumed cavaliers and
ruffled dames pacing the corridors, or surrounding
the groaning board. Katherine of Aragon, Anne
Boleyn, Katherine Seymour, and others, flitted before
me; and, living in the past, almost unconsciously my
imagination was cultured and my mind imbued with
a love of history and poetry." [1]

The beach was another favorite haunt. The recep-
tive and dreaming boy roamed up and down the
sands, or sat in physical idleness but busy thought,
watching the white-winged ships, listening to the
moan of the sea—which, like himself, was subject to
ever-changing moods. Once he saw an East-India-
man wrecked on the shore before his very eyes, heard
the shrieks of the passengers, seven hundred in number, and gazed with horror upon their dead forms,
rising, falling, rising again, on the white crests of the
cruel waves, and finally washed up on the sands—a

---

[1] "Autobiography and Personal Recollections of John B.
Gough," 1871, pp. 20, 21.

sight which gave him nightmare-visions for weeks and months.

The people of Sandgate were fishermen—and smugglers. The duties on silks, laces, teas, etc., were so high, the coast of France was so near, the passage across was so easy, the fishing boats were so convenient, the margin of profit attendant upon landing dutiable articles surreptitiously was so large, the love of adventure among these amphibious folk was so strong, the nights were so often temptingly dark,—that virtue yielded to such manifold temptation. The beach was patrolled day and night by men-of-war's-men, armed to the teeth, to prevent smuggling. Many were the struggles between these guards and the Sandgaters, with various results; although for the most part the smugglers, aided and abetted by the whole population, got the best of it. But the snap of gun-locks, the whiz of bullets, the hurrying of feet, and sometimes the presence of death as the result of these skirmishes, were common sights and sounds in those days. On a certain occasion, young Gough went with a comrade up an adjacent hill to kindle a beacon-light as a signal to some smugglers in the offing to run in their goods. The boys then ran in themselves—Gough into the arms of his angry father, whose hard-earned pension he had imperiled by his escapade, and who, therefore, soundly boxed his ears.

The boy delighted in playing soldier with his father as captain. The elder Gough was nothing loath, and, with a broom for a gun, would drill the boy by the hour, and then end the lesson by telling stories of his campaigns. "Here," he would say, "was such

a regiment; there such a battalion; in this situation
was the enemy; and yonder was the position of the
General with his staff." The boy listened, as boys
will listen to such tales, and seemed to feel the excitement of the battlefield thrilling along his nerves, to
smell the smoke of war, and to swell with the pride
of victory. Thus he became at a tender age a veteran
by brevet. 'Tis surprising that the rampant militar-
ism of his surroundings—those outlying castles, the
constant recurrence of the petty conflicts between the
men-of-war's-men and the smugglers, and the object-
lessons of his father, who "showed how fields were
won,"—did not impel young Gough to become a soldier. Probably nothing saved him but the feminine
delicacy of his temperament, his dread of physical
pain, and his early withdrawal from the scene. A
soldier he did become, after all, though of a grander
type—a moral hero, whose campaigns were as real
as they were bloodless, and whose peaceful victories
were " no less renowned than war."

John was a fun-lover and a fun-maker from the
start. Some of his practical jokes, however, brought
him into trouble, one in particular, which he shall
relate: "A dapper little man, a tailor by profession,
attended the Methodist chapel, where my father worshiped; and his seat was directly in front of ours.
He was a bit of a dandy, a little conceited, and rather
proud of his personal appearance, but was a sad
stammerer. He had what was called a 'scratch wig'
—a small affair that just covered the top of his head.
One unlucky Sunday for me, as I was sitting in the
chapel, with his head and wig right before me, I
began playing with a pin, and having bent it to the

form of a hook, found in my pocket a piece of string,
tied it around the head of the pin, and began to fish,
with no thought of any particular mischief, and doing
what boys often do in church when they are not interested in or do not understand the service. So,
with one eye on my father, who sat by me intently
listening to the discourse, and one eye alternately on
the minister and my fishing-line, I continued to drop
my hook, and haul it up again very quietly—when,
becoming tired of fishing, I gathered up the line, and
resting the pin on my thumb, gave it a snap; up it
went; I snapped it again and again very carefully, till
one unfortunate snap sent the pin on Billy Bennett's
head; it slid off. Then the feat was to see how often
I could snap it on his head without detection. After
several successful performances of this feat I snapped
it a little too hard, and it rested on the 'scratch wig'
too far forward to fall off. So I must needs pull the
string, and as my ill fortune would have it, the pin
would not come; I drew it harder and harder, very
cautiously, till it was tight. The pin caught somewhere. Now, I knew if detected I should be severely
punished. The temptation was so strong to pull off
that wig that it seemed to me I must do it, my fingers
itched; I began to tremble with excitement, I looked
at my father. He saw nothing. All were attentively
listening to the preacher. I must do it; so, looking
straight at the minister, I gave one sharp, sudden jerk
—off came the wig. I let go of the string; poor Billy
sprang from his seat, and, clasping both hands to his
head, cried, 'Goo—Goo—Good Lord!'—to the astonishment of the congregation. But there in our pew
lay the wig, with pin and string attached, as positive

evidence against me. One look at my father's face
convinced me that 'I had done it' and should 'catch
it'; and 'catch it' I did. My father waited until
Monday, and in the morning conducted me to Billy
Bennett's and made me beg his pardon very humbly.
Billy was good-natured, and actually tried to beg me
off; but my father declared he would 'dust my jacket
for me.'. And he did; or at any rate would have
dusted it most thoroughly, but he made me take it
off—so that the jacket was none the better for the
'dusting,' though my shoulders and back suffered
some, and it served me right." [1]   This passage in
John's life, like many another, illustrates the saying
of the French philosopher, that "opportunity is the
cleverest devil."

Occasionally the boy was sent to mill with a bag
of grain—red-letter days these were. The horse of a
neighbor was borrowed for the nonce, a blind, lame,
raw-boned animal.   Mounting this Bucephalus, he
would make the circuit of the village, win the admiration of the envious boys, then amble off to the mill,
and, on returning, be laid up a couple of days to recover from the lameness caused by the joint action of
the beast's case-knife backbone and cobble-stone trot.

On returning from school in Folkestone one day,
Gough received his death-blow, actually. He was
playing stage-coach, and pretending to drive four
spirited horses in the presence of four even more
spirited boys. "Get up! go long!" and away they
went, pell-mell. Just then the team and driver
passed a laborer who was in the act of throwing up a

---

[1] " Autobiography and Personal Recollections," pp. 38–40.

spadeful of clay from a trench beside the road ; the sharp edge buried itself in the side of John's head. He fell, bathed in blood; remained unconscious for days, and was expected to die, or, if he lived, to lose his reason. Sad, anxious days they were in the cottage of John and Jane Gough. The boy was spared; but he never got over that blow. Fifty years afterwards he said: "To this day I feel the effects of it. When excited in speaking, I am frequently compelled to press my hands on my head to ease the pricking and darting sensation I experience." Eventually that same "pricking and darting sensation" struck him dead.

Among the formative influences of Gough's childhood we must certainly mention the annual fair, held towards the end of July, on the village green, directly opposite his home. The gaudy booths, the flaring-painted canvas, the gaping crowd—John himself among the gapers, we may be sure—the scene made an indelible impression upon the young mimic; and some of the characters he portrayed so graphically in after life he saw and absorbed in front of his own door-sill. He describes the sights and sounds—the mermaid, the pig-faced lady, and spotted boy from Bottlenose Bay, in the West Indies, the calf with two heads; the "ambiguous" cow that can't live on land, and dies in the water; the greatest saw you ever saw saw in all the days you ever saw; the swings, the merry-go-rounds, the climbing of the greased-pole, the donkey races (the slowest donkey to win, and no man rides his own donkey); the clowns, the harlequins, the pantaloons, the columbines, the whole being spiced with the music of drums, fifes, penny-

whistles, cat-calls, hurdy - gurdys, bagpipes — the
dread of mothers and paradise of children.[1]

But events like these were only the dessert in the
dinner of life; the chief part of the meal was composed of much less dainty and appetizing morsels,
according to a boy's conception. John had his
studies, his chores, his duties, in a word, which, like
Banquo's ghost, would not "down" at his bidding.
His temperamental tendency to day-dreaming, when
he was not engaged in mischief, was measurably held
in check by the prosaic demands made on his time
and attention by school and work. The narrow
means at home drove him early to help eke out the
family resources. His main recourse for this purpose
was Purday's library—the news center of the village.
Here he made many a sixpence as an errand-boy, and,
perhaps, quite as often as a show-reader. One day
he earned five shillings and sixpence in this way.
Rushing home with it to show his mother, he found
her in tears. The larder was empty, the husband and
father was absent seeking employment; the poor soul
had walked that day to Dover and back (eight and a
half miles each way), striving in vain to sell some
lace, the work of her own deft hands, and now it was
night—there she sat, tired out and hysterical.

The eager boy made over his small fortune to his
mother gladly, although this disposition of it spoiled
his "Arabian Nights'" visions of a millionaire's position and expenditures, and, kneeling down with her,
thanked God for the timely provision. Then Mrs
Gough gave her son half a penny for himself. With

---

[1] "Autobiography," pp. 43-44.

this he hurried across the street to the store of Mrs. Reynolds, and cried: "Now, Mrs. Reynolds, I want a farden's worth of crups (a kind of cake) and a farden back." The experiences of that memorable day, his half-crown piece, his willing gift of it to his mother, his contented exchange of it for the half-penny, and Mrs. Reynolds's "farden's worth of crups," with the "farden back," were stamped indelibly upon Mr. Gough's memory. He often told the story, and has given it a permanent record in his book of personal recollections.

One summer, the celebrated and excellent William Wilberforce, who had made the emancipation of the slaves in the West Indies his life work, and who, as Lord Brougham said, "went to heaven with eight hundred thousand broken fetters in his hands," came down to Sandgate for an outing. The elder Gough took his son to a prayer-meeting held at the lodgings of the distinguished visitor. After the meeting, John was called upon to read something, which he did, winning the approbation of Wilberforce, who gave his praise tangible expression in the shape of a book, which he inscribed, and his blessing, which he laid upon the lad's bowed head. The book Gough lost. The blessing he kept.

PART II.

The Emigrant

I.

THE ·DEPARTURE FROM HOME.

POVERTY is only less cruel than sin. It was now about to force a boy of twelve away from his father's house and his mother's arms across the sea. For those situated as the Goughs were life was hard at best. The present held no comfort, the future no hope. Daily bread was a daily battle. Happily, this world-old and world-wide struggle teaches self-reliance, promotes diligence, necessitates economy, stirs enterprise, and is intended to build character. This is the real explanation of its existence in the order of divine Providence. Most of the strong-featured characters that have marked their own age and molded succeeding time have been disciplined in this stern school. "I thank God," said Edmund Burke, "that I was not coddled and dandled into being a legislator." Lincoln floated into the White House on a Mississippi flat-boat. And the heather is in the poems of Burns, because it was under his eyes while he held the plow in Ayrshire. But, however sweet the flower, the bud has a bitter taste.

John Gough, Senior, had his pension. This was the raft under his feet—afloat, though always wet. John Gough, Junior, had nothing. He could aspire

3

to nothing higher than the position of a gentleman's servant.   Even a trade was beyond his reach, for that could be learned only by the payment of a premium. Many and anxious were the conversations between his father and mother regarding this matter.   It all ended in an act of self-immolation on Jane Gough's part.   Her boy was her life.   She loved him so utterly that she consented to send him away to America with a family of neighbors who were about to immigrate, and who ageeed, in consideration of ten guineas of the King's money, to teach him a trade and give him a home until he should come of age. She consented to this—not without an agonizing struggle with herself.   But her son's welfare seemed to demand the sacrifice.   A useful and honest life was promised beyond the Atlantic.   The fact that her judgment and conscience conquered her heart is further proof of the strength and excellence of her character.   A good mother is a true saint.

John thought it was a lark—the realization, alas, came later, and made a lifelong tumult in his breast.

On the 4th of June, then, in 1829, behold him as he mounts the night-coach with his new guardians preparatory to setting out for London, whence the party expected to sail.   The four shining horses paw the ground impatiently.   The guard in scarlet livery lifts the bugle to his lips.   The ostlers drop the bridles. The driver cracks his whip.   They are off !   Presently, as they reach the bathing-houses on the sands half a mile away, John sees a crouching figure behind the hedge and recognizes his mother, who had hurried thither while the coach was being loaded in order to catch one last sight of the hope of her life.   She had strained him to her heart, held him off at arm's length, and then clasped him again, times without number, ere he left the house.   Now she caressed him with her eyes !

It was a night ride up to "Lunnon," this of which we speak.   In the excitement of the journey, the boy soon forgot (forgot only to remember for ever) that heartbroken mother weeping beside the road.   He had been on a mail-coach once before when eight years old, and had gone with a schoolmate, whose father was the driver, as far as Maidstone, half way to the metropolis.   But that was four years ago—a century to a boy ; and now London was the destination ! How fast the horses went !   How their hoofs rang out on the hard road !   How proud John felt, perched up there on the top of the lumbering vehicle, as the women ran to the windows to look, until their eyes were blinded by the dust.   They made ten miles an hour.   The horses were changed every seven miles. This was fast traveling in the year of grace 1829— remember that, reader, spoiled by the experience of fifty miles an hour ; which, by-the-by, will, in its turn, be antiquated as the stage-coach jog when the electric railroads are perfected.   At each relay there was a tavern where driver and guard took an "'alf-an'-'alf" —and others, also, both male and female.   Then the bugle blew, and the coach was off again.

London was reached safely the next day.   With all a rustic's curiosity, John gazed around him in open-mouthed wonder.   What crowds, what endless lines of houses, what smart shops!   Stop, here is a candy-shop.   Where are those pennies ?   They were not plenty in his pocket in those days.   All the *free* sights he took in during the tarry of four or five days in town. For the rest he was like the Peri in "Lalla Rookh," at the gate of Paradise—outside !

On the 10th of June they sailed in the good ship *Helen.* Off Sandgate the ship was becalmed—a joyful occurrence for the boy, already homesick, for his father came out in the afternoon ; and in the evening his mother and sister, spending more than they could afford in boat hire. These two had been absent from home in the afternoon and did not know of the *Helen's* presence in the offing until night fell. There was another sad leave-taking. As his loved ones dropped down the ship's side and floated away in the darkness John's heart sank. With a lump in his throat and tears in his eyes, he "turned in" and cried himself to sleep. The poor mother, we may be sure, did not sleep at all. During the night a breeze sprang up, and in the morning Sandgate was miles and miles astern.

The strange experiences of the voyage filled the time and held the attention of the young emigrant, who proved to be an excellent sailor, and who, with the happy facility of boyhood, found in change and novelty an antidote for sorrow. The scrubbing of the deck, the shifting of the sails, the "yo hoy" of the seamen, the phosphorescent trail of the vessel, the flapping wings of the sea-gulls flying about the rigging and around the hull, the appearance of an occasional porpoise tumbling and rolling in the waves —were an endless source of amusement to this quick and sharp observer.

He left many friends behind him in Sandgate. He soon made many new ones on shipboard, and became a general favorite. One of these sadly reduced his small capital. "I had," he tells us, "like other capitalists, negotiated a loan with the black cook, to whom I advanced an English crown; the principal and interest remain unpaid; not an uncommon occurrence, I have been told since, in regard to foreign loans."

In the gray dawn of August 3d land was sighted; and soon everybody was on deck—all but poor John, who was kept busy below blacking the shoes of his master's family preparatory to landing, much to his disappointment, while the delighted comments of the company on deck, as the *Helen* sailed up the lovely bay, sounded in his ear. Thus he learned that he was no longer a petted boy at home, and that life meant disappointment.

The people to whom he had been intrusted went ashore that afternoon. He remained on board the ship until the next day, when he, too, waved a good-bye to the friendly seamen and that insinuating cook, and set foot for the first time upon the soil of America.

THE FARMER'S BOY.

GOUGH'S "master," to use the English term, remained in New York City two months, which were devoted by him to "prospecting," and by the lad to sightseeing, as opportunity offered. They then went to Utica, in New York State, where the Englishman bought a farm of about one hundred and fifty acres, which lay a few miles out of town, and whither the family removed.

The journey up the Hudson river by steamboat to Albany, the diversified scenery, the jaunt on the canal-boat to Utica, and the wagon ride thence to the farm,—were all noted by the young traveler. His new home was on the frontier. For in 1829, the western march of civilization had scarcely reached central New York. There were settlements beyond that point, but they were few and far between. Hence life on the Oneida farm was like life in the Indian Territory to-day. Hard work, and plenty of it, was necessary in order to comb out the country. The boy from Sandgate became a drudge, "gee-hawing" the oxen, caring for the stock, hauling wood, driving the plow, running on errands, and enacting the *rôle* of Jack-general-utility.

He did not like the American weather. One day it

was so warm that he worked in his shirt sleeves. The next there was a heavy fall of snow. Such sudden changes dazed him—as they have many others before and since. Indeed, our climate resembles Pope's description of Villiers, the Duke of Buckingham,— "everything by starts, and nothing long." As the winter deepened, Gough's clothing proved insufficient. No matter, when he felt cold he warmed himself by extra exertions. When he came to explore his chest he found fresh evidences of his mother's love and care. She had pinned on almost every article a bit of paper containing some text of Scripture, written in her own dear penmanship. His Bible, too, was marked throughout, the second, third, fourth, and fifth chapters of Proverbs being especially over and under scored.

As soon as the rough duties of his new life would permit, he wrote to his mother a long and remarkable letter, full of Goughiana, minutely describing the scenes and incidents of the emigration, and proving unconsciously to himself that he must have improved to the utmost those hours in school which abruptly ended when he was ten years old. The penmanship is good, the spelling immaculate, and the grammar and style worthy of a collegian. The gift of expression was his by nature—the pen spoke, less graphically but not less clearly than the tongue. We put in evidence a few extracts from one and another of his letters:

"The farm is very comfortable, and has a dwelling-house, where we live, and a nice log-house. There are also a wood-house, a wagon and sleigh lodge, three hog-pens, a granary, a stable,

two barns, two cow-lodges—but master talks of having eighteen
or twenty cows in the summer; two horses, three fatting hogs,
seven pigs, fifty sheep, a bull, and a calf. I like driving our
team about. A team in this country is two horses. Our
wagon is not so heavy as the English one. The horses are put
in as you put them in a pair-horse coach." [1]

Later on he writes again:

" I have enjoyed pretty good health since I have been here.
I have learned a great many things.   I can hold the plow, and
thrash, and plant and hoe corn, plant potatoes, make cider, and
do a great many things that I knew nothing of before. I was at
the harrow with the oxen, when I heard there were some letters
for me, and soon after Elizabeth brought a packet to me in the
field. But I could not work any more all day for joy. I like
the Yankees pretty well. They are open, free, and generous.
They much use the word 'guess.' Thus, if they meant to say,
'I shall go to chapel,' they would say, 'I guess I shall go to
chapel.' Yesterday I went to camp-meeting, which is held once
a year by different societies of Methodists. It is generally held
in some of the woods. When we arrived at the entrance to the
woods where this meeting was held, we heard a confused noise,
but the first thing that struck our attention was a great number
of tents or booths, such as are used at fairs. The next was
the voice of prayer in every direction. About fifteen engaged
in prayer to God at the same time at different prayer-rings,
which consisted of about fifteen or sixteen men and women
met together, with a log to separate the males and the females." [2]

Mark the accurate observation and minute description here. Plainly Gough was Gough even at the
age of twelve.

We subjoin one or two extracts from Mrs. Gough's

---

[1] "Autobiography," p. 58.   [2] "Autobiography," p. 60.

letters, which exhibit at once her intelligence, her piety, and her motherhood :

"I wish, my dear, when you write again you would let me know if you have committed to memory any of the chapters I mentioned to you in the letter I put among your clothes. You will find them of great use to you; more especially if you are employed in the fields, where, perhaps, you will be much alone. Then you will find it a pleasant and profitable employment for your thoughts to be able to repeat to yourself portions of the Word of God. I speak from experience, my dear. I have often passed pleasantly many an hour of hard work by repeating to myself passages of Scripture committed to memory, and I can now remember those best that I learned before I was your age.

"We long to know, my dear boy, how you got through the severe winter. It was very severe here; but I suppose you will find the summer as hot as you have felt the winter cold."[1]

Again :

"I do assure you we all of us remember you with unabated affection; and the 9th of the month brings forcibly to my mind the time when I parted from you ; and I hope, if it be the Lord's will, that we shall meet again in this world, if our lives are spared. You have been gone now nearly two years, and the time will wear away.

"Your father was pleased that you had taken time to write your last letter so well. He wishes you to practise your writing whenever you have opportunity ; and also your ciphering, as it may be of great use to you in your future life.

"I hope, my dear boy, you are earnestly seeking after the one thing needful. You know the Lord has said, 'they that seek shall find.' It is, my dear boy, the earnest wish of both your parents that you may in early life be devoted to the Lord;

---

[1] "Autobiography," pp. 55, 56.

that you may be His servant—serve Him—and so, my dear boy, keep close to your Bible." [1]

Here a loving Christian mother's heart throbs in every word. Admonitions like these sometimes seem to be forgotten—they never are. Waywardness and sin may overlay them ; but, like that long-lost portrait of Christ by the old Italian painter, done on the wall and covered by neglect and ignorance with whitewash, which was finally discovered and restored, the divine features drawn by a mother's hand in a child's consciousness will eventually reappear in undimmed beauty and with force unspent.

At the end of his second year on the farm, John resolved, if possible, to leave it. He had two reasons for this. First, he was being dwarfed into a mere "hand." There was neither time nor opportunity for schooling—not even for Sunday-school study ; and he knew and respected his parents' wishes on these points. Churches were infrequent, but he did attend one or another of them occasionally; and, indeed, in a revival, had united with the Methodists upon probation. Second, some one had told him that in New York City he could learn a trade without the payment of a premium—the necessity in England which had driven him into exile. Filial feeling led him to write home for permission to make the change. Postage in those days was high, and he sold his penknife to buy the stamp. The consent came. Gough laid down the shovel and the hoe, picked the hayseed out of his hair, and started for Gotham.

---

[1] "Autobiography," p. 56.

III.

THE YOUNG BOOKBINDER.

THE English lad is now out of tutelage, and

"Lord of himself—that heritage of woe!"

His parents are three thousand miles away. His recent guardians have been left behind up in Oneida County. He has just landed from the steamboat, and stands at the corner of Cortlandt street, in New York City with a baby trunk (plenty large enough to hold all his possessions) at his feet, fifty cents in his pocket, and fourteen years on his head.

"Carry your trunk, sir?" said a voice.

He started, for he had been standing panic-stricken in the rush and roar of the human stream.

"Carry my trunk," he repeated; and then asked himself—"where?" He realized now the full meaning of solitude in the midst of multitudes—the dreariest loneliness of all.

Well, it would not do to be standing here in a brown study. Like "Poor Joe" in Dickens's story, he must be "movin' on." Some one directed him to a cheap hotel. There he lodged. Next, he was directed to seek work at the Methodist Book Concern, then in Crosby Street. He did so, and was engaged as errand-

boy in the bookbindery, with the promise of being
taught the business. What were the wages? They
were $2.25 a week. How much did he pay for board?
He paid $2 a week. The magnificent sum of 25 cents
was left for clothing and incidental expenses.

He first boarded in William Street (long since
wholly given up to business), and found that the landlady had placed him in the same room and bed with
a poor Irishman who shook all night with the fever
and ague. The next day Gough asked for a separate
bed. That night he slept on a "cat-tail" bed up
under the rafters in the same room with the sick man,
whose groans kept him awake, and who presently gave
a gasp, a moan—and died. Poor Gough was frightened out of his five senses. He sat there with eyes as
staring and mouth as much a-gape as the dead man's,
until morning dawned, when by a mighty effort he
overcame his catalepsy, rushed from the stifling den,
and aroused the landlady. She was as composed as
he was agitated—the man's board was paid! "This,"
remarked Mr. Gough, "was my first experience in a
cheap boarding-house in New York, but not the last
by any means. For lack of comfort, for want of all
that makes life enjoyable, a cheap boarding-house
stands preëminent." Here, beyond dispute, is the
secret of much of the dissipation prevalent among
men in great cities. The saloon is a-glitter with light,
offers companionship, in attractive contrast with the
dingy, six-by-nine lodging-house; and usually stands
between the brothel and the theater, opening impar-
tially into both.

For a time, however, Gough escaped these pitfalls.
As he worked that day he began to cry—the scene of

the night before, his lack of sleep, and a sense of his forlorn situation flooded his heart with woe. A young woman near by saw and pitied him, learned his story, and said:

"Poor, distressed child, you shall go home with me." He did so. Her mother received him most kindly; he had a mother and a sister once more. Unhappily, he did not remain long with these good Samaritans. He went from them to board with Mr. Anson Willis, his class-leader in the church which he attended. The future looked bright. His new friends were interested in him, and, indeed, proposed to educate him for the ministry. He wrote to inform his parents of these prospects, and received their glad sanction. For some reason, the educational project fell through, Gough left the church, quitted the Book Concern, and changed his boarding-place—a social revolution. This passage in his life he treats in his "Autobiography" with reticence, and obscures it by a reference to "circumstances." In so far as his immediate future was concerned these "circumstances" were most unfortunate; although the

> ". . . divinity that shapes our ends
> Rough-hew them how we will "

meant from the evil to educe a compensating good.

With the improvement in his condition, the tugging at his heart towards home increased. As he could not go there, why not bring home here? He wrote urging his parents to leave Sandgate for New York. The father, unwilling to lose his pension, remained in England in order to arrange for a commutation, hoping to follow later, and meantime sent his wife and daughter on ahead in response to this appeal.

John was now sixteen, had learned his trade, was earning $3 a week, and felt quite a man. When his mother and sister arrived, he met them, received their compliments upon his appearance, responded to their affectionate caresses, and, the three went off to set up that home of which John had been dreaming. It was lowly—but it was theirs! The meals were frugal— but they were prepared by mother! They all thought the three rooms in which they kept house quite palatial, the three cups and saucers a grand show, and the shabby furniture good enough for anybody.

"Be it ever so humble, there's no place like home."

IV.

MRS. GOUGH and her daughter had reached New York in August, 1833. The weeks and months which followed were like so many pages out of a fairy-story, when, in November of the same year, the dream burst, and fairyland was exchanged for prosaic privation. Hard times came on ; snap, snap, went the cords of business. Firm after firm failed. John lost his place. His sister, who had secured work as a straw-bonnet maker, lost hers. The breadwinners were both idle. The Goughs retrenched by giving up two of their rooms, and thus reduced their rent from $1.50 to 50 cents a week. But, where was this to come from? And how about food, and fire, and clothing?

The battle for bread which they had found desperate enough in England, proved to be even more desperate in America. The winter seemed interminable. One by one the pieces of furniture were disposed of— eaten up. One by one their articles of wearing apparel were carried to the pawnshop. John roamed the streets in search of something, anything to do; sometimes succeeding, more often failing to get even a light job. Mrs. Gough and her two children went hungry to bed, rose hungry in the morning, remained hungry through the day, as an habitual experience.

The agony of it who can tell, save those who know!
These were moments when meek-eyed patience folded
her hands in despair.

Self-respect kept the Goughs through that dreadful winter from applying to the poor-fund of the city
for relief. The worthy poor have to be sought—they
seldom seek. There was then no organized charity;
charity was individual and sporadic. Moreover, these
people were unsophisticated, strangers in a strange
land, human chips on the Niagara rapids of a great·
city, and unskilled in the wretched art of self-asser-
tion. Had they been less worthy and more brazen,
they had fared better in a world which often gives
from a motive no higher than to "get rid" of a
beggar.

· As the wintry days brightened into spring and then
warmed into summer, these privations continued.
The necessaries of life were precariously gotten and
enjoyed. The boy and girl bore it better than might
have been expected. They had youth on their side
and health. Nor were they haunted by memory, nor
racked by anticipation. Mrs. Gough grew thinner
and thinner. She became so weak that she could
hardly drag herself about the garret. But for the
children's sake she forced a semblance of cheerfulness
to her face. The daily portion of Scripture was
unfailingly read. A blessing was asked on every
starvling meal. Like Milton, when poor and broken
and blind, she " bated no jot of heart or hope," but
submitted with the unmurmuring resignation of a
Christian.

It was the ·8th of July, 1834. The day was hot.
Late in the afternoon John went off to bathe in the

East River. He was in unusually good spirits, and
sported in the water like a fish, while his companions
laughed merrily at his antics. At eight o'clock he
returned home, reinvigorated by his bath, and leaped
up the stairs two steps at a time, whistling. His
sister met him at the door of their room, and exploded
in his ear the bombshell announcement:

"John, mother's dead!"

At first he was stunned—then he became hysterical.
As soon as he could command himself he went in.
There she lay—dear, dear mother—her eyes closed,
a handkerchief around her head and chin,—so cold, so
still, yet so sweet and beautiful to look at—not like the
staring-eyed and open-mouthed dead Irishman in that
other garret, three years before! The boy's genius for
observation enabled him to grasp these details at a
glance. Then a tempest of sorrow beat within his
heart. Meantime, he sat there beside the unre-
sponsive form, as calm himself, physically, as the
dead. He took the passive hand in his palm, and
held it until it seemed, as in life, to give him pressure
for pressure. Thus he sat all night, thinking, thinking, devoid of fear and frozen with grief. He recalled
his mother's love and care—her life of hardship—her
meek and holy fortitude, and felt almost glad to
know that she was now in heaven, where such as she
belonged.

At break of day, a wild mood seized him. He rushed
from the house. "Mother is not dead," he said to
himself; "she shall not die!" Then the reality of it
shook him like an aspen leaf. He wandered down to
the river. There he sat thinking,—ever thinking,
taking no note of time. By-and-by he went home.

4

They told him his sister had been cared for by neighbors on the floor below; told him, too, how his mother had been found by some one who passed the open door of their room, stretched lifeless upon the floor, where she had fallen, struck down by apoplexy while in the act of preparing his supper, which was found burned to a crisp in the saucepan on the stove—her last thought and effort expended for him!

Entering the room once more, John learned further that a coroner's inquest had been held, and that orders had been left to bury the body before the next day noon. But how? Where? He plunged into the streets again. On, on he went, anywhere, nowhere, without a purpose save to keep in motion.

Involuntarily he drifted back to the house, and discovered that the city had sent a cart, a pine box, and two men, and that the precious dust had just started for the Potter's Field. Hastening with his sister after the vehicle, which was soon overtaken, the two "mitherless bairns" followed on to the grave. This dear saint had been tumbled into the pine box, with her shoes on her feet, without a prayer, without the reading of the Scriptures she loved, and was now dumped in a shallow trench, which was hastily refilled—all was over. Such was the pauper funeral of poor Jane Gough!

This experience made a practical atheist of Gough for many years, and paved the way for his moral downfall. "If there were a God (so he reasoned), would He neglect His children? Did my mother ever desert me? Was not she a saint? See where she lies now—in the Potter's Field!" Having thus stabbed Providence with interrogation points, and

put over him an exclamation mark for a tombstone,
he proceeds to rail at the Church and at ministers.
"Mother was a consistent Church member, yet she
died unsuccored, and was carried to a pauper's grave
without a prayer!"

We do not quote his words. But these bitter feelings were locked-up in his heart as he turned over
these mysteries which have perplexed profounder
minds that his, and which have been discussed endlessly since they were mooted in the days of Job
under the tents of the Idumean Emirs. Happily,
deeper views of the creation, a wider knowledge of
human nature, a juster conception of Providence, and
a better understanding of death—of the release and
reward it brings to the righteous—eventually brought
him back to his mother's Bible and his mother's
God.

As it regards Gough himself, this pathetic passage
in his life by-and-by softened his heart, made him
infinitely pitiful, and gave him for the poor and
miserable a sympathy which enabled him to speak
for them and to them with redemptive power, and
with the persuasiveness of personal fellowship.

Moreover, his early poverty allied him with some
of the greatest of men. What did Dante owe to
Florence but exile, confiscation, and persecution?
Lord Bacon is said to have been reduced to beg a
mug of beer in his old age—and to beg in vain.
Otway was choked to death by a morsel of bread
swallowed too ravenously after a long fast. Johnson,
after the publication of his dictionary, was released
by his publishers from the debtor's prison. Gold-
smith, more than once, took refuge from actual

starvation among the beggars of London. Nay, the Divine Nazarene Himself was so poor that He "had not where to lay His head."

This boy of sixteen was thus far in good company.

PART III.

The Inferno

"O thou invisible spirit of wine, if thou
hast no other name to be known by,
let us call thee — devil!"
— SHAKESPEARE, *Othello*, Act II. Sc. 3.

I.

ADRIFT.

UPON returning from the funeral of their mother to the garret, where she died, and which had been their home, John and his sister seated themselves in utter desolation. They would not, could not remain where the associations were so sad. The few articles which had stood by them in their poverty until now, were now numbered among the assets of the pawnbroker, and with the pitiful proceeds the children changed their abode and paid for new lodgings a month in advance—for the credit of homeless orphans is seldom good! Then John, weakened by sleeplessness and long abstinence (he had eaten nothing since his mother's death), was taken seriously ill, and required medical attendance, which the city furnished. When convalescent, he went to the Oneida County farm to visit the people with whom he had emigrated; his sister going to board near a place in town where she had at last secured work. After an outing of several months, he returned to New York and went into the bookbindery of John Gladding. Two years and more ticked themselves away, month by month, week by week, day by day, hour by hour, minute by minute, second by second, into eternity. How did the young bookbinder spend the time? Recklessly! He joined one of those volunteer fire-engine companies which were a feature of New York fifty years ago—trap-doors of perdition, too. This was a first downward step. He made the acquaintance of a fast set. This was a second step downward. He soon began to frequent questionable resorts. This was a third step in his moral descent. Low he went, and ever lower, slowly, surely; illustrating in real life the scenes which Hogarth has immortalized in his cartoons of "The Rake's Progress."

Talent is to a man what beauty is to a woman—ofttimes a fatal gift. Gough sang finely, especially in the comic vein. He was a natural actor. Story-telling was his forte. Add to all, a social disposition; and 'tis easy to understand why the young fellow should have been the center and charm of those loose circles.

In such companionship drinking was a matter of course—and excessive drinking. Gough's temperament was intense. Whatever he did was done to the full extent—whether it was work or play, folly or repentance. He was also excessively nervous; and a single social glass would set his brain aglow and inspire his genius. This his friends knew. Hence they would give him a "starter," and off he dashed like a racer at the word "go!"

Story ever old and ever new! Wretched delusion, to imagine that happiness is to be enjoyed by indulging instead of in controlling appetite!

Nevertheless, Gough is more deserving of pity than of blame. Think of his youth—of his exposure—of his sordid lodgings—of his isolation—of his peculiar constitution. Had his mother lived she would have supplied him with what he lacked, a home, the oversight and restraint of parental affection and religious guidance. In losing her when and as he did, he lost God, the Bible, the Church, every wholesome influence.

One morning in the late winter of 1837, while at breakfast in a Grand street boarding-house, he was told that there was a fire down the street. He had been out late the night before, and was surly, as young men are with nerves on edge after a carousal.

" Let it burn, it wont hurt me."

It did, though, for it was the bookbindery of Mr. Gladding that was on fire. He was out of work again. Not long, this time, but his " boss " went to Bristol, Rhode Island, and as he wanted John to go with him, the young man was *burned* out of New York and into New England.

ON THE STAGE.

In Bristol, Gough changed the scene but not himself. Bad always tends to worse. His drinking habits grew stronger, and his companionships more dubious. Within a twelvemonth Mr. Gladding failed. John went to Providence. Being an excellent workman, he easily found employment. The trouble was not to get it but to keep it. His new employer liked him. All that he needed was steadiness. Before he became familiar with his new surroundings, a theatrical company billed the town. Gough sought their acquaintance. They praised his singing, admired his acting, and laughed at his stories.

"Say, young man, why don't you go on the stage?" said one of these Thesbians.

This question pleased his vanity. An actor—why not?

His mother had taught him to look with horror upon the theater. For years he never passed one without a shudder. Now he had become a confirmed play-goer; another proof that

> "Vice is a monster of so frightful mien,
>   As to be hated, needs but to be seen;
>   Yet seen too oft, familiar with her face,
>   We first endure, then pity, then embrace."

The theater to-day is prurient enough. Histrionic geniuses, like Edwin Booth and Charlotte Cushman, have striven in vain to purify it. From the same stage the serious face of *Hamlet* and the half-nude form of the shameless *danseuse* have been exhibited. Hyperion here, a satyr there. Sensuality claims and dominates the boards. The plays that draw the best and pay the most are of the type of the "Black Crook"—moral monstrosities. It sometimes seems as though the days of Congreve and Wycherly had come again. The license of Charles the Second's time, when the loosest verses were put into the mouths of women; when hard-hearted and swaggering licentiousness prevailed; when every wife was represented as a bawd and every husband as a dupe; when Shakespeare's *Viola* was changed into a procuress, and Molière's misanthrope became a ravisher; when vice was the fashion and virtue a joke,—these gross indecencies of the restoration disfigure the last decade of the nineteenth century. We badly need another Jeremy Collier.

Not long before his death, the late Edwin Booth wrote to a stage-struck young friend well-placed in life as follows:

" I have known many who, like you, gave up home, friends, and a respectable position for the glitter of the actor's calling, and who now are fixed for life in subordinate positions unworthy their breeding, education, and natural refinement. I beg you, as your friend and sincere well-wisher, to abandon the mistaken resolve, and enjoy the drama as a spectator, which pleasure as an actor you will never know, and retain the family, friends, and happy home that now are yours. Had nature fitted me for any other calling, I should never have chosen the stage ; were I able to employ my thoughts and labor in any other field, I would gladly turn my back on the theater for ever. An art whose professors and followers should be of the very highest culture is the mere makeshift of every speculator and boor that can hire a theater, or get hold of some sensational rubbish to gull the public. I am not very much in love with my calling as it now is (and, I fear, will ever be); therefore you see how loath I am to encourage any to adopt it. I know you will take my advice, as it is meant, in sincere kindness, and believe that my only wish is to spare you the sorrow that must follow the course you would pursue."

When young Gough became an actor things were even worse. The theater was an outlaw. No pretensions were made to decency. When the plays were not frivolous, they were dissolute. Coarse vice disported on the stage, and drunkenness hiccoughed in the green-room. A worse environment for a young man with habits already bad could not be found.

Gough soon showed the effects of his new way of life. He drank more, swore more, gambled more than ever. The line of characters he portrayed was the lowest of the low—profligate buffoons. A certain success attended his representations, for he had in unusual measure the talent required. Nor was he quite a novice. Before leaving New York he had sung successfully in the old Chatham street theater, under the assumed name of Gilbert—a last tribute to his past; for now, quite shameless, he acted under his own name.

The players in Providence soon ended their season in bankruptcy. Gough got nothing for his service. Out-at-the-elbow, down-at-the-heel, his eyes red, his face bloated, he was thrown penniless upon the streets. From Rhode Island he wandered to Boston. Here he played in a drama entitled, " The Temperance Hoax," concocted to lampoon the cause afterwards so dear to him, in which the coarsest fun was poked at Dr. Lyman Beecher and Deacon Moses Grant, two of his best friends in the near future. Again the season ended in financial loss. Again he was out of employment and unpaid.

Years afterwards, when the now bankrupt young actor was mature and disillusionized, he thus throws a flash-light back upon these experiences:

" I shall never forget the sensation on my first visit to the theater. It was the Old Bowery. The play was ' The Apostate'—Mr. Booth, the elder, as *Pescara;* Mr. Hamblin, the manager, as *Hemeya;* and Miss Vincent as *Florinda.* The afterpiece was ' The Review; or, The Wags of Windsor"— Mr. Booth as *John Lump;* Mr. Hamblin as *Looney McTwolter.* Between the tragedy and the farce I cried and laughed. I was thrilled by the tragedy, and convulsed by the farce. It was a new world. How beautiful were the women! how noble were the men! Even *Pescara,* as his eyes flashed with malignant hate, was like a creature above the mere human. The gorgeous dresses, the music and lights dazzled me. I went home to my lodgings fascinated, carried out of myself. How mean and poor was my little bedroom, and what a dreary monotony of life mine was, plodding in a shop to learn a trade! Trade, profession, occupation, business—all was tame, slow, groveling, compared with the glorious, the grand, the bewildering pursuit of the actor. Again and again I enjoyed the delicious enchantment, and fully determined that I must be an actor—I must strut my hour upon the stage. I envied the poor stick who came on to remove the tables and chairs—the poor, despised supe; even the doorkeeper was an object of interest. Yes, I was smitten.

With what awe and reverence would we stage-struck boys

watch some celebrated actor in the streets. It was an event worth recording. 'I saw Forrest to-day.' 'I saw Booth to-day.' I have even followed them and set my foot on the same stones they had trodden. Remember I was but sixteen years of age. These boys had each his favorite actress, for whom he would fight, aye, and throw down the gantlet to all comers in her defense. How we would crowd around the stage-door to see some actor or actress pass in or out! Madame Celeste was a great favorite; we were never weary of singing her praises or seeing her performance. I should hesitate to say how many times I had seen her in ' The French Spy.'

"All this led me to neglect the duty that lay before me. I eagerly devoured any plays that I could lay hold of—learned parts. I could repeat and spout *Jaffier* in ' Venice Preserved.' From tragedy to comedy, from farce to melodrama; I even contemplated writing a play. I have carried a play-book surreptitiously to my work-bench, and learned the whole play while at my work, and then would mouth it and tear it in pieces in the most extravagant theatrical style." [1]

In speaking of the engagement in Boston, which ended his theatrical career, he says:

" I had now been regularly engaged on the staff of artists in a regular theater. Surely, I was at the summit of my ambition. Before it had been an occasional appearance to fill up a gap at a temporary place of entertainment. Alas! I found the gold to be tinsel. Here I acquired a thorough distaste for all theatrical representations, and all the genius and intellect displayed by the most famous actor has not, and never can, reconcile me to the sham, the tinsel crowns, the pasteboard goblets, the tin armor, the paltry spangles, cotton for velvet, all make-believe, the combats, and the sham blood. Even the nightly disguise became an annoyance; the painting the face, corking the eyebrows, penciling the wrinkles, the doing up with

---

[1] " Sunlight and Shadow," pp. 527, 528.

false whiskers, hair, mustache, the French chalk, the rouge, the burnt cork, to say nothing of the habiliments, rendered the whole thing at the last odious to me ; and I never felt meaner, or had less self-respect, than when I was bedizened to do some character. How men of ability and common sense can submit to this caricaturing night after night, passes my poor comprehension.

"In the theater I found some men of education in the higher walks of the profession ; but, oh ! the disenchantment ! The beautiful women were, some of them, coarse and profane ; the noble gentlemen often mean, tricky, and sponging. In fact, the unreality of it, the terrible temptation to the lower forms of vice, especially to those of the nervous, excitable temperament, increased by the falsehood and fiction involved in their profession, in seeming to be what they never were or could be, studying virtue to represent it on the stage, while their lives were wholly vicious, repelled me. Mark me well, I do not say this of all actors. I only speak of the special temptations of this special profession."[1]

In looking back, he affirms that even then he was glad he failed in that vocation—that the way was closed, and marked, "No thoroughfare." God did not mean Gough to wear the mask of Momus on the mimic stage. He was to act a more real part in a nobler drama.

---

[1] "Sunlight and Shadow," pp. 529, 530.

III.

ALTHOUGH he had the appearance of a hard drinker, Gough had been able to persuade himself until now that he was not a drunkard. Conscience accused him of it; but he played the special pleader in the court of his mind and cozened the jury into bringing in a verdict of acquittal. After his failure on the stage, he went back to his trade. He was soon dismissed on the avowed ground that he was a drunkard!

A disagreeable truth is resented. Gough was angry. He kept sober for a whole week in order to show himself that he did not deserve the opprobrious title. The next week he was drunk from Monday morning until Saturday night in celebration of his sobriety! Upon recovering from this debauch, poorer and shabbier than ever, he heard that a book-binder was wanted in Newburyport, Mass., and that $6 a week might be earned there. He went to New-buryport, in January, 1838, got the job, and remained sober for an unwonted interval. Then trade fell off, and he shipped on a fishing-smack for a voyage to Chaleur Bay. The captain carried no liquor; so that Gough was temperate on ship-board by compulsion. Every time the vessel touched along shore, however, he went on a spree. On one such occasion he lay drunk at the bottom of the yawl as it was rowed back in the darkness to the vessel at anchor a mile away. She was reached. The oarsmen scrambled aboard, not missing him. The yawl was then hauled on deck by the prow. The first jerk threw the poor drunkard against the stern. The blow aroused him. He cried out, and was caught just as he was about to be dumped into the sea. This narrow escape he treated as a good joke. The next time he went ashore he treated his rescuers, and got drunk again in their company.

Off Cape Sable, as the fishermen were homeward bound, they ran into a terrific storm. The rough sea-faring men did not expect to weather it. Crash went the masts. Another crash, the deck was broken in. Gough, made callous by dissipation, and calm in the midst of storm, occupied himself in taking mental kodak pictures of the scene—the tossing vessel, the shrieking wind, the upheaving waves, the frightened sailors. After a wild day or two, they ran into Sherburne Bay, Nova Scotia, for repairs; and sailed thence for home, which they reached without further adventure.

Gough describes one incident of this storm in a manner so characteristic that we quote it:

"We had a man on board so notoriously wicked that we called him the Algerine. His habitual profanity was frightful. Utterly ignorant, all he knew of prayer or Scripture, was the first verse of the first chapter of Genesis, and the first clause of the Lord's prayer. During fair weather, he was a great braggart and bully; when the gale so increased that we were really in danger, he began to show signs of fear; and soon we heard him muttering—'In the beginning God created the heaven and

5

the earth—oh!—oh!—Our Father shart in heaven—oh! we're
going down—oh! d—— the luck—In the beginning—oh! murder—d—— the luck—Our Father shart in heaven.' When the
jib blew away he was ordered by the captain to go out with
another sailor on the bowsprit. ' No, I wont—Our Father shart
in heaven—no—I wont—d——d if I do,'—and there poor Jake
lay prone on the deck. ' Get up, you lubber!' roared the
captain. ' Our Father shart in heaven' — continued Jake.
' You need to be started with a rope's end,' said the captain.
' In the beginning God created the heaven and the earth'—
' You fool! get up! you'll be washed overboard,' said the captain. ' Oh! oh!—Our Father shart in heaven,' said Jake as he
crawled to one of the rings by the hatchway, and clung to it
with both hands. Poor Jake! I think I see him now, as, in
spite of the tremendous sea and our personal danger, we could
but laugh. Utterly powerless with terror, all we could get out
of him was—' In the beginning'—or, ' Our Father shart in
heaven '—with an occasional ' d—— the luck,' interspersed with
the most dismal ohs and groans. And so it was till the storm
abated. When we were safe in Sherburne harbor, seated at a
table with coffee and doughnuts, one of the men said : ' Jake,
what was that about your Father?' another: ' Jake, tell us
what was it in the beginning?' and the chaffing commenced
and continued, till he was almost beside himself with rage, and
so threatened us that we thought it advisable to let him alone.
But the slightest allusion to Jake's ' Father ' or ' the beginning '
was sufficient to put him in a fury of passion ever afterwards." [1]

When a man is a fool in one way he may be safely
relied upon to prove himself a fool in various other
ways. At this time Gough married! He could almost support himself; probably he thought it would
be a poor woman who could not help a little. The

---

[1] " Autobiography," pp. 88–89.

singular part of it is that any woman should have
taken the same view. "Why are you women such
fools?" asked Napoleon of Madame de Staël. "I suppose, sire," replied she, "that God made us to match
the men." Gough's wife, poor thing, paid dearly for
her folly. Perhaps she married him to reform him.
If she did, she soon realized her error. She did not
lift him up; instead, he dragged her down—not into
drunkenness; that last disgrace was spared both of
them,—but into poverty and wretchedness.

> "Of all sad words of tongue or pen,
> The saddest are these—it might have been."

This marriage " might have been " happy. But in
order to that there was need of what Gough at the
time lacked, stability, sobriety ; in one word, character. Instead of altering his habits, he drank more,
if possible, neglected his home for his former evil
associates, and was habitually out of work. His
divinity was not his wife, but the bottle.

Soon his very associates grew ashamed of him.
They cut him in the street. The men who had
hounded him on along the road to ruin, now that he
had reached that destination, turned from him with a
curse. He became cheap in the estimation of the
"respectable " revelers, who wore good clothes and
held any social position. "Here comes that drunkard," they would say ; and then pass him without a
nod. These were men about town who had not long
before laughed loudest at his drolleries and applauded
his recitations.

Drunkard though he was, he was cut to the quick.

For it is a mistake to imagine that even the lowest of
the low is destitute of feeling or indifferent to social
outlawry. Gough has himself said, in referring to
this period in his career: "To speak of a drunkard's
pride seems absurd ; and yet drink does not destroy
pride and the desire for better things. The sting of
his misery is that he has ambition, but no expectation ; pride, but no energy. Therefore, the possession of these very qualities is an addition to his load
of agony. Could he utterly forget his manhood, and
wallow with the beasts that perish, he would be comparatively happy. But his curse is that he thinks.
He is a man, and must think. He cannot always
drown thought or memory. He may, and does, fly
for false solace to the drink, and so stun his enemy
in the evening ; but it will rend him like a giant in
the morning. A flower, a half-remembered tune, a
child's laughter, will sometimes suffice to flood the
victim with recollections that either madden him to
excess, or send him crouching to his miserable room,
to sit with his face buried in his hands, while the hot,
thin tears trickle over his swollen fingers."[1]

A self-respecting employer feels pride in his em-
ployés. Who wants a sot in his workroom ? Gough
could not get work. As he stood drinking at one of
the Newburyport bars he confided his situation to the
rumseller who had served him.

"Why don't you start a bindery of your own?" he
asked.

Gough laughed, surveyed his rags, and said:

"If I can't get work, how can I get credit?"

---

[1] "Autobiography," p. 117, *sq.*

"Well, Gough, I'll furnish the tools, and you can pay me in installments."

The offer was accepted. The tools were supplied. The bindery was opened. He was much impressed by this act of kindness.

"People say liquor-dealers have no heart. See what this man has done—when no one else would lend me a helping·hand!" Thus he thought. He actually kept sober long enough to repay the debt. Presently, however, his opinion was modified when he learned that his "friend" had secured the tools on credit, taken the money for them from him, never settled for them, and left him to be dunned for double payment!

How can a man who will not keep sober enough to work for others successfully manage a business for himself? Gough's venture ended, as it was sure to do, in failure. When he should have been in his bindery, he was in a grog-shop. Books that were promised were not delivered. Patronage ceased. The shop was closed.

The unhappy man was now constantly under the influence of liquor. He kept it in the house, drank every little while, until his brain was always in a dizzy whirl, and his hands trembled so that they lost the power to work at a trade requiring delicacy of manipulation, as bookbinding did.

In desperate straits, he joined himself to a strolling company of minstrels, and set out on a local concert tour. In one of those proverbs which concentrate the wisdom of ages, we are told that "a rolling stone gathers no moss." Gough's musical peregrinations brought him more applause than money. But, like the " Wandering Jew," he was in motion—which he craved.

Rum revolutionized the nature of this young man. He was naturally religious—he dethroned the Lord in his irreverent thought, and seated whiskey " as God in the temple of God." He was naturally affectionate—he withdrew his heart from his wife and gave it to drink. He was naturally truthful—he lied without scruple to get liquor. He was naturally frank and open—he became a sneak under the influence of the bottle, and dodged down alleys and skulked under the shadows when searching for a dram. The fatal vice emphasized every weakness and paralyzed every strength. Generosity became meanness. And, like Milton's Satan, he seemed to say: " Evil, be thou my good ! "

All this to tickle a little spot in the throat not an inch wide. " Oh, that men should put an enemy in their mouths to steal away their brains ! "

IV.

DELIRIUM TREMENS.

SINCE his separation from his sister in the autumn of 1834, soon after their mother's death, Gough had not lived with her. She was now married, and resided in Providence, Rhode Island. One day he received a letter from her in which she told him she was ill, and requested him to send his wife to her for awhile. He consented—a welcome respite to her, no doubt.

Having seen her off, he returned to his home. Her absence depressed him. A house without a wife in it is like a body from which the soul is gone. He sat down promising himself that he would go to work in earnest. It was in the morning. Soon he espied a bottle of West India rum. "Ah," said the toper, "here is consolation." He took a glass, another, then another. He lay down in a stupor. Late in the afternoon he staggered to his feet. A sense of loneliness drove him out in search of companionship. He found a neighbor with kindred tastes. Together they returned to Gough's room, and made a night of it. In "the wee sma' hours," the visitor hiccoughed a good-night, and stumbled away. Gough was so intoxicated that in groping his way back from the

door he fell over a table, broke the lamp, and lay on
the floor in the dark. By an effort he rose, found the
bed, and, without undressing, threw himself upon it.
But not to sleep. A horrible drowsiness put its fingers on his eyelids and pressed them down. A horrible wakefulness pried them open. Every sense was
preternaturally acute. His mouth seemed to be
stuffed full of dry flame. A furnace flamed in his
stomach. Dawn looked in at the window. Gough
rose, steadied himself, and sallied forth to replenish
his stock of rum. With a fresh supply he returned,
and for three days he lay on the bed nursing the bottle. During all that time he ate nothing, nor did he
sleep. He rose, got a pipe, and went to bed again
with it lighted between his lips. He dozed. His
face became hot. He half awoke. The pillow was
on fire! He dashed it to the floor and sank into a
heavy stupor. From this state he was aroused by
neighbors who had been attracted by the smell of
fire. The straw on which he lay was smouldering
and in a few moments more must have burst into
flame! He was between two fires, unconscious of
either.

The fright sobered him—just enough to enable him
to crawl out for more rum. He continued to drink,
until his nervous system gave way. Alarmed now,
he begged for a physician, who appeared, diagnozed
the case as one of alcoholism, and banished all stimulants. Then came the drunkard's remorseless tor-
turer, *delirium tremens*. Gough himself describes it:

"For three days I endured more agony than pen can describe, even were it guided by the mind of Dante. Who can
tell the horrors of that malady, aggravated as it is by the con-

sciousness that it is self-produced ? Hideous faces appeared on the walls, on the ceiling, on the floors; foul things crept along the bed-clothes, and glaring eyes peered into mine. I was at one time surrounded by millions of monstrous spiders that crawled slowly over every limb, whilst the beaded drops of perspiration started to my brow, and my limbs shivered till the bed rattled again. All at once, whilst gazing at a frightful creation of my distempered mind, I seemed struck with sudden blindness. I knew a candle was burning in the room, but I could not see it—it was so pitchy dark. I lost the sense of feeling, too, for I endeavored to grasp my arm in one hand— but consciousness was gone. I put my hand to my head, my side, but felt nothing, although knowing my frame and head *were* there. Then the scene would shift ; I was falling, falling, falling, swift as an arrow, far down into some terrible abyss. So like reality was it, that as I fell, I could see the rocky sides of a shaft where rocking, jibing, fiend-like forms were perched ; and I could feel the air rushing past me, making my hair stream out by the force of the unwelcome blast. Then the paroxysm ceased for a few moments, and I would sink back on my pallet, drenched with perspiration, utterly exhausted, and feeling a a dreadful certainty of the renewal of my torments." [1]

For awhile this descent into the inferno startled Gough into abstinence. He was young. He recovered rapidly. All that was necessary to make and keep him hale and hearty was a temperate life. Alas, no sooner did he feel like himself again than he returned to his cups like a dog to its vomit. His wife came home. With a drunkard's penchant for celebrations, he memorialized the event by getting drunk. What a welcome !

Now began another series of wanderings. Travel-

---

[1] "Autobiography," pp. 103, 104.

ing with a Diorama of the Battle of Bunker ("the British were here; the Yankees were there; and old Pat said: 'Dont fire, boys, till you see the whites of the Hessians' eyes!'"), he came to Worcester, Mass., a city destined to be for ever associated with his name. Here Mrs. Gough joined him. Worn out by destitution and racked by anxiety, she was in failing health. In giving birth to an infant she died. The child followed her. Gough was "alone, in poverty," but not like the old saint, "with God."

He was drunk when his wife and child died; drunk at the funeral; only less squalid than his mother's; drunk for weeks afterwards and unable to travel. He left the Diorama, or was left by it, and had recourse to his trade. Hutchinson and Crosby, bookbinders, gave him employment, in Worcester, and he worked when he was not drunk—and sometimes when he was. Indeed, nowadays he was always under the influence of liquor; it was only a question of more or less. His employers dismissed him. He pleaded for reinstatement on the ground of utter destitution on the edge of winter.

"Gough," said Mr. Hutchinson, "I'll tell you what we'll do. You shall come back, provided you'll let us keep your money and buy for you what you need. If you don't have money you can't get drunk."

Necessity cannot dictate terms—it accepts them. But after twelve years of self-support, Gough resented the passing under tutelage. He records this as among the bitterest of his humiliations. He had been out-at-the-elbow and down-at-the-heel. By the present arrangement he was clothed (though not "in his right mind"). He had been frequently in need of food—actually hungry. He was now sure of his meals. He had been shelterless. A roof and a bed were now secured to him.

The lack of money for the purchase of rum kept him sober, did it not? Not a bit of it! It only the more keenly aroused his appetite and developed his inventive faculties. Whatever household possessions remained to him were speedily drunk up. Then, in the evening, when the shop was shut, he sought one and another of the lowest groggeries, amused the bummers and loafers by his songs and stories, and took his payment in "treats." He chuckled to himself: " How finely I'm outwitting old Hutchinson!"

Poor fool! as though Hutchinson had any interest in the case aside from Gough's own good.

On a certain evening when "exhilarated" and ripe for mischief, Gough, accompanied by a group of rowdies, adjourned from the tap-room to a neighboring church in which second advent services were being held in anticipation of a speedy end of the world. The church was noisy with fervor. Amid a fusillade of glorys, hallelujahs, and amens, the tipsy actor seized a huge, square, wooden spittoon, filled with sawdust, quids of tobacco, and refuse, and passing down the aisle, said: " We will now take ρ a contribution for the purchase of ascension robes." [1]

Amazement quieted the audience. Then the sacrilegious clown was hustled out of doors and handed over to the police. The next day he was fined for disturbing public worship. An anonymous friend

---

[1] "Autobiography," pp. 119, 120.

paid the fine—he never knew who, and thus saved him from jail.

Again came *delirium tremens*—again the descent into hell—again the tortures of the damned. Pale as a ghost, weak as a child, Gough crawled out of the house, stopped at a drug-store, bought laudanum, proceeded to the railroad track, put the bottle to his lips, and was about to make an exit from life through the door of suicide. His courage failed. He dashed the poison to the ground, and barely escaped self-murder.

Every morning he resolved to reform. Every evening he treated resolution. He became hateful to himself, because he knew he was an object of universal contempt. True, he might, and often did, change his locality. He carried his environment with him, however, was despised as soon as known, and might cry with the fiend in "Paradise Lost":

> "Me miserable! which way shall I fly?
> I cannot fly—myself am hell!"

PART IV.

Recovery and Relapse

" For to will is present with me, but how to
perform what is good I find not. For the
good that I would, I do not ; but the evil
which I would not, that I do."
— ST. PAUL, Rom. vii.: 18, 19.

I.

THE KIND TOUCH ON THE SHOULDER.

IT was in October, 1842,—the last Sunday of the month. The air was tonic. Late in the afternoon, a poorly clad figure, surmounted by a flushed face, came out of a house in the mechanic quarter of Worcester and started off uncertainly down the street. The man was in that middle state between sobriety and intoxication when the senses are acute while the spirit is melancholy. Hating the drink which had unmanned him, he was, with the curious inconsistency characteristic of his kind, proceeding to a rum-hole in Lincoln Square to get a dram.

He felt a kind touch on the shoulder.

The wayfarer turned and saw at his side a stranger.

"Mr. Gough, I believe," said he.

"Yes," was the answer, "but you have the advantage of me."

"My name is Stratton—Joel Stratton. I'm a waiter yonder in the Temperance Hotel. You've been drinking to-day."

Mr. Stratton's manner was so evidently considerate and friendly that Gough could not take offense.

"Yes," confessed he, "I have."

"Why don't you sign the pledge?"

"I have no will, no hope, no future—nothing. The drink has eaten out my soul. Alcohol which preserves snakes destroys men. I couldn't keep the pledge if I took it. My dreadful condition is that I at once hate rum and crave it."

Mr. Stratton took the young man's arm and walked slowly on with him.

"You were once respectable," he said; "wouldn't you like to be so again? To have friends, to be a useful member of society?"

"I should like it first-rate," retorted Gough; "but I have no expectation that such a thing will ever happen."

"Only sign our pledge," remarked the Good Samaritan, "and I will warrant it shall be so. Sign it, and I will myself introduce you to good friends who will feel an interest in your welfare and take pleasure in helping you to keep your good resolutions. Only sign the pledge, Mr. Gough, and all will be as I have said; aye, and more, too."

Hope stirred the embers of his lost manhood.

Hope—it had been lost for years.

"I will sign the pledge."

"When?" asked his friend.

The devil-appetite suggested delay. "You've done enough in reaching a good resolution. Coddle this good resolution; treat it once more," whispered this devil. Gough hesitated a moment, then said:

"I can't do it to-night. I *must* have some more drink presently; but I certainly will to-morrow."

Mr. Stratton looked at him sharply. The glance convinced him that Gough was already whirling in the maelstrom of drunkenness—that should he sign now it would be only to break the pledge.   He showed his practical wisdom by not insisting.

"We have a temperance meeting in the town-hall to-morrow evening," said he; "will you take the pledge then?"

"I will!"

"That is right," was the hearty response.   "I will be there to see you."

"You shall," said Gough.   And they parted.[1]

What an enigma human nature is!   The sot who had just resolved that he would be temperate, went straight from the "valley of decision," on this blessed Sunday afternoon, to the dram-shop in Lincoln Square, which had been his objective point before he met his resurrectionist.   He gulped down glass after glass of liquor.   How good it seemed—never had it tasted so delicious as now, when it was about to be dropped for ever!   Again he was in the streets.   They were filled with church-goers.   He had already worshiped, with Bacchus for a god, and the bar for an altar, and the cup for a Bible, and the liquor-seller for the officiating priest.   He staggered to his room, and fell on the bed, dead drunk.

On Monday morning he arose, pressed his hands to his swollen, aching head, washed the stupor out of his eyes with trembling hands, and, without breakfasting, hurried away to the shop.   We do not know, but we suspect that his work was ill-done that day.   His mind was not on it.   While he handled the wonted tools of his trade, his thoughts were elsewhere—in distant Sandgate by the Sea—on the Oneida County

---

[1] "Autobiography," pp. 127–129.

6

farm—with his sainted mother—reflecting upon his
vagabond life—centered on his dead wife and baby—
and at last enmeshed in baser associations. "John
Gilpin's," famous ride was a quiet amble compared
with this wild, reminiscent gallop of the mind, as the
poor mechanic stood there in front of the work-
bench.

All the while the consciousness of the temperance
meeting called for that evening, when he had promised to sign the pledge, was ever present. A hundred
times he said to himself, "I won't sign it!" Just as
often he gritted his teeth, and said, "I will!" He
fought numberless Waterloo battles with himself on
that day.

It was noon. He decided not to go to the meeting.
It was afternoon. He resolved to go. Night fell.
He left the shop with his mind made up: "I'll not
sign away my liberty!" He ate no supper—thought
was too busy. Up in his room he said: "I'd like to
go to the town-hall, but I'm too tired—I've eaten
nothing to-day." He looked at the clock. It was
near the hour. Without waiting to think longer, he
seized his hat, buttoned his overcoat over his rags up
to the chin, and fairly rushed away. He entered the
hall and seated himself. There was a call for the
relation of experiences. Acting under impulse,
Gough rose and told his wretched story. This was
his first speech on temperance.

Joel Stratton was there. When the prodigal ended
his narration, he brought him the pledge and gave
him the pen.

Gough signed it—"in characters almost as crooked
as those of old Stephen Hopkins on the Declaration

of Independence." It was his declaration of independence!

Did that scrawl of a signature emancipate this slave of the bottle? Not so. Nor did the Declaration of Independence free America; it took eight years of bloody warfare to do that. So Gough's pledge merely initiated his freedom, won only by a terrific succession of moral Bunker Hills, and Valley Forges, and Yorktowns.

Miserable days and nights succeeded. Many times he was on the eve of giving up the struggle. "To be weak," says Milton, "is to be miserable, doing or suffering." His will had been rotted by alcohol, as acid rots cloth. His nerves, deprived of their accustomed stimulants, racked him like so many inquisitors. His stomach loathed wholesome food, and rejected it. Unwonted abstinence superinduced *delirium tremens* again. There were hours when Gough would have bartered his soul for one dram. But kind friends surrounded him. Their encouraging words helped him. Self-respect, long absent, returned to inspire the recovered outcast. A tedious sickness confined him to the bed, so that he could not get liquor. With time, appetite relaxed the vigor of its grip, though it did not die out—and never did.

Out of "the body of this death" he emerged alive, and only alive. "Those who saw me," he remarks, "might have said as was said of Dante, when he passed through the streets of Florence:

"There's the man that has been in hell."[1]

---

[1] "Autobiography," p. 138.

II.

SMALL BEGINNINGS OF A GREAT CAREER.

THE drunkard is proverbially tattered and torn; has no regard for cleanliness and decency of apparel. Sobriety restores manhood; and, *presto!* the shoes are blackened, the wardrobe is renovated, the hair is combed, the inward change expresses itself through these significant outward signs. For seven years (from eighteen to twenty-five) Gough had neglected his person. Having signed the pledge, he straightway new-clothed himself. This was not vanity; it was self-respect.

In those days a temperance meeting was held every Monday night in Worcester. The reformed mechanic became a regular attendant. The week following the signing of the pledge, the president of the club observed him, and asked how he was getting on. Gough rose and said:

" I am getting on very well, and feel a good deal better than I did a week ago." [1]

This was his second temperance address. The Demosthenes of total abstinence had a genius for oratory, but this was not displayed at once. At the weekly meetings referred to he usually said a few words, making speeches which were *speechlets*. Gradually he enlarged upon the theme, kindled it with

---

[1] " Autobiography," p. 140.

passion, seasoned it with humor, enforced it with
pathos.   Ere long the nascent orator was invited to
repeat the story of his experience in outlying towns.
Thus he became in a small way a temperance circuit
rider.   He had as yet no idea of making a business
of lecturing.   Nor did he extemporize his reputation.
Like everything else of value, this had to be acquired.
Months of practice in schoolhouses; countless verbal
repetitions of his biography, aided in the development of the great advocate's powers.   His custom
was to work at the bench in the daytime, and then
ride or walk in the evening to his appointments in
the neighborhood.   He had been a notorious case.
The report of his reformation soon spread throughout
the locality.   The audiences, therefore, were large.
Gough was a natural speaker.   Continual practice
did the rest.

These meetings were usually held in schoolhouses
or town-halls, a number of speakers taking part. At a
gathering in West Boylston, Mass., Gough first occupied the whole time, and earned his first lecture-fee,
$2, so that the occasion was doubly memorable.[1]   As
the weeks passed the local demands for his services
increased so that he took off his apron, left the bindery, and the new life absorbed him.

And now as the apostle of temperance begins his
labors, it should seem proper to review the history of
the cause.

Our English temperance comes from a Latin word
which means self-restraint, viz., *temperantia*.   Its
present sense restricts it to abstinence from intoxi-

---

[1] "Autobiography," p. 142.

cants. Nor is there lacking classical authority for
this use. "By abstaining from sensual indulgences,"
remarks Aristotle, "we become temperate." Xeno-
phon declares that the term temperance means,
first, moderation in healthful indulgence, and,
secondly, abstinence from things dangerous. Plato
devotes the first two out of the twelve books of his
Laws to a discussion of temperance legislation, and
reaches the conclusion that there is a distinction
between food and intoxicating beverages—that the
one should be used in moderation and the other prohibited. This, too, is the conclusion of Herodotus, and
of Thomas Acquinas, and the mediæval schoolmen.

The vice thus banned is as old as authentic history.
It began with Noah, and went with his sons, Shem,
Japhet, and Ham, through Asia, Africa, and Europe.
Drunkenness disfigures the Patriarchal era, the Mosaic
dispensation, the Egyptian, Persian, Greek, and
Roman militarisms, and the Christian economy—all
hiccough and stagger. The classics are foul with
intemperance; Anacreon is the poet-laureate of the
ancient pot-house. And English literature up to
within a hundred years is similarly poisoned. Pages,
which otherwise laugh with wit, like those of Field-
ing and Smollet, have to be expurgated into decency
before we dare place them on the center table.

Tacitus paints the ancient Britons as gluttons and
sots, and the Roman is confirmed by the Venerable
Bede. Our German ancestors, before they streamed
out of their primeval forests into civilization and
Christianity conceived of heaven as a drunken revel.
With such an origin is it any wonder that drunkenness is in the Anglo-Saxon blood?

The inebriating principle in liquor is alcohol—a modern name for an old devil. We have borrowed the designation from the Arabs, one of whose chemists (Albucasis), in the eleventh century, discovered an artificial method of producing it—although the Chinese knew the secret long before that, and anathematized the inventor, Iti. The chemists of the Middle Ages called alcohol *aqua vitæ*—water of life. It has proved to be the water of death. 'Tis, in fact, the juice of decay, naturally produced by fermentation, artificially produced by distillation, which simply hastens decomposition.

Distillation cheapened alcohol, and so when it came into general use, enabled the poorest to have a "familiar spirit." The result has been especially disastrous in Europe and America. By the close of the seventeenth century drunkenness was national and international. Great Britain suffered worst of all. The use of distilled spirits, and the resultant evils, attracted universal attention. Hogarth's shocking cartoon of "Gin Lane" was tame compared with the actual fact. The historian Smollet, referring to London, says: "The populace were sunk into the most brutal degeneracy by drinking to excess the pernicious spirit called gin, which was sold so cheap that the lowest class of the people could afford to indulge themselves in one continuous state of intoxication, to the destruction of all morals, industry, and order. Such a shameful degree of profligacy prevailed that the retailers of the poisonous compound set up painted boards in public inviting people to drink for the small expense of one penny, assuring them that they might be dead drunk for twopence, and have straw for nothing.

They accordingly provided cellars and places strewed with straw to which they conveyed those wretches who were overwhelmed with intoxication. In these dismal caverns they lay until they recovered some use of their faculties, and then they had recourse to the same mischievous potion, thus consuming their health and ruining their families in hideous receptacles of the most filthy vice, resounding with riot, execration and blasphemy." [1]

Nor was drunkenness the peculiar vice of the lowest—the highest were transgressors. Bolingbroke, at the head of affairs, Addison in the Department of State, Walpole, the Prime Minister, at once set and followed the bad example, and Oxford, otherwise a high character, went frequently intoxicated into the very presence of the Queen—and went without rebuke!

In contemporaneous America the situation was as bad or worse. The colonies were soaked in rum. Liquor-selling was a branch of other and reputable lines of trade. Everybody drank, and almost everybody got drunk. Independence, which brought political relief, did not affect this evil. Through the eighteenth and the first half of the nineteenth centuries people drank as they ate, as a matter of course. A decanter stood on every sideboard. The guest who did not pledge his host, the host who did not drink the health of his guest, was deemed uncivil. Farmers supplied their "help" with grog as they did with bread. Was there a house raising? It was signalized by a free provision of rum and a general carousal. A

---

[1] " History of England," Vol. III., chap. 7.

funeral ? The attendants were "treated " as part of the
ceremony. A lawyer, like Daniel Webster, was not
singular when he held on by the rail in order to stand
and argue a case, half drunk, in the Supreme Court
of the United States. Famous doctors went drunk
to their patients. Clerical conventions were opened
and closed with a glass of grog as regularly as they
were with prayer; the one was as orthodox as the
other. Religious denominations were noted for
" never giving up a ' pint ' of doctrine or a pint of rum."
The entrance to a hotel was sure to lie through the
bar-room. Everybody ordered wine for dinner,
whether it was drank or not—not to do so was
thought " mean." In those days three-quarters of the
farms of Massachusetts were sold under the hammer
for rum debts.[1] That is to say, liquor was regarded
as a necessary part of private and public provender.
The man who did not drink was exceptional—was
tabooed as unconvivial. He who could tip the largest
number of bottles and lie last under the table, was
looked upon as the truest gentleman. To be carried
habitually drunk to bed was a patent of nobility.
" As drunk as a lord," is a proverb inherited from
those times.

Was nothing done through all these ages to antidote this poison ? Various remedies were suggested,
some few were attempted, but these were only palli-
atives. Acts of Parliament in England, statutes
in America, were framed in the interest of restric-

---

[1] Wendell Phillips's " Review of Dr. Howard Crosby's ' Calm
View of Temperance,' " pub. by Am. Nat. Tem. Soc'y, New York
City, 1881.

tion, but were vitiated by some form of license, construed into sanction. In 1785, Dr. Benjamin Rush published his essay against ardent spirits, and thus began a period of preparation. More than a quarter of a century later (in 1825), Dr. Lyman Beecher added his magnificent contribution in " Six Sermons on Intemperance "; each one a columbiad, whose detonation aroused the sleeping conscience of the Church. The evil was so present, so visible, that when their attention was called to it, other clergymen of prominence, like Dr. Justin Edwards, and Dr. Leonard Woods began to inveigh against it. Within two decades most of the clergy of New England had become abstainers. Temperance societies were organized—one of the earliest being the American Society for the Promotion of Temperance, in Boston, in 1826. Temperance newspapers were also founded. Of these *The National Philanthropist*, established by William Collier, a Baptist city missionary, in Boston, also in 1826, deserves special mention, as it was the first newspaper in the world which was devoted to the temperance cause and which advocated total abstinence. This sheet was the mate, in a kindred reform, of *The Liberator*, organ of the Abolitionists. And, significantly enough, Wm. Lloyd Garrison served an editorial apprenticeship in the office of *The National Philanthropist* before he graduated into *The Liberator*.

By the year 1834, the reform movement had spread to twenty-one States, and 5,000 local temperance societies had been organized, with a membership of 1,000,000 strong. Before the close of that decade, at least three States, viz., Tennessee (in 1838), and Mississippi and Ohio (both in 1839), had enacted prohibitory laws—advanced ground which they soon abandoned.

In 1840 the Rev. Matthew Hale Smith lectured in Baltimore, Md., on the evils of intemperance. One or two men heard him who were members of a mechanic's drinking-club, which met in the tap-room of an adjourning tavern. They carried back to the pot-house a report of the discourse. The question was hotly debated between the members. As the outcome, six of them went over to total abstinence, established an organization which they called "The Washingtonian Temperance Society," and started an active propaganda. These six original apostles were presently joined by a seventh, J. H. W. Hawkins, a reformed inebriate, who became the St. Paul of "the Washingtonians," as they were popularly called. Washingtonianism caught from town to town and kindled from State to State. Hundreds of thousands signed the pledge under its auspices, most of them drinking men.

In this wonderful movement there were two radical defects. First, it was based on mere moral suasion —upon what it called "the law of love," and discountenanced any appeal to prohibitive law. Second, it ignored religion—when it did not antagonize it. A movement thus operated by sentimentalism and infidelity could hardly be long lived, even though it sought to remedy an evil like intemperance. When the novelty wore off, Washingtonianism began to "dwindle, break, and pine." But while it lasted it started agents and agencies more potent than itself, which gather force as the years roll on.

It was in this temperance revival that John B. Gough was born again.

III.

TEMPTED.

MR. GOUGH was now fully occupied as a Washingtonian lecturer. His reputation and engagements were
as yet local. The first, however, waxed daily; and
as for the others, towns crowded one another in the
effort to secure his services.

He sadly missed at this time a wise and watchful
intimate to moderate his pace. Unused to the new
life, which was very exciting, deprived of a stimu-
lus to which he had been long wedded, he was in
grave moral danger. The peril was aggravated by a
feeling of self-sufficiency which now puffed him up.
Poor fellow! yesterday an outcast, to-day a favorite
—is it any wonder that his head swelled again as it
swelled of old, though from a different cause?

"Pride goeth before a fall." Gough needed to
fall in order to rise—to realize his weakness that he
might find his strength.

He had abstained for five months. He believed
his appetite conquered—and by himself. Knowing
little of medicine, he was not alarmed by certain
symptoms which were danger-signals—extreme rest-
lessness, occasional incoherence of thought and
speech, a sense of apprehension, and an intense nervousness which made the slamming of a door jar his

whole system. A good physician, observing these symptoms would have prescribed rest and quiet. *His* doctor gave him tincture of tolu, with opium—the worst prescription imaginable.

One day he dropped his engagements and took the cars to Boston, without a purpose, save to do something. It was a case of nervous prostration; *he* feared *delirium tremens.* Hallucinations already haunted him. In Boston he went to the theater— met some former associates—told them of his strange feelings—accompanied them to an oyster-house, and —took brandy!

He took it thoughtlessly. When he had swallowed it, he felt as Peter did after he had denied Christ, and the cock crew. To drown thought he drank repeatedly, but not to intoxication. From Boston the fallen lecturer went to Newburyport, drawn thither unconsciously by old associations. The news of his reform had preceded him—but not of his relapse. Friends of the cause urged him to speak there. He did, twice, though agonized by his false position. After a few days he returned to Boston, where he also stayed for several days, drinking in the meanwhile, and trying to make up his mind what to do. His temperance career was closed—there was no doubt of that. But he could be a sober man. He resolved to go back to Worcester, confess his fault, then depart to—no matter where.

Gough reached Worcester on a Saturday, went directly to several of his closest friends, told them what had occurred, resigned the pledge, and packed his belongings preparatory to leaving town. He was urged to wait and attend the well-known temperance

meeting on Monday night. He did; and in a pathetic
address which melted speaker and auditors, sobbed
out the story of his sin and penitence. Resolutions
of sympathy and confidence, were publicly adopted.
The sin was condoned. The penitent was reinstated.

Mr. Gough was an apt scholar. That relapse in
Boston led him to see that a change in the will is a
different thing from a change in the appetite. A depraved appetite lies couchant in the body, like a tiger
in a jungle, ready to spring out and craunch whenever the victim is unwary. He thus detected one fatal
defect in Washingtonianism which was based on moral
suasion. Reflection taught him, too, the absolute
necessity of religious principle. A higher power than
man sways is required to hold an infirm will to a
righteous purpose and the appetite in subordination.
Appeals to "manhood" tickle human vanity; but
while they please, they damn. One "hid with Christ
in God" is safe. And so, he preceived the second
philosophical error in the Washingtonian crusade—
its neglect of personal piety as the most stable founda-
tion in reform.

Strange, that a third great truth did not dawn
upon his consciousness, viz., the importance of
prohibitive law, as an indispensable safeguard.
When he went into the streets of the New England metropolis on that sad day; they were set
thick with pitfalls. A weak or depraved man was
almost sure to trip and fall into vice. Prohibition
would have closed those abounding doors, and made
the streets comparatively safe for feet like his to
tread.

Moreover, prevention is better than cure. Prohibitive law seeks to forestall temptation. It contemplates the salvation of the drunkard; but it does more—it aims at the preservation of unsoiled youth and inexperience. Under such a law Gough would not have become a drunkard—would have been saved from those seven years of sin and shame. Eventually, he reached this truth, also; but not as early as might have been expected.

The relation between these three great parts of temperance is obvious. Moral suasion in the wrecker's boat rowed through the surf to clutch from the fiery waves of alcohol the wretches who have made shipwreck of manhood. Religion nurses them back to health and strength after they have been brought ashore. Prohibitive law prevents further shipwrecks by removing the rocks or shoals which imperil the voyage of life.

Reformed inebriates sometimes imagine that, after a period of abstinence, they can begin again and drink moderately. There is no case on record of success in such an undertaking. And for the reason already mentioned—the will is weakened and the appetite depraved. Indulgence leads inevitably, invariably to excess. Moderate men may drink moderately, provided they have never been drunkards, although even they are in danger. But for those who have been down, and are now up, there is only one rule—total abstinence.

And so, as it concerns men whose temperament is nervous, susceptible men, pushing and shoving men, whose pulses throb with energy, and whose being is marked *plus*—for such total abstinence is the only safe practice. "I can abstain," said old Dr. Samuel

Johnson; " I can't be moderate." As for Mr. Gough, he testified, years after he had stopped drinking, that the mere smell of brandy gave him a raging thirst for it which God's grace alone quenched. His life was a battle. Like the bravos who skulked under the shadows in mediæval Venice, appetite and temptation dogged his footsteps with poisoned stiletto, watching for a chance to strike. He illustrated the saying of Goethe that " He only earns his freedom and existence who daily conquers them anew."

PART V.

In the Arena

"We do not take possession of our ideas,
but are possessed by them. They master us and force us into the arena,
where, like gladiators, we must fight
for them."
—HEINE.

I.

ON THE PLATFORM.

THE speed with which Mr. Gough got upon his feet after the fall in Boston is proof of his grit. Folding that experience he marked it "important," filed it away in his memory for future reference, and at once resumed his labors in the cause of temperance.

> "Possessed by the one dread thought that lent
> Its goad to his fiery temperament,
> Up and over the land he went,
> A John the Baptist, crying—' Repent!'"

During the earlier half of his first year in the work, he made his name and fame known in Worcester County ; in the latter half he became a magnet throughout New England. He was ubiquitous— indefatigable. "In three hundred and sixty-five days," he says, "I gave three hundred and eighty-three addresses, and received for them $1,059—out of which I paid all my traveling expenses ; traveled six thousand, eight hundred and forty miles ; and obtained fifteen thousand, two hundred and eighteen signatures to the pledge."[1]

Facts of this kind he habitually jotted down in a

---

[1] "Autobiography," p. 160.

vade mecum. He could have earned more money at bookbinding ; but his heart was set now upon something better than money. Sometimes, however, the meanness or thoughtlessness of his audience put him in straits. In 1843 his average pay for a lecture was $2.77 ! "Once," he writes, "after I had been speaking for nearly two hours, and had taken my seat, the chairman rose and proposed a vote of thanks, which was passed unanimously. As the audience were being dismissed I asked if that vote of thanks 'could be given me in writing? as perhaps the conductor on the train would take it for my fare.' The hint was sufficient, and a collection was taken up, amounting to $4."[1]

In September, 1843, Gough spoke for the first time in Boston. He had avoided that town, because he underrated his own ability and overrated Boston culture—which, like many others, he believed to be four feet thick on a level. Probably the American Athens was a formidable arena. Intelligence was as high there as anywhere in the New World ; and many of the most famous speakers of the day were Boston men. There Otis and Adams and Ames and Quincy had thundered ; there Webster and Everett and Choate and Wendell Phillips, were "names to conjure with." No wonder the young mechanic shrank from the ordeal.

At a temperance gathering in rural Massachusetts, in the summer of 1843, he met and made a lifelong friend—Deacon Moses Grant. This gentleman was a Bostonian, the son of one of the revolutionary tea-spillers, a wealthy merchant, and the president of the

---

[1] "Autobiography," p. 161.

Boston Temperance Society. Mr. Grant had traveled in Europe, and had been liberally educated in America. He was of a nervous, sanguine temperament, under the medium size, and had a habit of twitching the muscles of his face and shrugging his shoulders when specially interested—a peculiarity which Gough instantly detected. He wrote a sensible letter, made a practical speech, was peculiarly happy in his remarks to children, and was in demand as chairman on all philanthropic occasions.

It was this good man who had invited Gough to Boston. After no little hesitation, he consented to become Mr. Grant's guest, and to speak under his auspices.

A mortification met the young orator on the threshold. He was arrested for debt. During the Arab days, when drunkenness and poverty were his inseparable companions, he had "remembered to forget" to pay a board bill in Boston. The landlady saw the announcement of his lecture, recognized the name, found out where he lodged, and dispatched an officer to collect the debt ($20), or collar the debtor. From this dilemma Deacon Grant extricated the impecunious lecturer, and bore him off in triumph to the meeting in Tremont Chapel, under the Boston Museum.

Mr. Gough acquitted himself so satisfactorily that he was engaged on the spot to speak three nights more in Boston, which he did to ever-increasing audiences, and amid great enthusiasm. And ever after the announcement of his name was sure to crowd the largest halls in the city.

After a few weeks spent in circling around the

"Hub," "temperancing," as he used to say, and creating a *furore* everywhere—at Nashua, N. H. (where he spoke with Franklin Pierce, afterwards President of the United States, as a fellow talker); Concord, N. H.; New Bedford, Marblehead, and then down into the "Old Colony," in the neighborhood of Plymouth Rock—Gough ran back to Boston. Thence, on the 23d of November, 1843, he proceeded to Boylston, near Worcester, to be married.

Some time before this he had spoken in Boylston, and had met a certain lady destined to become another self—a feminine and, therefore, etherealized self, and a helpmeet in very truth. Her name was Mary Whitcomb. She was a New England farmer's daughter, a Yankee schoolma'am, physically strong, intellectually alert and appreciative, morally sweet and pure, and a devoted Christian.

> "A creature not too bright and good
> For human nature's daily food—
> For transient sorrows, simple wiles,
> Praise, blame, love, kisses, tears, and smiles.
> A perfect woman, nobly planned,
> To warn, to comfort, and command;
> And yet a spirit still, and bright
> With something of an angel light."

During their brief courtship of a few weeks, they talked of religion rather than of love; but is not religion love? "She took me *on trust*," remarks the husband, "with $3.50 in my pocket; but Mary was willing to risk it with me." [1]

---

[1] "Autobiography," p. 172.

Mary Whitcomb understood John Gough by intuition—his weakness, his strength; saw what he required to transmute the first into the last, and supplied the means. They were married on the 24th of November, 1843, by a ministerial mutual friend, in Worcester, with Spartan simplicity—"no bridal wreaths or gifts; no wedding-ring or cards; no bridesmaids or groomsmen—only they two agreeing to walk the journey of life together." From this date on for years, Mary Gough accompanied her husband everywhither, prolonging his life by her care, and doubling his usefulness by her inspiration.

Mr. Gough's manner of speaking was so exhausting (to him) that when he closed a lecture he dripped with perspiration; his clothes were wringing wet; his vitality was spent; he was in a state of collapse. Hours of attention were necessary in order to soothe him into quietude. He had to be recuperated with bath and food; nor did sleep come until long past midnight. His wife made herself his nurse—his "brave, faithful Mary!"

The young couple went from Worcester back to Boston; where the proud husband introduced the bride to Deacon Grant. The good deacon, realizing the fact that marriage makes or mars two lives, had been doubtful about the choice of his *protégé*. When he saw her he said:

"John, she'll do !"

And, Gough adds the comment a quarter of a century later, "nobly she *has* done."

They fixed their residence in Roxbury, now a division of Boston. The groom spoke that very evening in Roxbury on his favorite theme, rested on the Sunday which followed, and then went on with his work, spending the honeymoon and the weeks that succeeded, on the platform.

In the spring of 1844, with Mrs. Gough for a traveling companion, he visited New York City to attend the anniversary of the American Temperance Union, on the 9th of May. The meeting was held in the Broadway Tabernacle, an historic hall long since demolished. Gough's name was not as familiar then as it soon became. As he rose to speak, towards the end of a long session, many people rose with him— to leave; not a common practice in his experience, even then. But those who remained enjoyed a treat.

Various other points in the Middle States were visited on this tour—Brooklyn, Newark, Philadelphia, Baltimore, among the number. Then Boston was sought again, where a notable temperance celebration was held on the 30th of May, with the city dressed as gaily as Venice used to be when the doge wedded the city by the sea to the sea: stores closed, an endless procession in the streets, a monster mass-meeting on the Common, and a grand *finale* in the evening in Faneuil Hall, with Gough for the orator.

Off again: this time to deliver a series of thirty addresses in western New York (where Mr. Gough pointed out to " Mary " the Oneida farm)—compensation, $10 a lecture, the itinerants paying their own expenses. They were not likely to get rich on such terms.

" No matter, John," said Mary; " we are doing the Lord's work."

It was during this tour that the couple first saw Niagara Falls. " I thought," comments Gough, " that a parallel might be drawn between the stream, rapids, and cataract before me, and the stream, rapids, and cataract of drunkenness. Above the Falls of Intemperance the water is bright and smooth, thousands who embark on that placid stream, as it glides down and comes into the rapids, are swept on with fearful rapidity, and sent into the gulf at a rate of 30,000, 40,000, and 50,000 a year, a dreadful waste of human life. The friends of humanity see this terrible destruction; they station themselves above, and cry out to the people, 'Back! back for your lives: none escape who get into these rapids except by miracle.'"[1]

Upon reaching Boston again, now their headquarters, Mrs. Gough proved the strength of her influence for good over her husband by pursuading him to unite with the Church. She was already a Church member, and transferred her membership by letter to the Mount Vernon Congregational Church, in Boston, Mr. Gough coming into the fold upon confession of his faith. In the pastor, the Rev. Dr. E. N. Kirk, both found a warm and helpful friend, in full sympathy with their spiritual and moral aims. Dr. Kirk possessed remarkable pulpit gifts and graces, and was a tongue of Penticostal fire in his day.

With his feet thus set on the Rock of Ages, and set to stay, and with such a wife at his side, the young lecturer felt strong to do and dare for God and humanity.

The close of the year, 1844, was selected by the friends of temperance in Boston for another demonstration in Faneuil Hall. A vast audience assembled

---

[1] "Platform Echoes," pp. 617-618.

to hear and cheer Mr. Gough. It was on this occasion that he introduced his apostrophe to water, which soon became famous across the continent. Holding in his hand a glass filled with it, he said :

"Is not this beautiful? Talk of ruby wine. Here is our beverage—water, pure water; we drink it to quench our thirst. There is no occasion to drink except to quench one's thirst ; and here is the beverage our Father has provided for His children. When Moses smote the rock the people were thirsty, and it was water that came forth, not wine, or rum, or ale. Were you ever thirsty, with lips dry and feverish, and throat parched? Did you never lift the goblet of pure water to your lips and feel it trickling over the tongue and gurgling down the throat? Was it not luxury? Give to the traveler on the burning desert, as he lies perishing with thirst, a goblet of cold water, and he will return the goblet heaping with gold ; give him wine, rum, or ale, and he turns away in feverish disgust to die. Our beverage is beautiful and pure, for God brewed it—not in the distillery, but out of the earth."

The orator then described it as enveloping the earth in wintry mantle, as rolling up the valley in the cloud-mist, settling on the mountain-top, and descending in the rain; and painted it in the streamlet, in the rainbow, beautiful always and blessed; no curse in it, no heartbroken mother or pale-faced wife, no starving child nor dying drunkard to lament its existence, and he concluded:

" ' Give water to me, bright water to me,
It cooleth the brow, it cooleth the brain.
It maketh the weak man strong again.'

"Tell me, young men and maidens, old men and matrons, will you not dash from your lips the drink that maddens and destroys and take as your beverage the beautiful gift our Father in Heaven has provided for His children?"[1]

The apostrophe was seldom repeated verbatim. The speaker was always changing it, sometimes for the better, often for the worse; but it never failed to call forth a hearty response.

With the Godspeed of Faneuil Hall Mr. and Mrs. Gough proceeded to Philadelphia, where he opened the year 1845 under the shadow of another historic edifice—Independence Hall, in which the first Continental Congress met and the immortal Declaration was signed.

The reformer had spoken before in the Quaker City, but under poor management and to small numbers. He came now to fill an engagement with the Pennsylvania State Temperance Society, which gave him prestige. Besides, his reputation was now continental. His success was phenomenal. After speaking in several churches on successive evenings, he was driven at last to the immense Chinese Museum, and this also was twice crowded to suffocation.

At this period Mr. Gough spoke his biography, with numerous *asides*, both humorous and pathetic. He then sang a song or two (which will surprise those who heard him only in later years), and solicited sig-

---

[1] In his book entitled "Sunlight and Shadow," pp. 359, 360, Mr. Gough gives the apostrophe, and defends himself against the charge of plagiarizing it from Paul Denton.

natures to the pledge—quite after the fashion of an evangelist nowadays, exhorting converts.

In appearance, in these early years, he was pale and thin—the shadow of a man, and looked tall, though only 5 feet and 7 inches in stature. His hair was bushy, and he tossed it about as a lion does his mane. His coat was close-buttoned to the chin. The lithe form was always in motion, and needed a large platform for full effect. "The restless, eager hands, supple as India-rubber, were perpetually busy flinging the hair forward, in one character, back in another, or standing it straight up in a third; crushing the drink-fiend, pointing to the angel in human nature, or doubling up the long coat tails in the most grotesque climaxes of gesticulation, when, 'with a hop, skip, and jump,' he proceeded to bring down the house. Dickens says of one of his humorous characters that 'his very knees winked '; but there was a variety and astonishment of expression in every movement of Mr. Gough that literally beggars description." [1]

In the midst of what in another might have seemed extravagance, there was a steady self-command which enabled him to ride the storm he raised. He was not like *Falstaff*, who in a double sense made a *butt* of himself, first, by swallowing so much sack, and secondly, by conceit. Good sense and wisdom, elevation and enthusiasm, marked both wit and pathos. His description comprehended everything—character, mode of dress, peculiar gestures, different humors, style of speaking and writing, down to the last detail.

---

[1] Miss Frances E. Willard's description, quoted in " A Knight That Smote the Dragon," pp. 150, 151.

He was an animated photographic apparatus, talking and acting pictures. His transitions of mood were lightning-like in their rapidity. He amused and instructed, fired and sobered, by his coincidences, comparisons, combinations, in a single breath. The man was a galvanic battery, and electrified his hearers.

An English traveler, then in Philadelphia, was attracted to hear Gough while these meetings were in progress. He went—not expecting much, for he had heard the great orators of England. We quote a few words from his account:

"It was the most awfully interesting biography I ever listened to. . . . At one moment he convulsed the audience with merriment, then, as if by touch of an enchanter's wand, he subdued them to tears. It was a wonderful display of his power of the feelings and passions; and yet, with all, there was so much of humility, that one knew not which most to admire—the man or his matter. Mr. Gough is an admirable mimic, and tells a story with more point than, Charles Matthews excepted, any other story-teller I ever listened to. . . . Taken altogether, it may be safely said that he is one of those men whom the Almighty calls out, at certain periods, to wage His battles and effect great moral reforms." [1]

It was in 1845, that the first "Autobiography" appeared. Gough dictated it to a friend, a short-hand writer, as he paced the room—talked and walked it off. The booklet (it has less than 150 pages) ran through more than thirty editions. 'Tis admirably done, and cantains pathos and humor enough to make and preserve the reputation of the author, had he done nothing more.

---

[1] First "Autobiography," Boston 1855, p. 149, *sq*. Appendix.

II.

THE " DOCTORED " SODA-WATER.

THOSE who have lived for others, and striven to make the world better, have usually lived as martyrs. Mr. Gough appeared to be an exception to the rule. His popularity was so great from the beginning to the end, the crowds he drew were so enormous that many who saw him only on the stage of action thought his career was a *fête*, a generation long. Those who looked behind the scenes knew better. His enemies were among the bitterest of their ilk, and from the outset, detractors made him a target to practise at

Mr. Gough was of an oversensitive disposition. Enmity and detraction pierced his heart as though they had been arrows. He winced, and showed that he was hit—a fact well known in the camp of his foes, and of which advantage was taken to continue or inflame the torture. It is to the credit of the reformer that, though he winced, he did not swerve. He maintained the manner of life which brought him into inevitable collision with wicked men by disturbing their plans, or with selfish co-laborers by outdazzling their dimness.

His vulnerable spot was his former life—the heel of Achilles, whither the arrows flew. Human nature

is various, and some varieties *do* seem superfluous!
Certain critics of Gough really disbelieved in the
genuineness of his reformation, of any such reformation, and said that he had only added hypocrisy to
his original vice. Others pretended to disbelieve.
Lies swarmed about his pathway, most of them accu-
sations of drinking on the sly. A liquor-seller at
Newburyport, for instance, asserted that Mr. Gough
had stopped to drink in his restaurant on the way
from one of his temperance lectures to the train. He
was forced by a threat of legal proceedings to retract
this lie, and apologize for it. But where one liar was
caught, a dozen escaped, and lied on.

Worse yet; attempts were made to entrap him into
inconsistent and vicious conduct, and thus destroy
his reputation. One of these had well-nigh succeeded.

Mr. Gough went to New York City in the autumn
of 1845 to map down his route and arrange his dates
for the approaching winter. He arrived at 6:30
o'clock; went to a hotel; supped; left word at the
office that he might not return that night, as he was
going to Brooklyn to visit friends; strolled out upon
Broadway; entered a store or two, and made trifling
purchases; resumed his stroll; and was accosted by a
stranger.

"Good-evening, Mr. Gough."

It was now near eight o'clock. Mr. Gough did not
recognize the speaker, and said so.

"Well, I used to know you years ago, when you
worked in this city," said he. "My name is Williams
—Jonathan Williams."

The time referred to was several years back; the

man appeared honest. Gough was unsuspicious—
indeed there seemed no occasion for suspicion. The
lecturer made a cordial response.

"You have got into a new business since we worked
together," continued "Williams," as he walked on
beside the former bookbinder.

"Yes," replied Gough; "I'm giving my time to
temperance."

"I suppose," said "Williams," "you are so good
and proud now that you'd not drink a glass of soda
with an old shopmate."

"Oh, yes, I would," was the hearty answer.

They were then opposite a drug-store, and both
stepped in. There was a crowd around the fountain.

"Oh," said "Williams," "we can't get served here.
I know a better place."

They went out, sauntered down Chambers street
to Chatham, and entered another store. This time
they got their soda-water; "Williams," handing
Gough a glass, with his hand over the top of it, which
the latter thought rude, though he suspected nothing
at the moment. They left together and soon parted.
In a short while Gough, although out of doors, became
dazed, lost his way, and was abducted and secreted
for nearly a week, being found in a disreputable
house in Walker street, in a stupor.

Friends bore him away to Brooklyn, his objective
point when he quitted the hotel on the evening of
September 5th. Here, at the residence of Mr. and
Mrs. Hurlbut, he was tenderly nursed. Mrs. Gough
was sent for. The lost was found, and in good hands
again.

Of course, this dramatic episode caused wide-spread

comment. Gough's enemies were jubilant. A searching inquisition was made, however, by a committee of the Mount Vernon Church, specially appointed for the purpose; whose report completely exonerated Mr. Gough. The physician who treated him in Brooklyn testified that he found abundant evidence of drugging. The public press at the time generally denounced the abduction. Gough was robbed in that den—but not of his good name.

Probably, "Williams" followed his victim to New York, as he disappeared and was never detected. He "doctored" the soda-water when he passed it with his hand over the rim. Confederates watched the drugged man after the parting. When they saw him bewildered they plied him with liquor, and guided him to the place where he was finally discovered.

The case is painful. Circumstances of mystery still surround it. We have not felt called upon to go at length into it, because Mr. Gough has himself done so in documents easily accessible.[1] What was called his second "fall" gave his opponents an advantage of which they then and for years afterward availed themselves. But this was the last cloud on his name. His life for forty years, pure, noble, lived out in the sun, must be permitted to interpret this dark passage.

It should be added that Mr. Gough confessed to imprudence on this occasion, but never to any guilt. The wife stood by her husband and blamed herself, wife-like, for permitting him for once to go alone to New York.

---

[1] "Autobiography," pp. 195–209.

8

But even had this been a genuine "fall," surprise would be out of place. Temperance may be in the purpose when intemperance is in the conduct. Pathology and moral science show that the worst action of inebriety is on the will. It shatters the nerves, but it paralyzes the will. Hence, years are often needed for recovery—years marked by occasional lapses. The question with regard to a reformed man ought not to be—

"How many times has he fallen?"

It should be—

"How long has he stood?"

He who comes out of drunkenness and stands forty years, is a moral hero.

Through the rest of September and the whole of October and November, Mr. Gough lay at the point of death. It was not until the beginning of December that he was sufficiently strong to mount the platform.

Thus ended the year 1845.

" FOOTPRINTS ON THE SANDS OF TIME."

ANOTHER severe trial awaited Mr. Gough. As time passed he found himself more and more out of sympathy with Washingtonianism. He was sincerely attached to that movement, and had occasion to be, for it had rescued him. Its leaders were his close friends. He was its most eloquent exponent. But experience and observation taught him the insufficiency of its methods. He both felt and saw that piety alone clenched the nails which moral suasion drove in. The pledge started the inebriate toward manhood. Manhood itself, however, involved not one virtue, but many. The ultimate motive was the fear and love of God. This anchored character. Therefore, he introduced into his addresses religious appeals, and gradually animated the temperance reformation with a new spirit.

Keen ears and eyes heard everything he said, and watched everything he did. This departure was soon noted. His old associates stood aloof and denounced him. They believed in moral suasion, and in nothing else. They believed the mere wish to break-off intemperate habits signified in a pledge would save the drunkard. Men hardly steadied into sobriety assumed to be teachers instead of sitting as learners.

Such men led the crusade. Success was measured by the number of names signed to the pledge, rather than by the renovated lives that followed the signing. There was jealousy of the Church as a rival institution. The Washingtonians, as a rule, refused to open their meetings with prayer, disowned the Bible, scouted the idea of piety, and were, many of them, avowed freethinkers. Naturally, too, for they were converts of the tavern. A bar-room is a poor divinity hall.

In reviewing these facts at a later day, Mr. Gough said :

"Men became leading reformers who were not qualified by experience, or training, or education, to lead, and out of them a class sprung up who became dictatorial, and sometimes insolent. Irreligious men insulted in some instances ministers of religion who had been hard workers for temperance, reformed drunkards sneered at those who had never been intemperate, as if former degradation was the only qualification for leadership. . . . Any remonstrance was construed at once into opposition to the cause itself, rather than to their methods. . . . The temperance cause is not strictly a religious enterprise, it is a secular movement; but the religious element in it is the measure of its success, and the absence of that element is its decay." [1]

In the same connection he remarks :

"I heard the Hon. Thomas Marshall, of Kentucky, make a ten-minute speech in the Broadway Tabernacle at the close of an address of mine, in which he said : ' Were this great globe one chrysolite, and I were offered the possession of it if I would drink 'one glass of brandy, I would refuse with scorn ; and I want no religion, I want the temperance pledge.' With

---

[1] "Sunlight and Shadow," pp. 497, 498, and 501.

that wonderful voice of his he thundered out ' We want no religion in this movement. Let it be purely secular, and keep religion where it belongs.' Poor Tom Marshall, with all his self-confidence, fell, and died at Poughkeepsie in clothes given him by Christian charity."[1]

Apropos, the writer heard this same gifted man lecture on temperance one evening in New Haven, Conn., when he was so drunk he could not stand. He half sat to steady himself upon a table which served for a desk, swinging one leg as he hiccoughed out his sentences, brilliant as the rainbow. Presently, he lost his balance, and fell over the front of the platform to the floor four feet below, with the table piled on top of him. The fall sobered Marshall. He reascended the platform imperturbable and erect as a grenadier and continued his lecture ! The object-lesson was more effective than the address. Personal piety would have saved the eloquent Kentuckian.

The Washingtonians accused Gough of a further offense. He advocated a recourse to law—not then nor for long years afterwards, with any immediate purpose to apply it, but as a right within the legitimate scope of the State. He would occasionally utter sentences like these:

"Our work has been very much like a game of ten-pins. We have been very busy in picking up the pins, but directly we set them up the liquor-seller has begun rolling the ball to knock them down again. We have picked up the pins and said, 'It is a good work to set them up'; but the ball came rolling in again, and knocked them down in every direction.

---

[1] "Sunlight and Shadow," pp. 497, 498, and 501.

We have buried the dead wood, and new pins have been produced, and the game has gone on. But the cry has gone forth, it has gathered strength, and by-and-by it will be thundered in the ears of the Legislature, 'Stop that ball!'"[1]

To the Moral Suasionists such utterances were gall and wormwood. What fools men are — how blind when they have an opinion to maintain, or a prejudice to defend, or a party to serve! As though any weapon, every weapon should not be welcomed in such a war as this against intemperance!

Mr. Gough's popularity was now a source of discomfort to the antiquated reformers, who refused to go on and up to higher ground. They circulated stories to his detriment. One whom he had nursed through *delirium tremens* wrote a scurrilous pamphlet, entitled "Goughiana," moved to it by so-called temperance people. This was given to the public sometimes at the doors of Washingtonian halls. The orator was twitted with being a temperance man for "revenue only," his very fees being grudged him— although they were small enough in those days, heaven knows! The profits, when he lectured, were large. They went into the treasury of the cause. In 1846 his personal receipts only averaged $20.52, and he always paid his own traveling and hotel expenses.[2] To the lecturer who received only $3 or $5, this looked extravagant. One Washingtonian newspaper assumed to fix the maximum rate for such lectures for all time to come. "Anything above $5," said this political economist, "is too much, and only tempts

---

[1] " Platform Echoes," p. 618.   [2] "Autobiography," p. 247.

unprincipled and selfish men to advocate temperance for the sake of money."[1]

Mr. Gough was unnecessarily sensitive to these shafts. Criticisms of his manner (easily caricatured) always annoyed him. But taunts that touched character, as we have remarked in the previous chapter, hurt him beyond most men. No doubt, his remembrance of the past, of what he had been and done, aggravated this weakness. He was lacking in self-esteem, and had no vanity. Nevertheless, too often for comfort, he wore his heart upon his sleeve for daws to peck at.

With the bitter came the sweet, mingled as usual in life's mysterious cup. His fame went on rising. His lectures were ovations. Friends, good and true, rallied to his side. He was a king of hearts as well as of the platform. Tens of thousands already dated the commencement of a new life from one or another of his addresses.

In January, 1846, Mr. Gough was invited to Virginia. Richmond, Petersburg, Portsmouth, and Norfolk were his centers of work, though other towns were touched. In the latter town he saw what he had never seen before—a slave sold at auction, and thus describes the occurrence:

"Passing through the market, I saw a crowd surrounding a middle-aged colored woman who stood on a barrel, the auctioneer below her. I stopped to hear : 'Two hundred and thirty dollars—two—thirty, thirty, thirty, going ; two—thirty, going, going——gone!' Yes! there stood a woman, one of God's

---

[1] Lyman Abbott, in his Introduction to "Platform Echoes," p. 41.

creatures, a wife and mother, with arms folded and the tears rolling silently down her cheeks, as she quietly and meekly turned at the bidding of the men who surrounded her, to show her arms, her shape, her breast, her teeth,—till the sale was accomplished, and the poor creature stepped down from her position before the crowd,—transferred from one owner to another, body, mind, and soul for two hundred and thirty dollars. I turned and said to a friend: ' That's the most damnable sight ever seen in a Christian country.' I was told I must not say that, and was hastened away." [1]

Later in this same summer of 1846, Mr. Gough received an invitation to give ten lectures in Lynchburg, Va., signed by the Mayor and one hundred other citizens. In the evening after the first address, he was given a mock serenade in front of the hotel at eleven o'clock at night. Some of the party were arrested for disturbing the peace. Upon hearing in the morning that four of them were to be tried at the court-house, he started for that building; was intercepted by a mob; came near being torn in pieces as an Abolitionist; was forbidden to speak again in Lynchburg; avowed his purpose to lecture on temperance that very night; abashed the crowd by his firm attitude, and managed to retreat from the scene unhurt.

Night came. The church was packed. Every one expected an outbreak—but as Disraeli used to say, " 'Tis the unexpected that happens." The orator entered through a window. He seated himself. Prayer was offered. The chairman, a well-known clergyman of the town, introduced him. He rose and came

---

[1] " Autobiography," p. 213.

forward amid suppressed excitement. Entirely self-possessed, he said:

"I wish you to hear me patiently before you decide what to do with me. I am ready to leave your city to-night by the 12 o'clock canal-boat, or I will stay and fulfill my engagement. I was invited here by a committee of one hundred of your citizens, headed by the Mayor, to deliver ten lectures on temperance. On Sunday night, I asked for arguments on the other side, and got them—a brass horn, a tin-pan, an old fiddle, a triangle, a piece of sheet-iron, and one man apparently hired to swear for the occasion, who did his work faithfully. These arguments were almost as good as I expected. I have been threatened with whipping, with being run into the river, with vitriol in my face, and I have been called an Abolitionist. Now, just hear me while I say that there is no gentleman here whose opinion is worth having, who would not despise me heartily if I were not an Abolitionist. You all know I am, and you knew it when you sent for me. But you engaged me to speak on temperance, and I came for *that* purpose. I have not spoken of your 'peculiar institution' in public, whatever I may have thought of it. *You* have introduced the subject, not I, and I should receive and merit your contempt if I swallowed my principles, and told a lie to curry your favor."

This manly preface completely won the audience, which voted overwhelmingly that he should stay. The remaining lectures were given, and did much good, hundreds signing the pledge.

While in Virginia, Mr. Gough had an attack of brain fever, the result of incessant work, superimposed upon the nervous prostration brought on the preceding autumn by the adventure in New York. Before leaving the State he addressed several large

---

1 "Autobiography," p. 218.

gatherings of the colored people. In one of their churches in Richmond he spoke to 2,500 of them. There they sat—so black that one could not have seen them had they closed their eyes! Turning to a clerical friend, Gough asked:

"How shall I talk to them?"

"Just as you would to white folks," was the answer.

He did, and found them like any other audience, only more emotional.

"I said something of heaven," remarked Mr. Gough, "and a tall negro rose and commenced a song. There was a chorus:

> " I'm bound for de land of Canaan,
>   Come, go along with me;
> We'll all pass over Jordan
>   And sound the jubilee.

> " Den we shall see Jesus—
>   Come, go along with me;
> We're all gwine home together,
>   And will sound the jubilee."

"I am afraid to say how many verses they sang—it seemed like a dozen, and I had quite a rest. Just as I was resuming my speech, a man rose near the pulpit, and said:

"'Bredren, just look at me. Here is a nigger dat doesn't own hisself. I belong to Massa Carr, bless de Lord! Yes, bredren, dis poor ole body belongs to Massa Carr; but my soul is the freeman of de Lord Jesus!'" [1]

---

[1] "Autobiography," p. 219.

Gough adds: "The effect was magical, and the whole audience shouted: 'Amen!' 'Glory!' 'Bless de Lord!' I took the opportunity to say:

"'There is not a drunkard in the city can say that!'" [1]

Although he had seen slavery in its mildest aspect, the Northerner faced homeward hating the system more than ever.

An interesting and important part of Mr. Gough's work in these days was the talking to children. This is partly an art, partly a gift. There is danger of talking too high or else of talking too low. In the one case, they lose interest; in the other, they lose respect for the speaker. Mr. Gough was never happier than when before such an audience. He was a great boy himself and understood smaller boys. His graphic mannerisms, anecdotes, mimicry, always won the children, who were among his most enthusiastic auditors. He organized thousands and thousands of them into cold-water armies and similar temperance bodies.

In a characteristic passage he remarks:

"I have been often touched by the sorrows of the drunkard's child. Pitiful little things they are sometimes. I was asked by a gentleman at whose house I was dining in Washington, in the 'forties, What was the most pitiful sight I ever saw? After a little thought, I said: 'An old child; a child with wrinkles in its face, that is not yet in its teens; a child made old by hard usage; whose brow is furrowed by the plowshare of sorrow;—that is one of the most pitiful sights on earth.'" [2]

Mr. Gough's record for the five years commencing

---

[1] "Autobiography," p. 219. [2] "Autobiography," p. 226.

with 1847 and ending with 1852, was one of continuous lecturing through a dozen States, relieved only
by a few weeks' respite in each summer. He was
the man with a single theme. He could say of it,
however, as the Rev. John Pierpont did, when accused on account of his earnestness for temperance
of being a man of one idea,—" True, but its a whop-
ping big one ! " Moreover, he varied it so entertainingly, applied it so practically, connected it with current affairs so powerfully, and so vitalized it with his
own unique personality, that the people, like *Oliver
Twist*, in Dickens's story, never stopped clamoring
for " more."

To follow Mr. Gough in his journeyings would be
interesting, but endless as walking in the footsteps
of Sue's " Wandering Jew." Out of his budget of
experiences we select a few, as samples of the rest.

On Thursday night, October 21, 1847, temperance
was mobbed in Faneuil Hall. Liquor had been freely
distributed during the day to " lewd fellows of the
baser sort," two hundred of whom were gathered in
a corner of the old hall, intent upon mischief. The
floor of Faneuil Hall is not seated—the people stand.
Hence, it will hold twice as many people as could
otherwise get in ; and in a time of excitement, the
crowd sways to and fro like a field of grain in a
wind.

This meeting was held by the Boston Temperance
Society, whose president, Deacon Moses Grant, was
in the chair. After a prayer, he introduced Mr.
Gough. Instantly bedlam broke loose. Cheers and
counter-cheers for Deacon Grant and for some local
liquor-dealers, for Gough, and for Tom, Dick, and

Harry, were given with a will. Catcalls, singing, and, in a few minutes dancing in a ring formed yonder in rummy corner—made the "confusion worse confounded."

In this din speaking was impossible. A shout could not be heard across the platform. Mr. Gough made pantomimic appeals—in vain. Whiskey had come in for the purpose of mobbing temperance out.

Heated with liquor and instigated by their leaders, the rowdies passed from noise to violence. A rush was made for the platform, amid cries of "Throw Grant and Gough out of the window!" Members of the society on the platform met the assault resolutely, and pitched the assailants back to the floor as they climbed up. For a while a regular battle raged, with repeated assaults and repulses, as at Bunker Hill in '76—Gough was reminded of the Diorama whose crank he used to turn. Then the gas was cut off. Hostilities were suspended, but the war of shouts and jeers and oaths went on. After an hour of chaos, a large posse of police came on the scene. Comparative order was restored; the gas was turned on; the officers retook their places, and Mr. Gough spoke to an accompaniment of outcries and interruptions which would have embarrassed most orators, but which he met, parried, and turned against the mob with indescribable *sang froid*.

It was on this occasion that he told his famous stuttering story. One loafer, by his persistent interjections and profanity made himself a nuisance—all the more so, because a knot of rum-sellers under the gallery enjoyed the fun hugely and encouraged the fellow by laughing loudly at every impudent remark.

Advancing to the edge of the platform, and addressing him personally, Gough said :

"My friend, I pity you ; for you are doing the dirty
work of men who dare not do it themselves. You are
serving your masters and employers, who stand here
in this audience encouraging you in doing what you
would never dream of were you not set on by others.
You look like a sensible man, and I should like to tell
you a story of which you remind me."

The man broke in with, "Let's have the story."

"Well, a certain merchant who was a sad stammerer, had one joke which he related to every one who
would listen to him. His clerks had repeatedly heard
it and were familiar with it. One day, a stranger
came into the store. The merchant accosted him
with :

"'Can you tell me wh–why it was th–h–at B–B–B–
why it wa–was th–that B–B– wh–wh–why it was that
B–B——'

"Seeing his employer's difficulty, one of the clerks
said, 'He wants to know if you can tell him why
Balaam's ass spoke.'

"'Yes,' replied the stranger, 'I guess I can. I
reckon Balaam was a stuttering man, and got his ass
to do his talking for him!'"

The man laughed loudly with the rest, and soon
left the hall.

This was the last time temperance was mobbed in
Faneuil Hall; which, however, was the cradle of
mobs, as well as of liberty, when the Abolitionists
occupied it.

Mr. Gough's nervous temperament subjected him
to stage fright, of which he was the lifelong victim.

Fortunately, it always preceded and never accompanied his efforts. When he was announced to give his one hundred and sixty-first lecture in Boston, he had an attack of this kind which seriously frightened good Deacon Grant. Gough shook with apprehension all day—"he could not speak—would surely break down—had nothing to say—was talked out too *dry* even for a temperance man."

At night he baulked worse than ever—insisted that speaking was an impossibility. He told the Deacon flatly that he would not go to the meeting. After much persuasion he did go, and was introduced. He commenced thus :

"Ladies and gentlemen : I have nothing to say. It is not my fault that I am here to night. I almost wish I could feel as a gentleman in New York told the people he did when he addressed them—'I am never afraid of an audience,' said he, 'I imagine the people are so many cabbage heads.' I wish I could feel so——

"But no, I do not wish that. When I look into your faces, an assemblage of rational and immortal beings, and remember how drink has debased and dragged down the loftiest and noblest minds, I cannot feel so."

Having gotten an initial thought, he was off, and spoke gloriously for an hour and a half—a human cyclone, with tornado sauce.

When he sat down, Deacon Grant said rather sharply :

"Don't you ever frighten me so again!" [1]

In October, 1848, Mr. Gough's father arrived in America, his son having sent for him. For years the

---

[1] "Autobiography," pp. 235, 236.

two had lost sight and knowledge of one another.
A copy of his son's "Autobiography," had fallen into
the father's hands.   In this way a correspondence
was reopened, and now they were together—a meeting both sad and joyful. The pale, martyr face of the
wife and mother looked down upon the two, and
made a pathetic third.   And other ghosts of memory
and change revisited "the glimpses of the moon."
Henceforth until his death, in 1871, at the age of 94,
the elder Gough was supported by the younger.

John and Mary removed from Roxbury to Boston
in 1847.   In 1848 they wearied of the city, purchased
lands in Boylston, Mary's old home, and dear to John
as the place where they met ; and here at " Hillside,"
five miles from Worcester, they resided ever after
when at home.

'Tis a quiet, restful place.   The surrounding
country is diversified.   The house, a two-storied,
roomy building, surmounted by a cupola, stands at
the head ʋ a long approach, after the English
fashion.   Here, beyond the easy reach of men, but
accessible to those who wished to find them, the
Goughs browsed at delightful intervals in their busy
life ; and while Mary turned farmer, John went to
grass, like Nebuchadnezzar, or read yonder in the
cosy library, whose shelves he soon peopled with a
choice selection of 3,000 books. As an old bookbinder, Mr. Gough was specially fond of fine bind-
ings.   Many of his books he bound himself as a
pastime. His tastes led him in study to history, biography, essays, and art.   In these departments, therefore, his library was exceptionally rich.   The duties
which called this couple away from "Hillside" to

endure the discomforts of travel, the bare rooms of hotels, and the fatigue of life on the platform, had need to take sharp hold upon the conscience and the heart, else had they not budged from their bucolics.

Mr. Gough's habit at this period was to give, not a single lecture in a place, as in Lyceum days, but continuous courses of lectures; for instance, five at Rochester, eighteen at Buffalo, ten at Detroit. The number of lectures in any course was a matter of agreement. The average fee was less than $25 a lecture through the whole of the lecturer's first temperance decade.

In the fall of 1850 the Goughs spent some time in Canada, courses of twelve lectures being given in Montreal, eight in Quebec, six in Kingston, ten in Toronto, and seven in Hamilton. At several of these towns there were English garrisons. These Mr. Gough was invited to address. His father's long and honorable connection with the army drew his heart out toward these men, many of whom signed the pledge in response to his appeals—and kept it, too, as he learned long years afterwards. One day, in Boston, Deacon Grant asked Gough to call upon two young ladies who desired to see him—but let him tell about it:

"I went to the house, was shown into a room, and received by a young lady who motioned me to a seat. As I sat there for a few moments waiting for her to speak to me, I gave a glance around the room. There were evidences of better days 'lang syne,' though I shivered, for there was no fire in the grate, and the weather was cold. The young lady spoke:

"'Mr. Gough, my sister intended to meet you with me, but

9

she has sprained her ankle and is unable to see you. My mother has been confined to her room for many weeks, and to her bed for some days. Oh, sir, it is hard for a daughter to speak of a father's intemperance; but what can I do? I have sent for you as a last resort. My father is good and kind when free from drink; but when under its influence is cruel—he actually robs us of the common necessaries of life—and I would not ask you to sit in a cold room, had we materials for a fire.'

" I involuntarily glanced at the piano. She noticed it, and said quickly:

" 'You may think that pride and poverty go together; and they do. You wonder why I do not sell my piano. I cannot sell it. My father bought it for me on my birthday years ago. It is like an old friend. I learned to play on it. Mother loves to hear the tunes that remind us of days gone by—I fear for ever. My father has asked me to sell it; and suppose I did? It would but procure him the means of intoxication for a time, and we should be little better off.'

" I left them. Deacon Grant sent them provisions and fuel. In a day or two I called again. The father was there. After a short conversation, he said, to my surprise:

" ' Mr. Gough, have you a pledge with you?'

" ' I have.'

" ' I will sign it.'

" I immediately produced it; he at once wrote his name, and stood up, free! I watched the young girl, when he said ' I will sign.' She clasped her hands, and stood with eager eyes and lips apart, watching the pen. She seemed breathlessly anxious till the name was recorded;—then she sprang to him, twined her arms as well as she could around his neck (she was a little creature); and oh, how she clung to his breast. Then, unclasping her hands, she said:

" ' Oh, father, I'm so proud of you. Mr. Gough, he has signed it; and he'll never break it, I know him; he'll never break it. No, no, my father will live a sober man. Oh, father! Oh, father!'

" The tears were raining down her cheeks, as he passed his hand caressingly over her face. Then she said :

"'Father, you spoke of selling the piano. We can sell it to-morrow, and what it brings will pay what we owe, and we shall have something to start with again. Sha'n't we, father?'

" Yes, that poor heart was comforted. Now she would give up her piano—cheerfully. Why? Because her father would live a sober man." [1]

Early in 1851 Mr. and Mrs. Gough set out for Cincinnati, Ohio. It was in the early days of railroads. These annihilators of time and distance were as yet infrequent. The stage-coach and the steamboat, beyond the Atlantic seaboard, were still the reliance of passengers. At Cumberland, Md., our couple had to "stage it" to Pittsburgh, over a road deep with winter mud and slush. They intended to take the boat at Pittsburgh down the Ohio to Cincinnati. Opportunities for work unexpectedly opened in Pittsburgh, however, and detained them two weeks there and in Alleghany City, across the river ; and sixteen lectures resulted in the securing of between four and five thousand signatures to the pledge.

Thence they proceeded to Cincinnati, where they met and became intimate with that patriarch of temperance, Dr. Lyman Beecher, then at the head of Lane Seminary.

Mr. Gough spoke to the usual crowds. "Several times," he writes, " I was compelled to obtain an entrance to the church by the window. Once a ladder was placed against a window back of the pulpit. I hesitated as the feat of climbing seemed dangerous.

---

[1] "Autobiography," pp. 263-265.

Dr. Lyman Beecher said : ' I'll go first ; follow me.'
Encouraged by his success, I ventured.   It was
comical to see the doctor drive his hat more firmly on
his head as he prepared for the ascent ; but, taking a
firm hold, up he went, chuckling to himself all the
way." [1]

Wesley Chapel, the largest audience-room in the
city, was overfilled more than twenty times !   "I
spoke also," says the lecturer, " to firemen, to children, to ladies, and visited schools.   At Wesley College I made an address, and was asked by a young
lady to write the pledge in her ' album '; I did so;
when another and another brought albums—till I had
written in one hundred and forty-three of these
books.   I often in my travels see one of these albums
with the writing in it: and it recalls very pleasantly
the delightful afternoon I spent at Wesley College." [2]

Later in 1851 Mr. Gough delivered a course of nine
lectures in Halifax, Nova Scotia.   Here he addressed
a muster of the famous Forty-Second Regiment of
Highlanders.   In referring to it, he says :

" In passing through the city I had noticed a sign hung up
in front of a low drinking-house with a daub of a picture, representing a half-intoxicated soldier in the Highland costume, a
bottle in one hand and a pipe in the other, with the words
' The Jolly Highland Soldier,' in red letters beneath.   In the
course of my talk to the soldiers, I told them what I had seen,
and asked them if the publican dared to exhibit the picture of
a drunken lawyer, or doctor, or minister, or even a ' Jolly Highland Officer ?   No ! He associated the Highland *soldier* with
drunkenness.   It was an insult to them and to the ' garb of old

---

[1] "Autobiography," p. 271.   [2] 'Autobiography," p. 271.

Gaul,' of which they were so proud. The next day the sign disappeared! A deputation of the men had waited on the proprietor with a very emphatic request that the offensive sign should be taken down." [1]

In the course of an address at Colburg, Canada, the orator made a violent gesture and t—r—r—r—r—rip went his coat down the back from collar to skirt. Every one laughed but the speaker. He did not see the fun—at the moment. He could not speak without gesture. Now he did not dare to move his arms, for then the garment fell forward most absurdly. That torn coat quite spoiled his speech. Before he left town he was presented with a new one ; whereupon he said :

" I thank you for your gift ; and now as this is the result of my accident, I wish I had torn my trousers, too ! "

On another occasion, when he was speaking in the Church of Dr. Beman, in Troy, N. Y. (a giant of the pulpit, physically as well as mentally), a gas-burner began to blow. The good clergyman rose softly and stepped behind Gough to turn it down, just as he threw back his clenched fist; Dr. Beman received the blow full in the face. When Gough apologized, he said :

" Remember, sir, you are the first man who ever struck me with impunity."

These were the high-water days of temperance. Since 1843, when Gough signed the pledge, there had been a revolution in public sentiment. Drunkenness was no longer the rule, nor even the fashion. Liquor-

---

[1] "Autobiography," pp. 272, 273.

selling was disreputable.   Bars were screened.   Ob-
trusive decanters were banished from private *buffets*.
It was not high noon ; but it was 10.30 o'clock by the
pointers on the dial of reform, and the "good time
coming" seemed destined to chime twelve within
another decade.

In a free country social reforms are certain to work
into politics.   'Tis thus that results are funded, put
out at interest, and made to yield a revenue of righteousness.   So now the temperance convictions of the
people were stereotyped into statutes.   Local-option
laws were in force in Pennslyvania—had been since
1843.   In 1851, Neal Dow, a name synonymous with
prohibition, pushed the legislature of Maine to adopt
"the Maine Law," so-called, a law which has been
the pattern of prohibitory legislation ever since.
Massachusetts and Vermont passed similar statutes
in 1852.

It would be folly to ascribe these successes to any
one reformer.   The sources of a river lie in many
springs.   Multitudes of good men and true (some of
them "mute, inglorious Miltons," whose names are
"unhonored and unsung"), contributed to swell the
temperance tide.   Among them all, it is safe to say
that John B. Gough stands preëminent.   His advocacy made an epoch.   He transferred temperance
from the schoolhouses to the churches.   He attracted
to it influential names which had looked askance and
stood aloof.   He made it popular before vast assem-
blages, drawn together to laugh at Gough's stories,
but taught before they were dismissed to hate the
drink.

'Tis true that he did not then, nor until a good deal

later, set as much value as others did upon prohibitory law. He assented to the principle of prohibition. His motto was, "Kindness, sympathy, and persuasion for the victim—for the tempter, law." But he emphasized the first part, rather than the second half, of this motto. There were two reasons for this: one, philosophical; the other, temperamental. Mr. Gough was a good deal more of a philosopher than he got credit for being. He understood America and England. He knew that in either country a statute is not worth the paper it is printed upon unless it has behind it a friendly and executive public opinion. Law cannot execute itself. If the law officers evade it, and the people hold it in disfavor, of what use is the most wholesome statute? The laws against theft, arson, adultery, murder, are measurably enforced, because these offenses are under the frown of public opinion.

Hence he felt free to follow the temperamental impulses of his nature, and go on with his special calling, viz., the creation of temperance sentiment. This would not only make temperance law, but enforce it. A great speaker, he naturally gave himself, perhaps too onesidedly for awhile, to moral advocacy. It may be, also, that he set his mark too high, when he said: "Do not expect prohibition until you have four-fifths of the community on your side." At any rate, there must be a good working majority for prohibition before it can be made operative. Meantime, Gough's example is a good one to follow—work for the creation of that majority.

PART VI.

The First Visit to Great Britain

"England, with all thy faults I love thee still."
COWPER, *The Task*, Book II.

I.

FORTY years ago news did not travel quite as rapidly as it does in these electric days ; but it went fast enough to carry the name and fame of John B. Gough to those who were stationed on the watch-towers of public observation across the sea. Nor were American books and speakers as highly appreciated over there then as they are now. It was a flattering tribute to the ability of the Yankee reformer that the leaders of the temperance cause in Great Britain so quickly noticed the remarkable results attendant upon his career three thousand miles away ; and credit-able, also, to their own perspicacity.

The Macedonian cry, "Come over and help us," had been echoing from the other side of the Atlantic and sounding in Mr. Gough's ears for months. To these appeals he was long deaf. He was happy and useful here ; why go there? Could the need be greater abroad than it was at home? Besides, with habitual modesty, he thought his style of speaking would not please the English and Scotch people. They liked argument ; he was intuitional. He did not realize the splendor of his own powers. What men do with ease they seldom value.

For these and other reasons Mr. Gough replied to

the British overtures, as the Shunammite did to
Elisha, "I dwell among mine own people."

There is great virtue in persistency—and it is an
English virtue. The more he declined the more
pressing they became. Accordingly, like some young
ladies who say "Yes" to ardent swains, "to get rid
of them," Mr. Gough, in the spring of 1853, mailed an
agreement to visit Great Britain and spend the summer
vacation there, provided the London Temperance
League, whose committee had been in correspondence with him, would agree to pay Mrs. Gough's and
his own expenses to and fro, including one week in
Paris and another down at Sandgate. He thought
this proposition would not be accepted—further proof
of his modesty. It was, though, and eagerly. Thus
it was arranged that he should have a summer trip
abroad, and pay for it by six weeks' service to the
League.

The mercurial reformer had scarcely signed the
agreement before his heart failed him—he could not,
would not go—he was sure the Britons would dislike
him—failure was foreordained. Dr. Lyman Beecher
was visiting the Goughs at "Hillside" at the time,
and he laughed at and scolded John (as he familiarly
called him) by turns.

"Very well," said Gough ; "I will go, if I *must ;*
but I've borrowed $250 to make myself independent
of the League ; and if I do fail in my first speech, I
shall come back by the next steamer !"

Deacon Grant, too, and other friends, encouraged
the despondent advocate—and "Mary" was at his side.

They sailed in the steamer *America* on the 20th of
July, and reached Liverpool on the 30th, after a

pleasant voyage, during which the wife was seasick while the husband was not. On the tug which took them ashore they met a deputation of temperance friends, headed by Smith Harrison, Esq., a Liverpool merchant, who gave the visitors an English welcome, and escorted them five miles out of the city to the residence of a wealthy Quaker, Charles Wilson, where they slept that night in the prophet's chamber, senenaded by thrushes on the lawn, and couched in delicious peace.

The next day, August 1st, they took the train for London, over the Northwestern Railway, which runs through a picturesque country, typically English— "rich, green foliage; hedge rows, new to American eyes; clumps of trees artistically planted; agriculture in perfection; magnificent mansions of landed proprietors; cottage homes of laborers; and here and there a half-ruined castle, or the romantic remains of some fine old abbey." After four or five hours spent in the enjoyment of this beautiful panorama as it unrolled before their eyes—an experience "new and yet familiar" to John, new and unfamilar to Mary, but "linked sweetness long drawn out" to both—the travelers whirled into London.

Here, again, they were met, warmly greeted, and carried to the house of George Cruikshank, between whom and John Gough (as the English preferred to call him) in was a case of love at first sight. Mr. Cruikshank was then in the fulness of his fame as an artist, and was equal master of pencil and brush. As a caricaturist without a rival in his day, he displayed his fertile imagination and comic humor in illustrations each one of which would create a laugh under

the ribs of death.   He was, withal, a great friend of
temperance, and let the fact be known at a time when
temperance and fanaticism were synonymous.   His
moral courage equaled his genius.   Gough and
Cruikshank were drawn together by kindred tastes
and feelings.   One was the Gough of art, the other
was the Cruikshank of speech.   Gough owned and
showed at " Hillside " the finest collection of Cruikshankiana extant—more extensive even than the one
in the British Museum.

It had been arranged that Mr. Gough should enter
at once upon a temperance campaign.   He was to
speak first in Exeter Hall, London, on Tuesday evening, August 2d, the day after his arrival in London—
pretty quick work !   After this the list of engagements was continuous through the month, with the
Sundays alone set aside for rest.

The Executive Committee of the London Temperance League had engaged Mr. Gough on his American reputation.   Not one of them had heard him.
But they wisely determined that the responsibility of
failure, if failure there should be, should rest upon the
orator, rather than upon the committee.   They, therefore, advertised him magnificently—sent his "Autobiography" out by thousands of copies—arranged a
course of lectures on Gough's life and mission
by a competent English speaker, enlisted the press,
got the ear of *litterateurs*, secured the aid of the clergy
—and, in brief, stood the United Kingdom on tiptoe
with expectation.   Failure in such circumstances
meant ruin—success insured limitless opportunities
for usefulness.

How did Mr. Gough meet these high expectations?

To the surprise of the Leaguers, he did not seem to understand the situation. For example, he passed the whole of the 2d of August in riding about London on top of an omnibus, pointing out to "Mary" the Bank, the Mansion House, St. Paul's, Temple Bar, the Strand, Fleet street, Westminster Abbey, the Houses of Parliament, and a hundred other objects of interest as the 'bus rolled along ; in admiring a Punch-and-Judy show (of all things in the world); in undignified explorations and exclamations, which quite horrified the staid escort provided by the League—and this when he was to put his reputation to the touch that very night, "to gain or lose it all." There was consternation among the Leaguers. They did not know what to make of this "boy let loose from school"—nor of his female pal. They would have been better pleased had their protégé shut himself up in serious preparation for the ordeal that awaited him —and them as his sponsors.

Gentlemen, calm yourselves ! Your orator, had he been the profoundest of philosophers, could not have hit upon a better method than the one he used. His facts were all in hand. His speech was in his mind and heart. What he needed was recreation, the husbanding of mental and moral vitality, until he could pour it out in the molten lava of volcanic speech. Those loiterings amused him, and kept his thoughts off of himself and the impending *début ;* no matter, therefore, about the annoyance of the committee—they were not to lose or save the day.

Exeter Hall, where Mr. Gough had consented to begin his English work, was the headquarters of philanthropy in Great Britain. It occupied in London

the position held in Boston by Faneuil Hall. The
foremost orators of the Anglo-Saxon race in the nineteenth century had taught its echoes the sweetest of
all music—eloquent human speech. Here Brougham,
Canning, George Thompson, Henry Vincent, Daniel
O'Connell, and John Bright, had addressed popular
parliaments, to whose behests the official assembly
yonder in Westminster had been compelled to bow.
The air of the place was suggestive of the loftiest
names and aims in contemporaneous history—would
stifle a small man and inspire a great one.

Exeter Hall stands on the Strand, is entered through
a spacious door, beyond which a wide stairway leads
into the auditorium, where 3,000 people may be comfortably seated. On that 2d day of August, 1853,
the crowd began to gather as early as 4 o'clock P.M.
At 6 o'clock the doors were opened ; the hall was
filled in five minutes. At 8 o'clock, when the meeting
began, thousands were being turned away.

It was what the journals called a "respectable"
audience—meaning by that term that it was composed of prominent and influential men and women
—and this although London in August is as empty
of the "respectable" classes as any great American
city would be at the same season. Many had come
into town for the occasion. Representatives of the
best brain and heart of Great Britain were in the
seats and on the platform. The skill and success of the Executive Committee as advertisers
were abundantly vindicated. Now how about the
orator ?

J. S. Buckingham, the president of the League, was
in the chair. As the speaker came forward he was

received with a tumult of cheers—which Gough said
"took his breath away." He adds:

"While Mr. Buckingham was making the introductory
speech I reasoned within myself · 'Here are 3,000 men and
women wrought up to excitement and surely doomed to disappointment. They expect a flight of sky-rockets, and I cannot
provide it. No man can address an audience like this successfully while in such a state. Something must be done.' When
I was introduced I began to speak very tamely, knowing that
unless they were let down no living man could speak up to
their enthusiasm for an hour and a half ; so I continued in that
vein until I saw the enthusiasm fade away into disappointment.
Then I heard one on the platform groan audibly 'Ah!—h—h!'
another sighed loud enough to be heard—'This'll never do for
London.' Then I commenced in real earnest, laid hold of my
theme, and did the best I could." [1]

'Tis interesting to compare Mr. Gough's account
with the utterances of other competent judges. The
Rev. Dr. Campbell, the leading nonconformist of the
day, declares :

"Great as had been the expectations, Mr. Gough surpassed
them all. The vast multitude he swayed as with an enchanter's
wand. As he willed, it was moved to laughter or melted into
tears."

Newman Hall, who sat on the platform, a close
observer, said :

"Demosthenes could not have done more."

The newspapers the next morning devoted pages
to the speaker and the speech. As fair specimens of

---

[1] "Autobiography," p. 286.

these descriptions, we quote two—the first from the
British Banner :

"Mr. Gough is a well-adjusted mixture of the poet, orator,
and dramatist. His manner abounds in changes.   The absence of unmitigated vehemence is highly favorable to the
economy of strength, and a large measure of repose prevades
the whole exhibition.   Resting himself, he gives rest to his
audience, and hence both remain unwearied till the end. Mr.
Gough gave no signs of fatigue last night. At the close of
nearly an hour and forty minutes he seemed quite as fresh as
when he began, and quite capable of continuing till midnight,
cock-crowing, or morning! No heat even was apparent to
us; perspiration was out of the question; the handkerchief
was never, that we observed, once in requisition throughout
the whole of his surprising display. He resembled a clump of
Highland heather under the blaze of a burning sun—as dry as
powder! It is as natural to him to speak—and that on a scale
to be heard by the largest auditory—as to breathe. It ceases
now to be a matter of astonishment that he makes so little of
standing up to speak every night in succession, for weeks together, and traveling for that purpose one or more hundreds of
miles by day! There is an utter absence of all mental pertur-
bation; before he commences there seems no idea of his being
about to do anything at all extraordinary, or, when he has
finished, that anything extraordinary has been performed.   It
seems to be as much a matter of course as walking or running,
sitting down or rising up. His self-command is perfect, and
hence his control over an assembly is complete. Governing
himself, he easily governs all around him. It was impossible
for any man to have been more thoroughly at home than he was
last night. Like a well-bred man, once on his feet, there was
the absence alike of bashfulness and impudence.

"The address was entirely without order of any sort—nay,
for this the assembly was prepared at the outset by the inti-
mation that he had never written and never premeditated a
speech in his life! Last night the address was a succession of

pictures delivered in a manner the most natural, and hence, at one time, feeling was in the ascendency, and, at another, power. His gifts of mimicry seemed great; this perilous, though valuable faculty, however, was but sparingly exercised. It is only as the lightning, in a single flash, illumining all and gone, making way for the rolling peal and the falling torrent. Throughout the whole of last night he addressed himself to the fancy and to the heart. We cannot doubt, however, that Mr. Gough is in a very high degree capable of dealing with principles and of grappling with an adversary by way of argument, but he adopted a different, and, as we think, a much wiser course for a first appearance. The mode of address is one of which mankind will never tire till human nature becomes divested of its inherent properties. He recited a series of strikingly pertinent facts, all of which he set in beautiful pictures. Nothing could exceed the unity of the impression, while nothing could be more multifarious than the means employed to effect it. It was a species of mortar-firing, in which old nails, broken bottles, chips of iron, and bits of metal, together with balls of lead—anything, everything partaking of the nature of a missile—was available. The compound mass was showered forth with resistless might and powerful execution. The great idea, which was uppermost all the evening, was the evils of drinking; and, under a deep conviction of that truth, every man must have left the assembly.

"The conclusion to which we have come, then, is that the merits of Mr. Gough have been by no means overrated. In England he would take a stand quite as high as he has taken in the United States. There is no hazard now in saying that there will be no disappointment. He will nowhere fail to equal, if not to surpass, expectation; and his triumph will, among Englishmen, be all the more complete from the utter absence of all pretension. His air makes promise of nothing; and hence all that is given is so much above the contract. It is impossible to conceive of anything more entirely free from empiricism. From first to last it is nature acting in one of her favorite sons. Oratorically considered, he is never at fault. While the vocable pronunciation, with scarcely an exception, is perfect, the elocutionary element is in every way worthy of it. He is wholly free, on the one hand, from heavy monotony, and, on the other, from ranting declamation, properly so-called. There is no mouthing—no stilted shouting. His whole speaking was eminently true; there is nothing false either in tone or inflection; and the same remark applies to emphasis. All is truth; the result is undeviating pleasure and irresistible impression. His air is that of a man who never thought five minutes on the subject of public speaking; but who surrenders himself to the guidance of his genius, while he ofttimes snatches a grace beyond the reach of art.

" In Mr. Gough, however, there are far higher considerations than those of eloquence. We cannot close without adverting to the highest attribute of his speaking—it is prevaded by a spirit of religion. Not a word escapes him which is objectionable on that score. Other things being equal, this never fails to lift a speaker far above his fellows. In this respect, he is a pattern to temperance advocates. He did not, to be sure, preach Christianity; that was not his business; but the whole of his enchanting effusion was in harmony with its doctrines, always breathing its spirit, and occasionally paying it a natural and graceful tribute. At the close, in particular, that was strongly marked. He there stated that the temperance cause was the offspring of the Christian Church, adding that whatever was such was in its own nature immortal, and thence predicting the ultimate triumph of the cause in which he was embarked."

Our second extract is from the *Weekly News*, and is an equally excellent pen-portrait of the man and analysis of his power :

" He is dressed in sober black; his hair is dark, and so is his face; but there is a muscular vigor in his frame, for which we were not prepared. We should judge Gough has a large share of the true *elixir vitæ*—animal spirits. His voice is one

of great power and pathos, and he speaks without an effort.
The first sentence, as it falls gently and easily from his lips,
tells us that Gough has that true oratorical power which neither
money, nor industry, nor persevering study can ever win.
Like the poet, the orator must be born.   You may take a man
six feet high, he shall be good-looking, have a good voice, and
speak English with a correct pronunciation; you shall write
for that man a splendid speech, you shall have him taught elocution by Mr. Webster—and yet you shall no more make that
man an orator than, to use a homely phrase, you can 'make a
silk purse out of a sow's ear.' Gough is an orator born. Pope
tells us he 'lisped in numbers,' and in his boyhood Gough
must have had the true tones of the orator on his tongue.
There was no effort—no fluster—all was easy and natural. He
was speaking for the first time to a public meeting in his native
land—speaking to thousands, who had come with the highest
expectations, who expected much and required much—speaking by means of the press to the whole British public.   Under
such circumstances, occasional nervousness would have been
pardonable; but, from the first, Gough was perfectly self-
possessed.   There are some men who have prodigious advantages on account of appearance alone. We think it was Fox
who said, it was impossible for any one to *be* as wise as Thurlow
looked.   The great Lord Chatham was particularly favored by
nature in this respect.   In our own time. in the case of Lord
Denman, we have seen how much can be done by means of a
portly presence and a stately air.   Gough has nothing of this.
He is just as plain a personage as George Dawson, of Birming-
ham, would be, if he were to cut his hair and shave off his
mustache.   But though we have named George Dawson,
Gough does not speak like him, or any other living man.
Gough is no servile copy, but a real original. We have no one
in England we can compare him to. He seems to speak by
inspiration—as the apostles spoke, who were commanded not
to think beforehand what they should say.   The spoken word
seems to come naturally—as air bubbles up from the bottom
of the well. In what he said there was nothing new--there

could be nothing new—the tale he told was old as the hills; yet as he spoke an immense audience grew hushed and still, and hearts were melted, and tears glistened in female eyes, and that great human mass became knit together by a common spell. Disraeli says, 'Sir Robert Peel played upon the House of Commons as an old fiddle.' Gough did the same at Exeter Hall. At his bidding, stern, strong men, as well as sensitive women, wept or laughed—they swelled with indignation or desire. Of the various chords of human passion he was master. At times he became roused, and we thought how—

> " ' In his ire Olympian Pericles
> Thundered and lightened, and all Hellas shook.'

" At other times, in his delineation of American manners, he proved himself almost an equal of Silsbee. Off the stage we have nowhere seen a better mimic than Gough; and this must give him great power, especially in circles where the stage is as much a *terra incognita*, as Utopia, or the Island of Laputa itself. We have always thought that a fine figure of Byron, where he tells us that he laid his hand upon the ocean's mane. Something of the same kind might be said to be applicable to Mr. Gough; he seemed to ride upon the audience—to have mastered it completely to his will. He seemed to bestride it, as we could imagine Alexander bestriding Bucephalus.

" Gough spoke for nearly two hours. Evidently the audience could have listened, had he gone on till midnight. We often hear that the age of oratory has gone by, that the press supersedes the tongue, that the appeal must henceforth be made to the reader in his study, not to the hearer in the crowded hall. There is much truth in that; nevertheless, the true orator will always please his audience, and true oratory will never die."

It is evident that the excursion of John Gough, on the top of the omnibus, his flirtations with Punch and Judy, and his boyish delight in it all, did not destroy his chances on that Tuesday night in Exeter Hall.

We say to the apprehensive gentlemen of the Executive Committee, as Deacon Grant did to Mr. Gough on the occasion referred to in a prior page—

"Don't you ever scare us so again!"

"HOW DEAR TO MY HEART ARE THE SCENES OF MY CHILDHOOD."

THREE more monster meetings in London were addressed by Mr. Gough, another in Exeter Hall, and two in Whittington Club-Room, ere he entered the "provinces," as the the regions outside of the metropolis are indiscriminately named by our English cousins.

London is England; Paris is France; Berlin is Germany; Vienna is Austria. There is no city in this country which dominates America. New York is the financial center; and a New York reputation in art or literature, is an "open sesame" across the continent. But great names are made without the indorsement of Manhattan Island. Gough himself is a case in point. Indeed, only one illustrious American speaker of the past generation had any connection with New York (Henry Ward Beecher),—and he preached in Brooklyn.

Mr. Gough's London *début* preannounced him everywhere. Like Byron, he awoke to find himself famous, on the morning after that event. Traveling towards Scotland, he spoke at various places *en route*, and at Galashiels, in the neighborhood of Melrose and Abbotsford, faced his first audience of Scotsmen, after the lecture eating salmon "caught in the Tweed," and hearing "Burns's songs sung in the pure Scotch dialect." At Glasgow he spoke to thousands in the City Hall. It was not until the 1st of September, that he appeared before the people of Edinburgh. Here he had an ovation, and the visit was memorably punctuated by the presence of Dr. Guthrie, Professor Miller, and a host of celebrities—his firm friends for ever after.

This taste of Scotland taught the orator, spite of his dismal forebodings, that human nature is much the same in all lands, with due allowance for superficial differences produced by local causes; and that the English and Scotch, notwithstanding their supposed predilection for argument, take kindly and respond readily to men of the emotional and pictorial school.

Encouraged by this discovery, Mr. Gough, took the train at Edinburgh for Liverpool, where he passed a few charming days with Mr. Harrison, the gentleman who met him on the tug upon his arrival from America. Thence he went to. London, to attend a temperance *fête* in Surrey Gardens, and addressed 17,000 people—his largest audience up to that date.

The last week in September, he had so far filled his engagements that he felt at liberty to claim and enjoy that long-anticipated visit to Sandgate—"dear Sandgate, down in Kent." This grown-up boy entered it on top of one of those "Valyer" 'buses which had been the awe of his childhood, found in the driver one of his mother's former scholars, rode through the long street in a fever of excitement, as he read the familiar, Dickensesque names on the signs, just as he

remembered them a quarter of a century earlier,—
" Jimmy Bugg, the cobbler; Reynolds, the baker;
Draynor, the fishmonger,"—scarcely a noticeable
change in the whole drowsy stretch.

Best of all, *he* was remembered—and his *mother*, as
a kind of local divinity. The old friends and play-
mates of the past could not greet him warmly enough
to satisfy their good hearts, though they hugged and
kissed him—Mrs. Beatty, in particular, a dear old soul
who had comforted " Johnny " with milk and ginger-
bread on the eve of emigration. Five never to-be-for-
gotten days " Johnny " Gough, as they persisted in
calling him, spent among these humble folk and
homely scenes. He ransacked the house where he
was born from cellar to garret (an easy task)—found
the very nail on which he used to hang his coat and
hat—hobnobbed with the keeper of Sandgate Castle
now quite decrepit—roamed through the town and
over the hills to explore anew the haunts of boyhood
—walked to Folkestone, along the road by the " sad
sea waves," to look at the building where he had received his only schooling (but it was gone !)—got out
of the present and into the past, as an imaginative
and poetic nature could do without an effort—and
felt a mighty aching sense of grief at the thought of
the pauper grave in which *she* lay with whose memory
all these well-remembered scenes were so indissolubly
associated.

Soon he was joined by a party of notabilities from
London and elsewhere, to whom he pointed out these
same homely scenes and introduced these same
humble folk. His father, who had followed him from
America, was with him—which further helped to

complete the illusion and enchant the years out of to-
day and into yesterday. And his friend, Cruikshank,
mightily interested, and quite at home in such surroundings, sketched Gough's birthplace, and repro-
duced the landscape, as an artist might, in many
portfolio studies.

Mr. Gough's pride in his birthplace and fond remembrance of his boyhood friends, lowly though they
were, is not the least praiseworthy of his traits. Remember, he was in England—the home of snobbery.
He was famous—but near enough to the time " when
days were dark and friends were few," to be sensitive
on the subject. Here he stood, the admired center
of a circle of flatterers. One whose manliness was of
less fine fiber would have concealed those bygone
experiences, spoken little of Sandgate, and gone
thither, if he went at all, alone. This whole episode
stirs affection for this man, and reveals his moral
altitude.

But how proud the Sandgaters were of " Johnny "
Gough ! How they thronged over to attend his lecture at Folkestone ! How they laughed at his wit
and cried at his pathos ! What a great man he was
—as they always knew he would be !

This happening was an idyll in their lives and in
his life. And Mrs. Beatty ! Mr. Gough gave *her* on
the spot a crisp, new five-pound note—$25—in part
payment for the milk (of human kindness) and ginger-
bread (of affection) which she had given *him* so long
ago ; an amount which he never failed to send her
while she lived, at Christmas, in annual installments
on account of the " debt."

III.

HERE, THERE, AND YONDER IN THE BRITISH ISLES.

Upon the termination of his six weeks' engagement with the League, Mr. Gough was induced to sign a new contract, he agreeing to deliver two hundred lectures, commencing in London on the 3d of October; and they stipulating to pay him at the rate of ten guineas—about $50—a lecture and all expenses—the best terms he had made thus far. This programme disarranged his American plans; but he wrote home canceling all outstanding dates, and prepared to give twelve months to temperance in the British Isles. "You must remember, Mr. Gough," his friends said to him, "that you owe something to your native country." This argument, coupled wth the fact that he was accomplishing wonders, persuaded him, at the conclusion of this first year, to add another on the same terms ; so that his contemplated summer outing in 1853, grew into an absence of two years.

It is not easy work to give two hundred lectures in a year. It means the fatigue and exposure of constant travel, and the excitement and reaction of the platform four or five nights in every week until the advent of warm weather ends the professional season. In Mr. Gough's case there was the added strain of speaking always and everywhere on one subject—

in some instances scores and scores of times in one place and the same hall. The quality of his physical and mental constitution is shown by his endurance.

Nor did this professional talker merely talk. While his nights were given to the platform, his days were given to hand-to-hand work among the intemperate, He was a great believer in contact—in the gospel of hand-shaking. In almost every place he visited there was some hard case—too hard for local treatment ; and so this expert was called in for consultation. Thus his faculties were kept in perpetual tension.

Aside from the good he did to others in these daily excursions to seek and save, Mr. Gough aided himself. For he was ever enlarging his experiences, and always adding to his stock of incidents, comic and tragic ; and was thus enabled to work into his addresses fresh material which kept them up to date, and imparted to each a local flavor.

In referring to his labors in the homes of the intemperate, Mr. Gough says :

"I know the term 'brute' is often used in reference to drunkards, but they are not brutes—they are men—debased, brutalized, if you will ; but strip from them the influence of drink, and we find them men, in many cases with hearts as warm, feelings as tender, and sensibilities as keen as others possess. Dickens says of *Mrs. Todgers*, ' She was a hard woman, yet in her heart, away up a great many stairs, there was a door, and on that door was written, *woman.*' So in the heart of many a drunkard, away up a great many stairs, in a remote corner easily passed, there is a door. Tap on it gently, again and again—persevere ; remember Him who knocks at the door of your heart waiting for an answer till ' His locks are wet with the dew '—and be patient ; tap on, lovingly, gently, and the quivering lips and the starting tear will tell you you have been knocking at a man's heart, not a brute's. This power of drink to drain and dry up the fountain of love and affection in the heart is one of the reasons why we should hate it." [1]

In illustration of this truth, he tells this story :

"A man came to me at Covent Garden and said:

"'Mr. Gough, I want you to come into my place of business.'

"'I'm in a little hurry now,' I replied.

"'You *must* come into my place of business.'

"So when he got me there—into a large fruit-store, where he was doing business to the amount of two hundred and fifty or three hundred pounds ($1,250 or $1,500) a week,—he caught me by the hand and said:

"'God bless you, sir!'

"'What for?'

"'I heard you in Exeter Hall a year and a half ago, and signed the pledge. I was a brute.'

"'No, you were not.'

"'Well, I was worse.'

"'No, you were not.'

"'Well, I was as bad as I could be. Look at that cellar! I spent a whole Sunday in that cellar on a heap of rotten vegetables with a rope to hang myself by! Now sir, I lease that cellar and clear a hundred pounds a year. God bless you sir! See what a business I'm doing. Look here! See that woman in the corner? She's my wife. La! how I have knocked her about. Would you go and shake hands with her?'

"'I've no objection.'

"'Do, sir.'

"'I went up to her and offered my hand. She held back, and said, 'My fingers are so sticky with the fruit, sir.'

"'La!' said the husband, 'Mr. Gough don't mind sticky fingers.'

"'No, sir,' and I shook hands with her. Our fingers stuck

---

[1] "Autobiography," pp. 262, 263.

together! They were stickier than I expected. Again the man said:

"'God bless you sir! I wish to give you something. Do you like oranges?'

"'Sometimes.'

"He went to a shelf that was full of them, and began to fill a great bag.

"'That's enough,' I said.

"But he paid no attention, and went on filling the bag. Then he put it in my arms, and said:

"'There! Don't say a word; but go along. God bless you!'

"I had positively to hire a cab to take me home." [1]

As showing the redemptive power of temperance, and the significance of turning-points, he relates this incident:

"I had just spoken in the City Hall of Glasgow to 2,500 people. I was staying at the house of one of the merchant princes of that city, and when we came down stairs from the Hall his carriage was at the door—silver-mounted harness, coachman in livery, footman in plain clothes. You know it is seldom teetotalist lecturers ride in such style, and it is proper, therefore, that we should speak of it when it does happen, for the good of the cause. On reaching the pavement, the merchant said: 'It is so drizzly and cold you had better get into the carriage, and wait there until the ladies come down." I think I never had so many persons to shake hands with me as I did that night. 'You saved my father!' said one. 'You saved my brother!' said another, and a third said: 'I owe everything I am to you!' My hands absolutely ached as they grasped them one after another.

"Finally, a poor wretched creature came to the door of the carriage. I saw his bare shoulder and naked feet; his hair seemed grayer than mine. He came up, and said:

---

[1] Speech on "Drinking Usages of Society," pub. by Mass. Tem. Soc'y, 1861.

"' Will you shake hands with me ? '

"I put my hand into his hot, burning palm, and he said, 'Don't you know me ?'

"' Why,' said I, 'isn't your name Aiken ?'

"' Yes.'

"' Harry Aiken ?'

"' Yes.'

"' You worked with me in the bookbinder's shop of Andrew Hutchinson, in Worcester, Massachusetts, in 1842, didn't you ?'

"' Yes.'

"' What is the matter with you ?'

"' I am desperately poor.'

" I said, 'God pity you ; you look like it !'

" I gave him something, and obtained the services of Mr. Marr, the secretary of the Scottish League, to find out about him. He picks up rags and bones in the streets of Glasgow, and resides in a kennel in one of the foulest streets of that city. When the ladies came to the carriage and got in, I said, 'Stop, don't shut that door ! Look there at that half-starved, ragged, miserable wretch, shivering in the cold and in the dim gas-light ! Look at him !' The ring of that audience was in my ears, my hands aching with the grasp of friendship from scores, my surroundings bright, my prospects pleasant, and I said, 'Ladies, look there ! *There am I, but for the temperance movement!* That man worked with me, roomed with me, slept with me, was a better workman than I, his prospects brighter than mine. A kind hand was laid on my shoulder, in the Worcester street, in 1842; it was the turning-point in my history. He went on. Seventeen years have passed, and we meet again, with a gulf as deep as hell between us !' I am a trophy of this movement, and I thank God for it." [1]

Mr. Gough spoke in all the more important towns in England and Scotland; he and Mary putting such intervals of leisure as they had into sight-seeing.

---

[1] Speech on " Drinking Usages of Society."

Temperance in Great Britain, in 1853-4, was where it had been in America when Gough signed the pledge. Drinking was fashionable. Total abstinence was fanaticism. The Churches, as a rule, were on the wrong side. The clergy defended drinking out of the Bible. It was impossible to get churches to lecture in, or clergymen of repute to preside at temperance meetings. Oftener than otherwise, those who entertained Mr. Gough had liquor on the table, or if not, bunglingly apologized to the other guests for its absence as due to his "prejudice." There were many splendid exponents of the cause, like John Bright and Joseph Sturge and the Earl of Shaftesbury. But, though many by actual count, they were relatively few. Temperance sentiment was confined to the middle classes—the upper and lower ignored it.

The pledge, the great weapon of the temperance movement, was sharply and constantly attacked as "unmanly"—"a strait-jacket"—"fatal to self-respect"—and "destructive to character."

It was easy to show that the temperance pledge rests upon precisely the same philosophical basis as any and every other sacred promise—that all the transactions of civil society rest ultimately upon a pledge. In marriage the bride and groom promise to love, cherish, and honor one another—a pledge. On uniting with the Church the member enters into a covenant—a pledge. When he goes on the stand a witness in court swears to tell the truth—a pledge The grantor in a deed pledges himself by record. The funds of universities and libraries and charitable organizations are held under a pledge—a solemn promise to administer them in certain designated

11

ways. Do pledges of these kinds undermine character? If not, then why does a pledge to abstain from the use of intoxicating liquor as a beverage? Instead of undermining character, it rebuilds it and fortifies it, as hundreds of thousands can testify—reconstructs it as Nehemiah did the ruined walls of Jerusalem, in spite of the scoffs of Tobiah and Sanballat.

Mr. Gough thought the temperance cause at that time better organized in Great Britain than in America, and believed it to be on a more permanent basis. With reference to the societies then existing, he remarks:

"No one who attends their annual meetings, their festivals, their weekly assemblies,—can fail to be impressed by their earnestness, and I may say their pertinacity in carrying out the objects for which they are organized. Their boards of managers and standing committees are thorough, working men, who not only sympathize with temperance, but make it a special business to attend to the interests of the movement. I have been edified by the earnestness manifested at their business meetings, when I was privileged to attend them, and the carefulness with which they deal with minute details, as well as the broader operations of their societies,—the patience with which they master difficulties, and their self-denying efforts to achieve the greatest good effectually. There is, to be sure, some formality in the proceedings—especially in their public meetings—strange to us in America, and to some annoying; yet even this has its advantages; they make the business a serious and earnest one, and the very formality, in a certain sense, gives the proceedings a greater stability than if their arrangements were all carried on at loose ends." [1]

---

[1] "Autobiography," pp. 331, 332.

The sojourner was charmed with the hospitality of the people.   He got an inside view of their domestic life, warm, pure, sweet ; and discovered that they could not do enough for those whom they admitted to their firesides.   The very children were kindly. He says :

"One day, when strolling through Edinburgh, I saw a group of young girls standing in front of their school in the Canongate, looking toward me on the opposite side of the street. Soon they crossed and walked near me.   One of them said very modestly :

"'Mr. Gough ha'e ye ony objection to us lassies walking wi' ye ?'

"'Oh, no,' I responded, 'indeed I have not.'

"'We've heerd ye speak in the Music Hall, an' we're a' teetotalers.'

"Presently they reached the hotel where Mr. Gough was quartered.   Here one said :

"'We'll ye ha'e ony objections to shakin' hands wi' us lassies ?'

"As I took their hands, I heard in that sweet, low Scotch tone :

"'Ye'll soon be gangin' awa' frae Edinburgh, and we'll *weary* for ye to come back again.   Gude-bye to ye.'"[1]

Opportunities for special work sometimes presented themselves—as in addressing children, ladies, soldiers, and students—all eagerly embraced.   In the gray and mossy old university town of Oxford, the speaker had a sharp bout with the students who thronged the hall, and who came for fun.   For a time he was hard pushed ; but eventually he conquered them by his good humor and evident enjoyment of the racket—

----

[1] "Autobiography," pp. 335, 336.

they let him conclude in peace. A farewell *fête* was held in honor of Mr. Gough, in the grounds of the historic " Hartwell House," near London, on the 25th of July, 1855. The enthusiam was great, the sorrow over his impending departure was loud, and the temperance leaders and masses were assembled in vast numbers—Horace Greeley (then in Europe) being present as an invited guest. Good-bye speeches were made and suitably answered ; and, loaded down with a massive dinner-service for eighteen of pure silver, presented at the *fête*, and with numerous other souvenirs—Bibles, silver ink-stands, superb clocks, silver pitchers ; each one significant of some particular experience ; the spoils, not of war but of love—John and Mary Gough embarked for home in August, 1855.

It was the testimony of all that Mr. Gough's presence and advocacy had set the temperance reform forward in Great Britain beyond precedent. As for himself, we quote and adopt the language of Lyman Abbott :

" We doubt whether modern history records any case of an oratorical triumph more continuous and more extraordinary. Whitefield had the many-sided subject of religion, Mr. Gough but the one theme of temperance. Mr. Beecher's famous English speeches during the Civil War are unparalleled in the history of oratory ; but these were but six, and Mr. Gough spoke almost continuously for two years " [1]—between four and five hundred times in all ! And the eagerness to hear him was greater at the close than at the start. He only got away at last by promising to re-

---

[1] Introduction to " Platform Echoes."

turn again in two years for another long campaign in the British Isles.

Notwithstanding these unprecedented labors, and the exposure and excitement accompanying them, his health was good—better when he sailed for home than when he went out.

PART VII.

At Work in America Again

"Look up, not down; look out, not in;
and — lend a hand!"
— EDWARD EVERETT HALE.

I.

DEAR "Hillside!" how good it seemed to this "absentee landlord" to be at home again. Even the "Yankee twang" and the familiar "I guess," and "wal" were like the tones of old friends. Six restful weeks were passed in the lap of idleness. Then the trumpet sounded for battle, and the fray began.

Mr. Gough's British reputation, reëchoed to America. His services were in greater demand than ever. Each mail brought him urgent invitations from all quarters. He had never visited the great Northwest. He determined to do so now, the way having opened. At Philadelphia, on the 4th of October, 1855, he opened the season. That month was devoted for the most part to the State of New York. November was given to New England. On the 7th of December, he spoke. in Chicago, for the first time.

The census now shows a population of 1,600,000 in Chicago. The giant is 25 miles tall (along the lake, from north to south), with a depth of chest 10 miles deep (from the lake westward). Its head is cooled by the breezes of the north, charged with ozone. Its feet are planted broad and flat on the prairies, to the south. Its hands are busy with multifarious commercial manipulations. Its pockets are stuffed with merchandise, and its cheek is — words fail!

With prophetic vision, Mr. Gough foresaw the future in the past. Writing from Chicago at the date referred to, he said : " I found a population of more than 100,000; I have often wished that I could have labored there, and been identified, by my work, with the infancy of what is destined to be a giant among the cities of the world."

In the same connection he writes :

" This being my first view of the Northwest, my impressions were those of wonder, almost amounting to awe, at the vast resources and the certain improvement and power of that section. I leave it for others, who are able to write of its destiny; prophets all, and true, when they tell of its progress and swift-coming magnificence—for it grows before our eyes almost passing belief, and will grow year by year. Every Christian must look at the West with interest and deep anxiety for the enlightenment of the Western mind, and the establishment of the principles of a pure Christianity. West of the Mississippi what a domain is rapidly coming into settlement and cultivation! What millions must soon occupy the vast territory ! It is for Christians to decide whether these fertile lands shall be over-run with heathenism and infidelity, or be flooded with the light of Christian education. The field is immense—the opposing elements to good are powerful, the god of this world is marshaling his forces to ' go up and possess the land.' But if all who love righteousness will in Christ's name set up their banners, and come to the ' help of the Lord against the mighty,' the issues of the conflict are sure ; for ' greater is He that is for us than all they that be against us.' We may thus coöperate with God and holy angels in preventing sin, and in establishing His Kingdom in this great gathering-place of the nations. Men and women are laboring for this, full of faith. May our God speed their efforts !"[1]

---

[1] " Autobiography," pp. 382, 383.

Mr. Gough gave seven lectures in Chicago ; one each in Elgin, Milwaukee, Waukegan, Bloomington, Springfield, Alton; and then took the cars for St. Louis (also a first visit), where he lectured six times.

Returning to the East, he resumed work in New York, New Jersey, Connecticut, Rhode Island, New Hampshire, and Maine, besides speaking in all the large cities of the Atlantic seaboard. It was not until June 2d that he unbuckled the harness to enjoy a well-earned vacation at " Hillside."

When at home Mr. Gough usually attended church at Boylston. Worcester was conveniently near, but he felt that Boylston needed him. During the summer of 1855, the church there was without a pastor. He acted, *ad interim*, as pulpit supply, Sunday-school superintendent, sexton, and parson. Calling to his aid influential clerical friends, he agreed to "board and lodge them" if they would preach on designated Sundays. These offers were accepted, and Dr. Kirk (his Boston pastor), Dr. T. L. Cuyler, Dr. Dutton, and Dr. George Gould were successively heard in the Boylston pulpit. Between himself and Dr. Gould an intimacy sprang up like that between David and Jonathan—they were inseparable. A revival marked these Boylston labors, and the feeble country church was recruited and refreshed.

The idleness of an earnest man is fruitful. Rest comes from change. Mr. Gough, like Wesley, was " always at it."

II.

DURING the decade of 1855–65, in the United States, temperance touched the low-water mark. The tide was out—away out. Those Southern States which, a few years earlier, had adopted prohibition, seceded. In Maine itself the law, immortalized by its name, was repealed (in 1856), and superseded by license— as old as history, and as infirm as its age would indicate! The five other New England States retained the statute, but indifferently and spasmodically enforced it. In New York, rum-made and rum-paid judges declared the prohibitory law unconstitutional, and thus made dram-selling and drunkenness legal and equitable. This was the epoch of reaction.

There were three causes. For one thing, "no special moral reform agitation," as a philosophical observer remarks, "can be kept alive for an indefinite period. The public weary of it. They will not go to hear repeated for the fortieth time arguments whose conclusions they anticipate before they enter the hall, or experiences portrayed with which lectures and literature have already made them familiar."

In the next place, this inevitable falling away of interest seriously affected the temperance propaganda.

Public opinion was not made and inflamed as at the start.

Thirdly, and most important of all, the country was now preoccupied with another issue—newer—more angry—involving sectional feeling, interest, power—more clamorous—more hysterical, viz., the question of slavery, soon transferred from the forum to the battle-field, and debated with cannon-balls and grape-shot and bayonet charges for arguments; and with wounds, suffering, and death for practical applications, rhetorical pauses, and punctuation marks. The constitution of the human mind is such that it is impossible to interest it equally and contemporaneously in two exciting and absorbing questions. The present was what Wendell Phillips called "the negro's hour." Temperance was temporarily crowded into the background. The Civil War, in preparation or in operation, concentrated the thoughts and energies of the continent upon itself.

Mr. Gough was a close and accurate observer, as we have discovered. He was in constant motion, so that he knew the condition of affairs not only in localities but throughout the Union. And he was in close touch with prominent men everywhere—the men who make and reflect popular sentiment. Of course, such a man would speedily detect this lukewarmness, affecting as it did the cause to which his life was devoted, and visible as it was across the whole field of action. His spirit was apprehensive. His heart was heavy. He regretted his impending departure, feeling that he was needed at home. But he had signed an agreement before leaving for America to return to Great Britain in two years and give three years to the cause over there on the same terms as in 1853-4-5. His engagements were with the London Temperance League, and the Scottish Temperance League. The headquarters of the first were in London; of the second in Glasgow. But before Mr. Gough's second visit, the two were consolidated in " The National and Scottish Temperance League" (in 1856).

At this juncture, Neal Dow, the author of the Maine Law, one of the historic names of the nineteenth century, went to England to labor for prohibition in connection with the " United Kingdom Alliance," which was organized, in 1853, " to promote the total and immediate legislative suppression of the traffic in all intoxicating liquors as beverages." With this programme, Mr. Dow was in full accord. He was identified with it in and through the Maine Law; which prohibited the manufacture and sale of intoxicating liquor, except by specially appointed or permitted agents, selling for excepted purposes only, with provision for search, seizure, and forfeiture of liquors kept for illegal disposition.

When Mr. Gough heard that Neal Dow was going abroad in 1856, he said:

" I am sorry he is going this year, for I earnestly desire that his work there may be successful, and the English critics who are opposed to the law will say he has come to represent a failure, for the law is not now on the statute-books of his own State. If he would wait till it shall be reënacted with more stringent provisions, as it is sure to be, then, on the wave of a glorious success, his mission there would be doubly effective in aiding the friends to establish prohibition in Great Britain." [1]

---

[1] " Autobiography," p. 393.

On the 23d of March, 1856, Mr. Gough wrote to his friend G. C. Campbell in England:

"The cause in this country is in a depressed state; the Maine Law is a dead letter everywhere—more liquor sold than I ever knew before, in Massachusetts,—and in other States it is about as bad. Were it not that I feel desirous of laboring with you again, I should be inclined to ask for the loan of another year to labor here. I never had so many earnest applications for labor, and the field is truly ready,—not for the sickle, but for steady, persevering tillage; but we shall leave our dear home in July, with the expectation of laboring with you, as far as health and strength will permit, for the next three years. . . . I see Neal Dow is in England. I am glad. You will all like him; he is a noble man—a faithful worker. He can tell better than any other man, the state of the Maine-Law movement here, and the cause of the universal failure of the law to produce the desired results."[1]

This was a personal letter, not intended for publication. But as it recited certain facts which were of public concern, Mr. Campbell naturally and properly published it. Knowing the heated state of feeling existing at the time between the moral-suasion and the Maine-Law wings of the temperance forces, here and abroad, Mr. Gough regretted the publication, and remarked to his wife, when she showed him a copy of the British *Weekly Record* containing it. "I can see how it may make trouble, but I hope it will not."[2]

This hope was not fulfilled. It did make trouble, with a vengeance. The temperance press of Great Britain at once took sides. The American reformer was attacked with surprising bitterness, with per-

---

[1] "Autobiography," p. 392. [2] "Autobiography," p. 394.

sonal malignity, for this expression of opinion. He was defended with equal warmth. And that saddest of all controversies, one between co-laborers in a common cause, but divided into warring camps by differences regarding facts or methods—clawed and clamored, as though bedlam had broken loose. It was charged that Mr. Gough was "reckless"—that he was "prone to sweeping exaggerations"—that he was "not an honest prohibitionist nor an honest man"—that he was "subject to fits of the 'blues,' and had written this letter while under the influence of this malady"—that he "still drank, and took narcotics"—and so on to the end of a devil's chapter of rancor.

As he moved about the country, the lecturer took care to collect facts which corroborated his statements. These he forwarded to his friends and defenders in Britain—thus adding fuel to the fire.

The winter of 1856–57 he passed in the West. He spoke many times in many places—Chicago, Indianapolis, Cincinnati, Cleveland, Columbus, among the rest. In the spring of 1857, a farewell trip was taken. Great assemblies everywhere rallied to say "Good bye," notably at Philadelphia, in the Academy of Music, on the 21st of May, and at New Haven a month later. These were attended by the best and most representative men and women. On the 2d of July, a farewell picnic was held in a grove near "Hillside," where and when neighbors said, *bon voyage.* On the 9th inst., Mr. and Mrs. Gough sailed from Boston, in the *Niagara,* accompanied by a party of intimates, including Dr. Gould—to be gone three years.

PART VIII.

The Second British Tour

" A good conscience is to the soul what health
is to the body : it preserves a constant ease
and serenity within us, and more than counter-
vails all the calamities and afflictions which
can possibly befall us. I know nothing so
hard for a generous mind to get over as cal-
umny and reproach, and cannot find any
method of quieting the soul under them,
besides this single one, of our being conscious
to ourselves that we do not deserve them."
—ADDISON, *The Guardian*, No. 135.

12

I.

THE *Niagara* dropped anchor in the Mersey on the 26th of July, 1857. The "Yankees" were met and escorted ashore by a large party of waiting well-wishers, who saw their guests comfortably bestowed before they withdrew.

Mr. Gough instantly found himself the movable center of a circumference of personal detraction. Whenever, wherever he moved, it moved. Across the blazing borders of it he could not leap. All that was weak in his intemperate past was deepened into wickedness; all that was wicked was exaggerated into unpardonable sin. His reformation was denied. It was charged that he was worse now than then; for now he was a sinner masquerading as a saint.

All these reproaches came from the Pandora's box of that unfortunate letter to Mr. Campbell. The legal-suasian party in Great Britain chose to interpret the innocent missive as an affront to their policy. The orator was under contract to serve the interests of the moral suasionists—which added to the offense, since his popularity gave prestige to their rivals. The ill will and bad blood between the two temperance camps amazes the observer who looks back from the serene heights of distance and time. But it is clear

that a determined effort was made to blacken the
character and thus destroy the influence of John B.
Gough in the first year of his second British tour—
all on account of his identification with one of the
two then opposing schools of temperance thought and
action.

No, not *all* on this account: because personal
jealousies and petty spites, born of unsuccessful competition played a part in the farce-tragedy.

Or the day after landing in Liverpool, Mr. Gough
addressed a large meeting in Queen Street Hall.
He spoke nearly three hours, and in a vein of unusual
seriousness and philosophy. Replying to the current
criticism, he protested against the vituperation he
had received because of the expression of his opinion;
confirmed that opinion by documentary evidence;
paid a feeling tribute to "his noble friend and
coadjutor," Neal Dow, and expressed a hope that the
war between friends might stop—or be transferred
into the country of the common foe. A resolution
was passed, with substantial unanimity, at the close
of these remarks, expressing satisfaction with Mr.
Gough's statement and confidence in his character.
With this resolution in his pocket, and the contro-
versy quieted (as he hoped), he went up to London,
and took possession of his old quarters, at No. 32
Norfolk street, Strand, down by the Thames Embank-
ment, in one of the busiest parts of the city. His
engagements called for four months' work in Scotland and eight in England for three years. But a
week or more was given to breakfasts and *fêtes* before
the campaign opened.

George Cruikshank entertained the American on

one of these occasions. George had a brother Robert, also an artist, so that the two were often confused. At about the time of this visit an English review had discussed the relative merits of the two brothers, reaching the conclusion (which posterity has also come to) that "George was the real Simon Pure." Soon after, a German wrote a sketch of George Cruikshank for a German encyclopædia, in which he informed his readers that the subject of the memoir was an artist whose real name was Simon Pure, and in the index he wrote : " Pure, Simon—the real name of George Cruikshank." Mr. Gough never tired of laughing with and at his friend over this mistake, nor of telling the story on both sides of the Atlantic.

On the 25th of August, Exeter Hall again welcomed the "Yankee "—as he had been dubbed by his enemies, with a view, no doubt, to enlist national prejudice against the too-popular English-American. Thence, *via* Manchester and Preston, where large meetings were held, the travelers journeyed to Edinburgh.

Here a flat was rented; because the Goughs desired at least the semblance of a home while sojourning in " the land o' cakes an' ale." From this convenient center, they circled out through Scotland, making their orbit take in the Orkney Islands—treeless, windswept, barren, cold, shrouded in mist of heaven and mist of sea.

In January, 1858, they removed to London and began the English itinerary. They did in the South as they had done in the North—rented furnished apartments, and played at keeping house. Up and down, went the lecturer, informing and reforming multitudes, his comings and goings like a royal progress.

But during all these months the pitiless deluge of slander continued to beat down upon him; compared with this, the American abuse was as a passing summer shower in contrast with the rainy season in the tropics.

While in Scotland, an English associate, Mr. William Wilson, of Sherwood Hall, wrote Mr. Gough, stating that a prominent man had, in private correspondence, formulated specific charges against him. What were they?

" Your friend St. Bartholomew has often been seen narcotically and helplessly intoxicated. I believe him to be as rank a hypocrite and as wretched a man as breathes in the Queen's domains." Such were the alleged offenses, which the writer asserted he could prove by scores of witnesses. He challenged the "Yankee" to sue him for libel, and thus bring the question before an English jury.

Mr. Gough demanded, and finally got, the name of this libeler. It was F. R. Lees, Ph.D., a representative and lecturer of the United Kingdom Alliance.

Dr. Lees did not stop here. He dredged the sewers of slander in the United States, and imported the offal thus collected; he wrote to those who entertained Mr. Gough and asked these hosts to put their guest under espionage; and he hired and sent out lecturers to "expose" the "Yankee."

What was Dr. Lee's motive? Nominally, it was the vindication of a friend named Peter Sinclair, who had been sharply criticised in America, when he was there lecturing, and in Scotland, where he had been at work for temperance. Dr. Lees, without any proof, and against the truth, assumed that Mr. Gough had inspired their criticisms, and hence threatened him with exposure unless he should apologize for and withdraw statements he never made. The real motive was, no doubt, a mixed one—the spite of a clever lecturer overshadowed by a greater one, and intense partisanship.

The "Yankee" accepted the challenge of Dr. Lees. Suit was brought in the Court of Exchequer, before Baron Martin. The case was tried in June, 1858, Mr. Gough took the stand. He testified that, since the episode of the drugged soda-water in 1845, he had never tasted spirituous liquors of any kind; had never bought or eaten opium in any form, saving on that occasion, before he signed the pledge, when he contemplated suicide by swallowing laudanum; that he knew nothing about the articles reflecting upon Peter Sinclair; and that he had with him several memorandum-books which would show his whereabouts and condition during every day of the interval in question.

Here the plaintiff's attorney rested. It was now the turn of the counsel for the defendant to cross-examine the witness. He rose. He retracted the charges. He consented to a verdict for the plaintiff—with nominal damages, because Mr. Gough wanted not money, but a legal vindication.

Dr. Lees, a day or two later, repudiated the conduct of his counsel in this disposition of the case, which drew forth from his leading lawyer a letter, in which he confessed that there was nothing else to do—that his client was present in court and consented to the action taken, and had no evidence at all to substantiate his charges.

What shall be thought of a libeler who does not provide himself with evidence before he begins to utter the libel?

It has been shrewdly surmised that what really frightened off the defense in the famous case of Gough *vs.* Lees, was the fact that the plaintiff had with him in court those memorandum-books, which traced his life from day to day and place to place, with dates and witnesses of his state set down in black and white. Lyman Abbott, in referring to the matter, says: "From that day to Mr. Gough's death, slander against his good name never rose above a whisper. Neither envy, malice, nor even partisanship dared face that diary."[1]

Mr. Gough felt this abuse keenly. "It was a terrible ordeal," he writes; "they intended that I should suffer, and I did; and, if it is any consolation for them to know that they caused me and mine such pain as I would not inflict on the meanest of God's creatures, I give them the information here. Still, through all this, I did not miss an appointment, but kept steadily at work."[2]

Had he been less sensitive and more worldly-wise, the orator, living upon publicity, would have gotten comfort from the reflection that his enemies were giving him free advertisement. For months his name

[1] Introduction to "Platform Echoes," p. 63.
[2] "Autobiography," p. 403.

was in every journal and on all lips on both sides of the
water. The daily press behaved admirably. Scurrilous matter, offered in abundance was rejected. The
actual facts were speedily detected and published.
Editors took up the cudgels for Mr. Gough; and Dr.
Lees, *et. al.*, were belabored as lustily as though all
the parties were engaged in a shindy at " Donnybrook
Fair." Excepting when animated by political passion
or interest, the newspapers of England and America,
alike, may be relied upon in every case to secure fair-
play and announce righteous judgment.

LEAVING the Court of Exchequer with a sigh of relief, Mr. Gough resumed work, and divided the autumn and winter of 1858–59, and the ensuing spring and early summer, according to agreement, between England and Scotland. So far from injuring him, the assaults upon his character, now banned by an acquittal in open court, served but to increase his audiences and animate his friends. He became the hero of the hour; a position which his modesty enabled him to hold without growing dizzy with conceit. Small men look smaller on a pedestal ; great men need one.

The long strain, however, told upon him. He resolved to take a vacation, and to spend it on the Continent. With his wife and a small party of relatives and friends, he left London on the 22d of July, 1859, for Paris, where he arrived after a pleasant run of eleven hours.

Mr. Gough did not like Paris. He appreciated and acknowledged its beauty, but the atmosphere of the place did not suit him. The *genius loci* was not congenial. The reason is obvious—he was an earnest man—a man with a mission. Paris is the capital of pleasure. It is laid out in the interest of " the lust of the eye, the lust of the flesh, and the pride of life." 'Tis the city of sensual enchantments. Its boulevards, its broad spaces, populous with bewitching statues, its architectural splendors, its kaleidoscopic movement and glitter, appeal to the æsthetic rather than the moral nature. Lotus-eating is there the serious business of life. The city is love-sick with music and poetry. The luxurious citizens, melted in baths and perfumes, and lounging in delicious languor, in front of the cafés, or in the foyers of the operas or theaters, mock at the severe precepts of Christian virtue. Lyres and easels are preferred to Bibles and churches. Paris is the apotheosis of earth. Beautiful? Yes; but "earthly, sensual, devilish."

A week in Paris, passed in sight-seeing, was enough for Mr. Gough, and that ex-Yankee schoolma'am, his wife, two Puritan souls out of harmony with their environment. On the 29th they deserted the French capital for Geneva, where they rested on the Sunday and attended church, their habit always and everywhere. On the Monday following they set out for Chamounix. The day was clear. The experiences were new. Each one made an indelible impression. Mr. Gough thus describes his first glimpse at Mont Blanc:

"Soon after noon we arrived at Lallenche, and, while waiting for dinner and a change of *voiture*, I strolled out with Dr. Gould; my wife, being weary, remained in the hotel. Standing together on the bridge, I said, 'How new all this is to me—the mountains, valleys, waterfalls, picturesque villages, chalets—all new and strange; the sky so clear and blue, the clouds so pure—it is all glorious! What a peculiar cloud that is behind those hills! so white, so clearly cut, it appears like—why it is—yes—no—George, that *is* the *mountain*—that *is* Mont Blanc! I *know* it!' And as I caught the first view of the

monarch of the Alps I trembled with excitement. With tears
in my eyes, and my heart full, I turned away to hurry Mary out
to enjoy it with us. We traveled the well known route to the
Valley of Chamounix. As we passed through it toward the
village, the sun sank behind the hills, and left us in shadow;
but the gorgeous coloring of the snow clad mountains filled us
with delight. Ever-changing, ever-beautiful—wave after wave
of glory seemed to roll over the summit, growing more and
more subdued until, with one flash of exquisite beauty from the
sun's last beam, the wonderful outline of mountain tops stood
relieved by the dark blue sky—white, cold, chastely beautiful." [1]

A few happy days of excursionizing in and around
Chamounix succeeded this elect day of entrance, the
weather holding fair and favorable. Then the tour-
ists proceeded through the magnificent *Tête Noir* and
Brunig Passes to Lucerne—another dream of delight. Thence the route lay through Basle, out of
Switzerland into Germany, to Mayence, down the
Rhine to Cologne, and from Cologne, by way of Lisle
and Calais, across the channel, to England and London.

Amid the pleasures of travel, Mr. Gough did not
forget his life-work. He says:

" I had heard so much of the sobriety of wine-growing countries, and so many propositions to introduce wine in America
as a cure for drunkenness, that I determined to make what personal observations I might be able during my brief sojourn on
the Continent. On the boulevards and the Champs Elysées I
saw no more drunkenness than in Broadway or Fifth Avenue ;
but in the narrow by-streets back of the main thoroughfare, I
discovered as many evidences of gross dissipation as in Baxter
street, New York, or in Bedford street, Philadelphia. I took
a survey of the low cabarets, and found the same bloated or

<hr>

[1] " Autobiography," p. 447.

haggard faces, the same steaming rags, the same bleared and blood-shot eyes, the same evidence of drink-soaked humanity in its degradation, as in any of the grog-shops in the United States. In Geneva—the same; we were kept awake by the bacchanalian revels of intoxicated men in the streets all night. In Vevay, I saw more evidences of drunkenness than in any town of its population in America. In Mayence, a fair was held while we were there, and I saw more drunken men on the streets and in the squares than I believe were to be seen on the streets during the whole five days of the 'Peace Jubilee' in Boston. In Basle and in Cologne, it was the same; and my impressions are, from personal observation (not very extensive), that drunkenness prevails in wine-growing countries to as great an extent as in any portion of the United States that I have visited."[1]

Mr. Gough relates how he and his wife were shown, at Cologne, the skulls of the ten thousand virgins— or at least *some* skulls, and says: "The attendant showed us a small cracked jar, carefully inclosed in a case, lined with crimson velvet, and told us that was one of the jars the Saviour filled with wine at the marriage in Cana. My wife turned away, and he said with a shrug:

"Americaine—hah! not moosh like relique."

He adds:

"This reminded me of the sword that was exhibited as Balaam's sword with which he slew the ass. One of the spectators said:

"'But Balaam did not have a sword; he only wished for one.'

"'Ah!' cried the showman, 'this is the sword he wished for.'"[2]

---

[1] "Autobiography," pp. 445, 446.   [2] "Autobiography," p. 450.

III

A DIP INTO IRELAND.

NOTHING is more fatiguing than sightseeing. It involves a double strain, of the body, on account of the incessant movement, and of the mind, through living on the *qui vive*, and thinking and talking in exclamation marks. Those breathless twenty-three days on the Continent made Mr. Gough, veteran traveler though he was, glad enough to rest a fortnight in London, before again turning

"... itinerant,
To stroll and teach from town to town."

But, as Tennyson says, "men must work." On the 30th of August the new season began, and the whole of September was spent in England. Then, on the 3d of October, the lecturer crossed to Erin, and stepped for the first time on Irish soil. At Dublin he was entertained by the Rev. Dr. John Hall, later of New York. Here three lectures were delivered to crowded and enthusiastic audiences. The responsiveness of the Celtic blood is proverbial. The Irish have quicksilver in their veins. Mr. Gough also spoke in Belfast, Londonderry, and Cork,—in the former four times, in the latter two cities, twice in each. These engagements took him quite through the island. The impressions of such a shrewd sight-seer are of value.

The Irish question was then, as it is now, has been for five hundred years, and will be until it is settled on the basis of political equity,—what the French call a burning question. Mr. Gough saw, what every traveler sees, abounding ignorance, poverty, and drunkenness—the very landscape squalid and tipsy. He found the people in a state of chronic insurrection and hating the name of England. They were at once the most religious and the most unconscientious peasantry in Europe. They went to mass, and then adjourned to engage in or watch a prize-fight. They talked honestly, and reduced thievery to a fine art in practice. They were grateful and ungrateful, in a breath. They worked, and were yet improvident. In wit no one could equal them, and in practical faculty they rated with the people of Dahomey.

Himself one of the most mercurial of men, Mr. Gough believed that these contradictions in the Irish nature were the result of a volatile temperament. He understood the Irish, because he knew himself. The lightning changes of mood, the heights and depths of feeling, the unreasoning and sometimes unreasonable states of mind which marked and marred his own disposition, he discovered in these dear, dirty, altogether enigmatical but delightful Irish folk—the admiration and despair of both friends and foes.

As for the existing ignorance and poverty, the apostle of cold water had no difficulty in tracing these to their sources. He was convinced that a vicious political system was one cause: a system so vicious that it gave over the land of Ireland to absentee owners, who had no interest in the tenants, save to squeeze out of them rent to the last farthing; made peasant proprietorship impossible, thus depriving the tillers of the soil of all inducement to improve the land, and of the sense of self-respect which comes from ownership; and discouraged manufactures, the only other available means of prosperity, because manufacturing England would not tolerate a rival on the other side of the Irish Sea.

The other plain cause of Irish pauperism he discovered in the drunken habits of the people. During the progress of Father Mathew's memorable temperance crusade, which began in 1838, 5,000,000 people, of both sexes, all ages, and all conditions, out of a total population of 8,175,124, took the pledge of total abstinence. Four years later, drunkenness had disappeared in many parts of the Emerald Isle, the public-houses were deserted, the distilleries and breweries were closed, and the criminal calendars at the assizes were almost blank. The annual consumption of spirits dropped from 11,595,536 gallons in 1837 to 6,484,443 in 1841, with an increased population.

This happy condition did not become permanent— why? Because it was not secured by a prohibitory law. A weak, moral purpose could not resist the allurements of temptation. Little by little, the liquor interest regained its temporarily lost supremacy. The public-houses, distilleries, and breweries resumed business under license. The number of gallons of ardent spirits consumed in a twelvemonth went up higher than ever; while the population entered upon a rapid decline—which has continued to this day. As for the courts, they soon found plenty of occupation, one person in every fifty-four of the population being annually convicted of habitual drunkenness.

Of these, and similar facts, we may be sure the temperance lecturer made telling use on the Irish rostrum.

Evidences of the awful famine of 1848, which America honored itself by shipping provisions to relieve, and in aid of which Mr. Gough had spoken more than once—were visible. Yet at that very time many million quarters of grain were diverted from the tables of the starving peasants to the distilleries, and thus destroyed for food and distilled into poison for the brain. "When children were found dead," remarks Mr. Gough, "with the seaweed they had been sucking for nourishment between their teeth; when, as I was told in Brandon by the rector, people dreaded to go out at night for fear of stumbling over a dead body; when thousands of poor creatures were fed every day in the yards of the well-to-do, and when such Good Samaritans were obliged to sprinkle the stones on which they sat with chloride of lime, for fear of infection from the famine fever which was raging;—at that very time the smoke of the distilleries was darkening the air and intensifying the famine."[1]

Mr. Gough spent a good many hours while in Ireland in looking around. The streets of Dublin and of Cork specially attracted him. He says:

"The best thing I heard in Dublin was said by a man to a woman. Two men were talking together, evidently belonging to the poorest class, when a woman short, thick, and dumpy, and

---

[1] "Sunshine and Shadow," pp. 152, 153.

13

shockingly dirty, came up and interrupted them. ' To the divel I'll pitch ye now, if ye're not away,' said one.

"Still she annoyed him, when, with an indescribable contempt in tone and gesture, he said:

' Go away with ye now ; you're for all the world like a *bad* winter's day—*short* and *dirty !* ' " [1]

In referring to Cork, he says:

" I followed two ballad-singers for nearly an hour to note the people. The ballad was rough, the singers were rude, and not very musical. The theme was the loss at sea of the *Royal Charter.* I was very much touched by the sad, sympathetic faces of the listeners, a crowd of whom surrounded the singers. The description of the storm, the striking of the ship, the cry of the passengers, the prayer that was offered by those on deck,—all received a share of notice and sympathy. When the name of God was spoken, every man's hat was off, and every woman bowed her head. I saw tears streaming down the cheeks of some, and heard such expressions as, ' Ah ! God be betune us an' all harrum '; and, ' Oh ! the cruel, cruel say, to swallow them all up.' It was to me very interesting." [2]

Ireland is the most beautiful of islands. It should be the happiest. Its rock-bound coast is a fringe of grandeur on an emerald robe. Its soil is as fertile as the sod is green. Its lakes are mirrors of heaven. Its hills and vales are flowery with romance and hoary with legend. The whole landscape is a smile of God.

Alas! though the mother of the people is genius, their father is squalor. They are housed in the hovel of drunkenness. A poor-house, couchant, and a distillery, rampant, should be quartered upon the Irish coat-of-arms.

---

[1] " Autobiography," p. 487. [2] " Autobiography," p. 485.

IV.

THE more salient of Mr. Gough's Continental and Irish impressions have been noted. We jot down in this chapter some of his views of British morals, manners, and men.

He observed and commended the judicious slowness of the English mind,—its dislike of novelty,—its constitutional conservatism,—its stubborn determination to hold on to what it has until it is sure of something better,—its preference for an acre on earth rather than a principality in Utopia,—its deliberate investigation and debate of every measure of proposed reform, from Magna Charta down, and desire to be assured of its practicability, before moving to adopt it. But he noted that when once convinced, movement follows, and what is gained is gained for ever. Lord Chesterfield, several generations ago, expressed this truth by implication, in an epigram addressed to a French acquaintance: "You Frenchmen erect barricades, but never any barriers." When the French see or suspect an abuse they are furious, sing the "Marseillaise," and upset the Government. The next week a reaction sets in, and the abuse reappears. In Britain the abuse is named, a meeting is called, proofs are offered, public opinion is informed, and reform follows as a matter of course, and stays. This takes time, and is galling to certain nervous and sanguine spirits. But arguments are better than bombs. And progress is surer when made by popular consent, than when imposed either by a mob or by a Cabinet. Many times hasty people go away from Britain only to come back after a series of misadventures to slow up with the country.

It was his knowledge of this mood of the British mind which made John B. Gough so patient and persevering in his use of moral suasion. He saw that what the people needed was information and direction— the actual preception of ardent spirits as an abuse that required reforming and could be reformed. "The great difficulty experienced in advocating temperance there," he writes, "is, or was, the dogged, arbitrary condemnation of the principles involved, a stolidity of perception, and an expressed belief in the impossibility of establishing those principles among them. And yet the temperance movement is steadily increasing in power and influence. Some of the leaders are far-seeing men, and look not only to the direct results, but to the future development of the harvest of which they are patiently sowing the seeds. I know no men who are more deserving of all praise than the steady, persevering advocates of reform— political, ecclesiastical, and moral—in Great Britain."[1]

Mr. Gough bears glowing testimony to the "large amount of good effected in England by self-denying women," and adds:

"Let any person read 'English Hearts and English Hands,'

---

[1] "Autobiography," pp. 506, 507.

or 'The Missing Link,' and he will see what women are doing in Christian work among the destitute classes. Read 'Haste to the Rescue,' or 'Ragged Homes, and How to Mend Them,' or 'Workmen and Their Difficulties,' and you will gain an insight into this sphere of labor that will convince you that their work must be successful in the end. No discouragements hinder, no opposition checks them ; their purposes seem strengthened by blasts of adverse criticism. I met the men and women who have been gathered in the 'Kensington Potteries' by Mrs. Bailey, and I spent a few days at Shrewsbury, as the guest of Rev. Charles Wightman, whose noble wife has accomplished a wonderful work among the denizens of Butcher's row —uncleanness, degradation, sin alleviated. . . . In many places where I was a guest, I found the ladies of the family busily and earnestly engaged in endeavoring to ameliorate the condition of the poor, by inculcating temperance, visiting them, reading to them, and teaching them cleanliness and habits of thrift." [1]

This work is not confined to the temperance classes. Thoughtful people generally are addressing themselves more and more to the study and solution of the complicated problems which tax and vex modern civilization—so he testifies.

Mr. Gough's remarks regarding society are interesting :

"Society in Great Britain is divided into three classes— nobility, gentry (among whom rank the clergy), and the public generally. These again are divided and subdivided, to an almost illimitable extent. My work brought me constantly in contact with the public generally, often with the gentry, and very seldom with the aristocracy. Though the reverence for mere rank is dying out, still there is a deference paid to 'my

---

[1] "Autobiography," pp. 510 and 512.

lord '; and to be seen on the sunny side of Pall Mall in the height of the season, arm in arm with a live lord, would repay some men for any amount of toadyism." [1]

Although toadyism results inevitably from the social organization in Great Britain, our critic is sure that there is a large element of it in human nature, and gives this sly dig at America :

"Though we in a republican country ridicule the flunkeyism of Great Britain, there is just as much here as there. Many Americans would feel flattered by attention from a lord, and bow as low to a title as any in England. How much planning and maneuvering there is to secure the presence of a lord at fashionable parties in New York and in other cities we all know." [2]

He might have made his case stronger had he cited the common sale of American heiresses for titles in the matrimonial markets of Europe—so much gold for so much title, with the girl thrown into the bargain !

Continuing in this vein, he goes on to say :

"I have heard of the great affability of the nobility, but I must confess, that in my limited experience of them I have found, with some exceptions, an indescribable sort of 'touch me not,' a kind of 'you may look but you must not touch.' Perhaps it is owing to my education and early experiences, but I could never feel as entirely at my ease with a lord as with a commoner." [3]

Mr. Gough was persuaded that the existence of a large, wealthy, idle, upper class, whose object in life

---

[1] "Autobiography," p. 456. [2] "Autobiography, pp. 456, 457.
[3] "Autobiography," p. 457.

is pleasure, stands toward vice in the relation of cause
to effect.   On this point he says :

"While I was in London, a testimonial was presented to a.
man who has dared, perhaps more than any other, to make
vice attractive.   I speak of the manager and proprietor of the
'Argyll Rooms,' where music and dancing are carried on
every night—'admission, gentlemen one shilling, ladies free,'
and where no reputable woman enters.   Actually, a lord presided at the dinner and presented the testimonial! No wonder
London abounds in *Traviatas* in the parks, theaters, and
fashionable streets.   The terrible 'social evil,'like everything
else in London, is on the most gigantic scale; it is a question
that can never be tabulated.   And so long as women can barely
exist in virtuous industry—so long as there are rich and fashionable men to sanction vice—so long as young blood becomes
fevered by strong drink—so long as young men and women
dare not marry, as their parents did, and bravely and nobly
fight the battle of life;—so long will the 'social evil' in England, and in this country, continue to be a social blot, tainting
society—a frightful source of sin and misery." [1]

Mr. Gough says that the social divisions in Britain
were accurately marked by the prices of admission to
his lectures : First class, five shillings, or half a crown,
as it might be ; second class, one shilling ; working
people, sixpence.

In the manufacturing districts he found much to
deplore:

"No one can visit them without being struck by the contrast
between the operatives there and here. Go into a mill here and
you see the girls, as a rule, neat, clean, healthy—bits of looking-
glass placed on the walls, or posts, at intervals, and perhaps
some young girl 'doing up her hair' in her short leisure time,

---

[1] "Autobiography," pp. 463, 464.

or sitting for another to curl it. In many English factories you see heated, half-clad figures, thin, clammy hands, and pallid faces—girls, women, lads, men—all alike in their gaunt, ghastly weariness. Out of the mill you see abject slovenliness, only occasionally relieved by a faint attempt at smartness. Girls go without bonnets, with sometimes a shawl over the head from which they have not picked out the oily refuse that clings to them. In Scotland and Ireland they are universally bare-footed. In Lancashire they wear those wooden-soled shoes that make a peculiar and deafening *clatter, clatter*, when the mill hands are let out." [1]

Of all working people, however, "the Yankee" found the miners and the agricultural laborers the most ignorant and neglected—but a step above the yahoos or thugs. The miners being out of sight (underground) are out of mind. With regard to the farm hands, he remarks:

"We are told that 'nature is a great educator.' I do not be-lieve it. I found men and women who were born and reared, and who lived in the most lovely rural districts, where nature laughs in all the perfection of beauty, who are among the most stupid, boorish, and unintellectual beings in human shape. Their employment requires no thought; one is a plowman, and does nothing but follow the plow; another a hedger or ditcher, etc. I have tried to converse with them, but found them wo-fully ignorant. The last words of a dying Lancashire boor are recorded: 'W'at wi' faath, and wat wi' the 'arth turning round the soon, and w'at wi' the raalroads a fuzzen and a whuzzen, I'm clean moodled and bet.'" [2]

Mr. Gough is sure that Dickens and Thackeray and Kingsley have not drawn and could not draw an

---

[1] "Autobiography," pp. 470, 471.   [2] "Autobiography," p. 472.

exaggerated picture of the ignorance of these people.
He writes :

" When visiting Bedfordshire, where Bunyan lived, preached,
and was imprisoned, and Cowper's residence when he was so
long with Mrs. Unwin—I went with a party to see the Church
in which Scott, the commentator, once preached. A woman
accompanied us to show us the place, and at every reply to
our questions, with her arms folded, she would duck down in
an attempt at a courtesy. I said to her once :

"' Please, ma'am, do not bob at me so, when I speak to you.
I do not like it.'

" We noticed a row of hard-looking benches—reminding me
of the seats in old-fashioned New England schoolhouses. I
asked :

'" What are these benches for ?'

"' Please, sir, they gits the colic, sir.'

"' The colic ! good gracious ! what do they get the colic
for ?'

"' Please, sir, they are obleeged to, every Sunday morning,
sir.'

"' Well, well, I never heard of such a thing ; obliged to get
the colic every Sunday morning ?'

"' Yes, please sir, all of them is obliged to get it.'

" I must confess for a moment I had a vision of a set of
wretched children on hard benches in a high state of inward
disturbance—when one of the party laughed heartily and said :

"' She means they are compelled to learn the *collect* (prayers
for the day in the English Church liturgy) every Sunday
morning.'

" That was, probably the extent of their religious education." [1]

In Scotland the helpers about the farm were called
hinds—a word which defines their status. In Wales,
Mr. Gough saw women and young girls working in

---

[1] Autobiography," pp. 478, 479.

the brick-yards—their dress simply a coarse frock. All these unfortunates were boozy with beer or fuddled with gin.

This was a generation ago. Things have somewhat mended since then. But we have already quoted Mr. Gough's testimony regarding the slowness of the British mind. What need amid such surroundings for the heart of Christ and the zeal of Paul!

Mr. Gough's vocation brought him in contact with the celebrities of the day, and especially with such as wrought in the field of philanthropy. Many of these meetings by the wayside of reform ripened into charming intimacies. The Established Church was then unfriendly to teetotalism, so that its clergy were not in touch with him. But the great Nonconformists leaders coöperated zealously against the drink. Of several titans he makes offhand sketches, commencing with Dr. Guthrie:

"One of the most fascinating preachers I ever heard was Dr. Guthrie, of Edinburgh. In 1853–55 and 1857–60 I listened to him often. It was difficult to get into the church, every inch of room being occupied that could be made available either for sitting or standing. The doctor kindly gave me a pass, and my wife and myself always found a good seat. The audience was composed of the literary, philosophical, scientific, and intellectual, with a fair show of the commonplace; for the preacher had a marvelous power of adapting his discourse to the gratification of the intellectual and to the understanding of the common mind. The Duke of Argyll was often there, together with professors from the University. Truly, the rich and poor met together, for Dr. Guthrie was almost worshiped by many of the denizens of the closes on High street, and no wonder ; for while he rebuked the sins, he sympathized with the sorrows of poor humanity. . . . After the preliminary services, which were very solemn and tender, the people settled down to listen. The first time I heard him he took the text : ' We all do fade as a leaf.' Then there was a pause amid the breathless silence of the congregation. See him with his noble forehead, and those magnificent eyes, as he tenderly looks over the large assemblage, his heart overflowing with tender sympathy and affection for those who were traveling to that ' bourn from which no traveler returns.' And then he went on and on with that magnificent voice, sometimes like ' a thunder psalm among the hills,' then like the sigh of the wind among the trees ; again like the sound of a trumpet, then like the Æolian harp ; at one moment, sharp, staccato, the next seeming to struggle through 'a mist of unshed tears.' Your eyes would fill in spite of yourself by the power of his pathos.

" The acquaintance and friendship I was permitted to enjoy with Dr. Guthrie, is one of the most delightful of my reminiscences. He presided several times at my meetings ; and I remember how amused he was when once the Secretary said :

"' The Rev. Dr. Guthrie, author of the " Sins and Sorrows of the City," will preside ; and Professor Miller, author of " Alcohol " will preside to-morrow evening.' "[1]

The Rev. William Arnot, of Glasgow, was another Scotch pulpiteer with whom the pleader for temperance became familiar—" very different from Dr. Guthrie, yet not one whit below him in influence or power, appealing to the intellect rather than to the feelings, yet at times very tender."[2]

Mr. Gough often heard, and greatly liked, Newman Hall, who preached in Surrey Chapel, where he spoke himself—his mother's first church home.

Among others, not of the clergy, but co-workers in

---

[1] " Sunshine and Shadow," pp. 383–389.
[2] " Sunshine and Shadow," p. 389.

good words and works, he recalls the Earl of Shaftesbury, a nobleman in fact as well as by title, who
carved his name in the hearts of England's poor ;
not an orator, but " whose presence was mightier
than speech." And John Bright is particularly mentioned, with whom he passed a week in one of those.
charming British country-seats (in Brymbo, Wales),
and to whom he listened for an hour (and could have
listened for ever), as he spoke there to an extem-
porized gathering of iron-workers upon the question
of " Capital and Labor," showing their inter-depend-
ence in words "incisive, clear as crystal," and of vivid
power.

With the Corn-Law reformers, too, he made an
acquaintance—and Richard Cobden, Henry Vincent,
and George Thompson were among the supreme
names in the estimation of this kindred spirit.

When in London his favorite resorts were the
Houses of Parliament, where history is made, and
Westminster Abbey, where history is preserved. But
the streets of the modern Babylon were, perhaps, his
chiefest haunt. Here he found human nature at first
hand—endless in its diversity—with tragedies and
comedies of actual life enacted on every corner—
Punch-and-Judy shows galore—heroism and coward-
ice, generosity and meanness, virtue and vice, elbow
to elbow in the procession of humanity.

The long term of the temperance advocate's voluntary exile drew to a close. His final round was made
in England, with the exception of eighteen days
given to Ireland, and a hurried trip to Glasgow for a
farewell address in that seaport, and to attend a
good-bye *soirée* there. On Wednesday evening, the

8th of August, he gave his last lecture in Exeter Hall. We quote his own account of this meeting :

" Several American friends were present, among them the Rev. Dr. George B. Chiever and the Hon. Ichabod Washburn, of Worcester. Those who had signed the pledge in Exeter Hall had subscribed for a Bible, to be presented on the last evening I should lecture there. I had spoken ninety-five times in that Hall, and on the ninety-sixth and last the Bible was presented. It was one of the largest audiences I had met there. It was very exciting to me, and I was more nearly overcome than I remember ever to have been on any similar occasion. My dear friend, George Cruikshank, presided ; Judge Payne, of the Court of Quarter Sessions, was appointed to present the Bible ; my first English friends, true, tried, and faithful, were there—dear Tweedie, Campbell, Howlett, the brothers John and Joseph Taylor, Spriggs, Hugh Owen, with many more from the London societies and from the provinces.

" When the Bible was presented, I rose to reply, and no schoolboy, on his first appearance, could have felt more embarrassed. At last I said : ' My dear friends, as I look at this splendid testimonial of your good will—rich in morocco and gold, beautiful as a work of art and skill—I think of another book, a little one ; broken, torn, ragged, and imperfect— you would hardly pick it up in the street ; but to me, precious as your gift is to-night, more precious is that little book. On the illuminated fly-leaf of this I read : ' Presented Aug. 8, 1860, to John B. Gough, on his leaving England for America, by those only who signed the pledge after hearing him in Exeter Hall, London.' On the brown, mildewed fly-leaf of the other book are these words : ' Jane Gough, born Aug. 12, 1776. John Gough, born Aug. 22, 1817. The gift of his mother, on his departure from England for America.' Two gifts, and two departures !

" As I began to review the past experiences since I left home, thirty-one years before, the flood of recollections came over me, combined with the tender associations connected with farewell, and I stammered, became nervous, and was unable to proceed. As I stood there, the unshed tears filling my eyes, Thomas Irving White rose, and taking me by the hand, said; 'God bless him! Give him three cheers!'

"And the audience started to their feet, and with waving of hats and handkerchiefs, gave them with a will. That unsealed the fountain, and I bowed my head and cried like a very boy."[1]

On the 10th of August, a large number of the reformer's friends gathered at the "Northwestern" Railway Station to see him off. Many brought, others had previously sent, parting gifts. Amid smiles and tears the train puffed away to Liverpool. In the evening of that same day, he spoke in Concert Hall, Liverpool, to another vast assemblage. On the 11th of August, 1860, the embarkation occurred, the good steamer *Arabia* started, and the second British tour became a memory. In summing up the figures, Mr. Gough states that during the first British visit he lectured 438 times, and traveled 23,224 miles; during the second, he delivered 605 addresses, and traveled 40,217 miles—making in all 1,043 public appearances, and 63,441 miles of travel.

The good he did is not so easily tabulated. But the Recording Angel may be depended upon for that record.

---

[1] "Autobiography," pp. 452, 453.

PART IX.

Renewed Usefulness at Home

" I pity the man who can travel from Dan
to Beersheba, and cry, ' "Tis all barren.' "
—STERNE, *Sentimental Journey*

I.

It so happened that Mr. Gough reached "Hillside" on his birthday, which was celebrated quietly but thankfully by all the inmates. A few days later there was a reception picnic in an adjacent grove; then a rousing reception in Worcester, at the Mechanics' Hall; and, finally, the truant was welcomed home by the clergy of the Commonwealth, at a great meeting in Tremont Temple, Boston; when an autograph-book, filled with the signatures (nearly five hundred in number) of those who had issued the address of greeting, with the inscription—"The Welcome of the Ministers of Massachusetts to John B. Gough, on his return from England in August, 1860,"—was presented, which called forth an appropriate and feeling response from the recipient.

Shadows lurk in sunshine. These public manifestations of esteem were saddened by private sorrows. Mrs. Gough learned that one of her brothers, Luke Whitcomb, had been killed in a railroad accident two weeks before her return. She found a remaining brother at death's door with brain fever, and within a fortnight saw him pass through the somber portals.

While doing what he could to comfort "Mary,"

14

the husband felt the shadow creep into his own heart
—the kind hand that had been laid upon his shoulder
to lead him to reform, was gone! He writes:

"On my return home from New York, October 26th, 1860, I
was informed that Joel Stratton was very ill. I at once proceeded to his home, and found him propped up by pillows in
his chair, for his disease was of such a character that he could
not lie down. The drops stood like beads on his forehead and
on the backs of his hands, for he was very weak. I said to
him,—'God bless you, Stratton; thousands are thankful that
you ever lived.' Feebly he whispered, 'Do you think so?'
'Think so! I have my English mail here,'— and I read him
some extracts from a letter I had received from a lady, who
wrote, 'How glad you must have been to meet your old friend,
Joel Stratton, for whom we often pray, and whom we all love.'
Looking at me with his pleasant smile, he said: 'When I laid
my hand on your shoulder that night, I never dreamed all this
would come to pass—did you?' 'No,' I said, 'but it has.' I
kissed him, and left him, hoping to see him again. I was engaged in Montreal on the 29th, and on my return found he was
dead. The funeral was to take place the next day, November 7th."

Mr. Gough spoke at this service, words of tender
affection and appreciation, a heart-throb in each one:

"I never knew him intimately, on account of his great modesty and diffidence. He always kept himself in the background.
He was always the last man to take my hand at the door at
my lecture when he was present. I owe to him all I am, since
I have been worth anything to my fellow men; and while I am
almost daily annoyed by letters from persons who knew me in
my former life, or who were acquainted with some who knew
me, asking of me some assistance, Joel Stratton never once

---

[1] " Autobiography," p. 521.

asked of me a favor. He never obtruded himself upon me; never alluded to his instrumentality in my reform; never appeared to pride himself upon it, as if it were a meritorious deed." [1] .

Mr. Stratton left his family in financial straits. Mr. Gough counted it a privilege to settle an annuity of $300 upon the widow, which he paid as regularly as the date recurred, during her life.

Now that he was at home again, he threw himself with his accustomed ardor into work—was here, there, and yonder, after the manner of what Wendell Phillips styled "a vagabond lecturer." Adventures were common. Once, while *en route*, the railroad was choked with snow; the train was hours late. "At a certain station," says Mr. Gough, "we took on board a large number of passengers who had been detained all night waiting for the cars, when one elderly, wo-begone man stood in the passage-way, and, looking about him—the seats being all occupied—said with a most lugubrious air and tone:

"'This is too bad! here I've ben *laying* on the floor in the depôt all night, and now I can't find a place to *set*.'

"A gentleman sprang from his seat, and said:

"'That *is* too bad; here's a place—*set* here!'

"Amid a noisy burst of merriment that surprised him, the man took the offered seat." [2]

The professional season of 1860–61 witnessed a new departure on Mr. Gough's part. Until now he had spoken invariably upon temperance. He was suffering in body and mind from this "harping on one string."

---

[1] " Autobiography," p. 524. [2] " Autobiography," p. 535.

He realized the need of variety in his labors if he would preserve his health and continue his usefulness. Thus far, he had acted as a guerilla in the lecture field. The Lyceum courses of the States had almost never announced his name in their annual lists of lecturers. The fault was not theirs, but his. He had preferred to remain an outsider. The Lyceum method was to engage six, eight, or ten different names, as diversified as possible; his was, to give courses himself. At this time he was besieged with applications from Lyceum committees—each mail brought them by the dozen, from all points of the compass. Often they asked for a temperance lecture; frequently the demand was for another theme. After prolonged consideration, Mr. Gough consented to prepare a lecture on "Street Life in London"—a taking caption, and a topic upon which he could speak *con amore*. Very reluctantly and timidly he set about his task. Even more unwillingly did he appear in public with the result, visible in the shape of a pile of manuscript laid before him, and before all, upon the table. It was in New Haven, Connecticut, and in the Library course on November 21st, 1860. The effort was a complete success. The notes did not interfere with his delivery; because, though he spoke from them, it was *away* from them! This New Haven success was repeated in Boston, Providence, Worcester, and elsewhere.

Encouraged by the approbation accorded to his maiden effort, the orator prepared another lecture— "Lights and Shadows of London Life," which was equally well received. Others followed on other topics, usually a new one each season; "Here and

There in Britain," "London," "Eloquence and Orators," "Peculiar People," "Fact and Fiction,"
"Habit," "Curiosity," "Circumstances," and many
more—all immensely popular, treated in a masterly
way, and combining entertainment and instruction
after the fashion characteristic of the author.

In entering the Lyceum Mr. Gough came in direct
competition with the great speakers of the country, as
he had not done before, in a way which inevitably subjected him to comparison. He lacked the classic finish
of Wendell Phillips, the rhetorical graces of Edward
Everett, the piquancy of Starr King, the magnificent
elocution of Dr. E. H. Chapin, the scholarly elaboration of Charles Sumner, the Addisonian style and
witchery of Geo. Wm. Curtis, the "Beecherisms" of
Plymouth Church's unprecedented Boanerges—but
he had a charm and versatility all his own, and was
and ever remained the only Gough! As for that
supreme test of popularity, the ability to draw, he
was from first to last the most reliable name on any
and every lecture list, from the Bay of Fundy to the
Golden Gate.

Like all men of strong personality and aggressive
earnestness, Mr. Gough had plenty of enemies both
within and without the pale of temperance. These
eagerly seized upon this change of base, and widely
heralded it "a desertion of the cause." The lie
refuted itself. For those who heard the new lectures
perceived that the lecturer invariably worked into
each prominent and repeated references to his old
theme. Moreover, he continued throughout his life,
whenever an opportunity occurred, to speak solely
upon temperance, and often at his own charges.

An idea of the demand for Mr. Gough's services
may be gotten from the fact that in some years he
refused upwards of one thousand applications. He
devoted eight months to the platform, now as formerly, and four to rest and preparation; and delivered from one hundred and sixty to one hundred
and eighty lectures in a twelvemonth.

It was said, as though it were a sin, that "Mr.
Gough grew rich on temperance." Supposing it
were true, did he not constantly assert that there was
more wealth in temperance than in drunkenness?
Should it have surprised anybody that the most popular speaker in the English world for forty-three
years, was well paid? How was it with successful
men in other spheres? Men of equal prominence in
the law got $50,000 and $100,000, in single cases.
Popular physicians had incomes of $50,000 per annum.
As for successful men of business, they became mill-
ionaires. In the smallest places visited by Mr. Gough,
there were sure to be men who had made fortunes
out of some patent for a sleeve cuff-button, or by an
invention to cut up hogs more expeditiously. Why
"should not a man who went about doing good," and
never spoke for nearly half a century without facing
a crowd that taxed the hall or church in which he
appeared, make money? Mr. Gough did not accumu-
late as he might have done, because he had many and
large demands on his purse. "Hillside" was a free
hotel. He supported a number of people wholly or in
part; some who had only a sentimental claim upon him.
He gave or lent (which he found equivalent to giving!)
to all who could trump up a decent story of desert or
want. These are not the roads to wealth. Hence, his

chief possessions were a generous heart and an open-hand—a few thousands only remained at the last to divide among heirs.

Mr. Gough was sensitive on this point. He made a detailed statement of his average receipts for lectures from the commencement of his career until the period of the war, which we subjoin:

Year.	Average per Lecture.	Year.	Average per Lecture.
1843	$ 2.77	1854	$48.46
1844	7.29	1855	50.14
1845	14.42	1856	63.73
1846	20.52	1857	62.90
1847	21.06	1858	47.88
1848	17.28	1859	49.32
1849	19.12	1860	60.10
1850	24.36	1861	88.37
1851	21.80	1862	90.83
1852	21.67	1863	104.94 [1]
1853	25.33		

Out of these sums, however, came all his expenses, including a traveling companion (usually Mrs. Gough, in earlier years, and, later, either an agent or a niece). From the year 1863 forward, Mr. Gough's fees were higher than the highest of the averages he tabulates. But it was money earned and merited, and satisfactory alike to the payers and the payee. In connection with his table of receipts, Mr. Gough says :

" Let it stand; leaving me to be glad that to the temperance cause will be given the honor of one of its advocates seeking to advance it according to his ability, and his family not ' asking bread' when he is laid aside—his work done. I have never

---

[1] " Autobiography," pp. 247, 248.

felt it an honor to the cause that its chosen workers should be so ill-provided for in its service, that the posthumous testimonial, or the earlier subscription paper, should be the only reliance of broken health, or support of beloved ones." [1]

The years immediately following the temperance advocate's return to America from his second British campaign for reform, were the most terrific in the history of the New World—the years of the Civil War. He was a loyal American, anti-slavery, freedom-loving, and therefore intensely sympathetic with the effort to emancipate the slaves and save the Union. He acquitted himself as a patriot should, and put voice and purse at the command of the country in "times that tried men's souls." We yield the floor to Mr. Gough, and let him summarize his connection with the historic struggle in his own language:

"I did what I could in aid of our noble soldiers who fought and suffered for the dear old flag, and the perpetuity of the Union. While memory serves me, I shall never lose out of it those years so full of thrilling interest, from the first cry of the 'bombardment of Fort Sumter,' that woke the echoes of the silent streets at midnight. Then followed the running to and fro, and men's voices were heard like the low mutterings of the coming storm. How I live over and over again that first dreadful, half-waked sense of the nation being suddenly called to suffer and sacrifice. Boys seemed to have become men, and men more manly in a night. Then came the tramp of armed men, not for review but service,—stern, hard service. How men sang 'Glory, Hallelujah!' in the streets as they marched, while women wept. How vivid is the remembrance of the sleepless nights, while our army seemed like endangered absentees from home,—of the first news of battle,—then of

---

[1] "Autobiography," p. 249.

disaster,—the terrible days in the Chickahominy,—the Wilderness,—the suspense about Petersburg,—the defeats that were but steps to victory,—hope and fear alternating,—then how the horizon grew brighter as we came to the Emancipation Proclamation,—and through all this the long lines of hospitals all over the land, full of suffering, and not seldom, too, of a glory not of this world,—the homes where sorrow came and staid,—the uncounted heroisms,—the shameful defections,— and the quiet, watchful, trustful attitude of the black race, on either side of which such powers were arrayed, and over whose rights this long conflict really raged, while the whole nation was learning to 'suffer and be strong.' Not until many years of peace shall we be able to estimate truly the times when every ear was strained to catch tidings from every breeze, and the years were full of the most sublime history." [1]

---

[1] " Autobiography," pp. 546 and 547.

II

FÊTE DAY AT " HILLSIDE."

MR. AND MRS. GOUGH had no children. They managed to keep their house full of little ones for all that. When Mrs. Gough's younger brother died, in 1860, he left his widow with five girls and a son. Five of these were domesticated at " Hillside." One of the girls (Mamie) died after a few years. The rest were fathered and mothered by John and Mary Gough, and trained for usefulness. "Since 1860," he remarks, "seven children have been members of our family; so if children are sunbeams, our home has been bright with them."

After the death of Mrs. Jane Gough, Mr. Gough's father had married again. A half-brother by this marriage had come to " Hillside " in 1848, at five years of age, and had been likewise looked after and settled in life. The orator's married sister had three sons. That family was prosperous, and required no aid. The half-brother resided in Worcester. The sister's home remained in Providence, whither she had gone at her marriage.

In 1868, November 24th, the twenty-fifth anniversary of the marriage of John and Mary Gough occurred. "Let us have a silver wedding!" cried the young folks at " Hillside." The couple immediately concerned, shook their heads—they would not come before their friends as beggars of presents, and wished the celebration to be confined to their own household. It was not so to be. The date became known. Friends in Worcester and in Boston insisted upon a demonstration. Other friends across the sea were reached and interested by correspondence. The Goughs finally agreed to keep open house on the occasion. Special express trains ran east and west, to and from Worcester for the *fête*. Free coaches were driven from the city to "Hillside" and back again. Hundreds of well-wishers thus appeared and disappeared. Refreshments were provided in abundance, and the tables, set both in the dining and the breakfast rooms, were occupied by a constant succession of guests. After extending their congratulations, visitors wandered through the house, admiring the nicknacks scattered around, each one a gift, and thus freighted with significance,—the silver ink-stand on the library table,—the set of English china, with a portrait of Mr. Gough on each piece,—the superb collection of Cruikshankiana (twelve hundred plates),—the endless photographs presented by different temperance societies,—the English farewell gift of plate, in 1860,—the welcome signed by nearly five hundred ministers of all denominations on his return to the United States,—the memorials signed by leading citizens on both sides of the Atlantic, in honor of John B. Gough at various times,—above all, the great volumes of signatures to the temperance pledge, procured by Mr. Gough himself, over one hundred and fifty thousand in number,—all were viewed, commented upon, and carefully replaced where found.

Public exercises were held in the " Hillside " gymnasium.   Addresses   were   made   by representative
men, valuable presentations of silver followed, and
one of the recipients, speaking for " self and Mary,"
replied at length.   We give his closing sentences:

"I must be permitted to say how gratifying it is to me on
this occasion to be surrounded by so many of my Worcester
friends.   You knew me, many of you, in the darkest days of my
life,—in my poverty and obscurity.   You have seen me among
you, going in and coming out before you these many years.
In Worcester I signed the pledge; in Worcester I married; in
Worcester I have lived and been known so long; and it is particularly gratifying to me to know that you who know me best,
should see fit to offer this splendid testimonial of your esteem
and confidence."[1]

The presents came from everywhere—across the
continent and across the sea.   They were very numerous and very valuable, and hence were kept in a
safe-deposit vault.   But their highest value lay in the
thought and esteem of which they were the visible and
beautiful expression.

A few days afterwards, Mrs. Gough uttered her
feelings in the following letter, addressed to the Committee of Arrangements, which we quote, because it
refers to and brings out a trait in her husband's character well worthy of emphasis:

"HILLSIDE," November 28, 1868.

"GENTLEMEN—As I return to the accustomed quiet of our
home again, after the stir and anticipation of our 'silver-
wedding' day, and live over in memory the brightness of that
event, I feel that we owe you no common thanks, for 'pleas-

---

[1] "Autobiography," p. 543.

ures of memory' beyond our thought, and for organizing an opportunity for such beautiful expressions of good will as met us then.

"Whenever we look over the receding years, it will henceforth always be that we must do so through that bright day in November, 1868, when yourselves and so many others recognized so delightfully both the toils and the results of those varnished years.

"It has given fresh impulse to our grateful remembrance of the God and Saviour who has led us so lovingly all the way; and we do not forget that He has ordered, that though a cool draught by the wayside-spring does not release from all sense of a toilsome path, it *does* so refresh as to strengthen for the 'hill difficulty' of the future.

"In all the kind things said and done that day for myself personally, there was one omission, and that inevitable under the circumstances. In the recognition of my husband's work and life in the past twenty-five years, none but myself could have said how much I was indebted for whatever of success has been my own in our united lives, to the generous trust and confidence, the unfailing regard, that have always recognized our interests as *one*,—which have left head and hands free,—made such a thing as a struggle for 'rights' unnecessary,—and rejoiced in such fruitage of that trust and love as makes the bond that binds us together so much stronger than twenty-five years ago, while losing not the greenness and freshness of its earlier time.

"With heartfelt thanks for all the wide and substantial sympathy expressed on that occasion, and with the hope that the truest peace may always abide in the homes represented at 'Hillside,' on that day, I am, gentlemen,

"Very gratefully yours,

"MARY E. GOUGH."[1]

Mr. Gough's little "Autobiography," prepared and

---

[1] Autobiography," pp. 543, 544.

published at the outset of his career, had been so
steadily popular and useful, that his friends urged
him to revise and enlarge it, and bring it down to date.
This task he was prevailed upon to undertake. The result was the large volume entitled, "Autobiography
and Personal Recollections of John B. Gough," which
Cruikshank partially illustrated, and which appeared in
1871. 'Tis intensely readable; but would have been better had some literary friend revised it. This, however,
was another of Mr. Gough's touchy points. He never
claimed any literary ability; but he *did* wish to be
thought the author of his own book. So much had
been said regarding the first " Autobiography's " not
being his own production, that he resolved to forestall all denial of his paternal relation to the second,
by keeping the manuscript and proof-sheets wholly
in his own hand. He thus secured his credit as a
writer, but injured his reputation as an author.

With regard to the disputed authorship of the
original life, he says:

" John Ross Dix, then calling himself John Dix Ross, was
an inmate of my family, and I, pacing the room, dictated the
matter to him, he being a good shorthand writer. When he
had copied it out, we read it together and made alterations;
and I wish to state that, excepting only three, or at most four,
instances, my language, not his, was used." [1]

The speaking and the writing habits are distinct.
Great speakers have seldom been great writers. The
elaboration and condensation, essential in composition, refine away and destroy the idiomatic energy
and fire which make the charm of popular oratory.

---

[1] " Autobiography," p. 545.

Addison said he could not think without a pen in his hand. A pen in the lips usually gags the most eloquent of men. Mr. Gough was not an exception to this rule. He wrote entertainingly, but often incorrectly. Inaccuracies, unnoticed in the rush of his utterances on the platform, insist on notice in cold type. However, the autobiographer never aimed at a literary reputation, and would probably have dismissed criticism, as Father Taylor, the famous pastor of the Boston Seamen's Bethel, used to do—"My verb has lost its nominative, but I'm bound for the Kingdom of Heaven!"

III

FOOTPRINTS OF RUM.

A RUMSELLER attended one of Mr. Gough's lectures at Portsmouth, New Hampshire, in the 'seventies. The speaker had referred to the "damnable results" of the liquor traffic.

"Mr. Gough," said the rumseller, " I've been in the business you denounce all my life—I never saw the 'damnable results' which you paint in such lurid colors."

"Well," was the reply, "suppose that, standing here in Portsmouth, you should take a gun and begin to fire it across the Piscataqua river in the direction of Kittery, on the opposite bank. Presently, some one rushes over here and says, 'Stop that firing! You've killed half a dozen people over there in Kittery, already,' 'Pshaw!' you answer. 'I've stood here and fired a good many times—I've never seen any dead folks.' 'No,' retorts the man from Kittery, 'because you are not where they are. If you want to know the facts in the case *go where the shots strike.*'" We propose in this chapter to follow Mr. Gough to the places where the shots strike.

He had been struck himself. He could and did speak from experience. He knew that the first "damnable result" of the drink is felt and shown by the victim. His nature is inverted. The will, the heart, the actions are all twisted from normal into abnormal relations. A rational being becomes irrational. A man is turned into a devil. Whiskey " sits as God in the temple of God." The drunkard's liturgy is *mania a potu*. Self-respect gone,—honor gone, —natural affection gone,—industry gone,—reputation gone,—property gone;—such are the common concomitants of drunkenness.

Mr. Gough tells of two clergymen of whom he had personally known. The first, was one of the best Greek scholars of the day. He began to drink; sank low and lower; and was one day dragged half-naked from under the bench of a dive. He was taken to the house of a friend, kept there four weeks, and sent away " clothed and in his right mind." While in the house of his benefactor he stole postage-stamps to exchange for liquor. And ten days after he went away, he was discovered *sans* hat, *sans* coat, *sans* shoes, *sans* everything,—drunk and begging for alms!

The second of this clerical brace was a man under whose ministry thousands once sat with profit. Drink brought him so low that he often preached one or another of his old sermons in the bar-room of a tavern to degraded men and dissolute women for ten cents !

" I saw an interesting little girl, who had hip complaint," says Mr. Gough. " Her mother sold her to a villainous tramp for two pairs of stockings—then sold the stockings and got drunk on the proceeds."

This leads us to call attention to a second " damnable result " of drinking, viz., its domestic ravages. Whatever deteriorates a man deteriorates his sur-

15

roundings, and especially his dependants. The
drunkard's family is, by common consent, the most
pitiable of objects. "I have witnessed scenes," remarks Mr. Gough, "that have haunted me for days.
In company with a friend, I once called on a man
who had formerly been a gentleman of position, but
who was now living on an annuity of $500—a com-
parative pittance saved from the wreck of his fortune.
His wife, a woman of refinement, had been very ill.
When we arrived we found the man drunk, sitting by
the fire, smoking, the wife lying dead on a miserable
pallet in the room. The drunkard was making a
great noise, and declaring she was not dead. The
gentleman with me laid his hand on him and said :

"'Now, you keep still ; your wife lies there dead,
and I will not permit this noise.'

"The drunkard sprang to his feet, exclaiming :

"'I'll let you see whether she is dead or not.'

"Before we could prevent, he sprang like a demon
to the bedside, and dealt on the upturned face of the
dead woman a terrific blow with his fist. Oh, I heard
the sound of that blow for weeks, at night and by
day !"

Here are some extracts from a letter written in
Philadelphia to Mr. Gough, revealing scenes in a
domestic tragedy in that city :

"Some few years ago I was in business at No. 30 Market
street, at which time a man named J—— C.—— applied to me
for work. He was quite genteel in appearance, and I gave
him work, which was satisfactorily done. For some time I
continued to employ him ; but he seldom came himself for or
with his jobs. His wife was in the habit of coming to the
store, and on one occasion I asked her why John did not him-

self bring in the work, when she reluctantly told me of her fears to trust him out, if it could be avoided, lest in his weakness he should drink to excess,_when he was sure to abuse her. So long as he kept from liquor, however, he was affectionate, industrious, and as good a husband as any woman could wish for."

After relating scenes of distress, imprisonment, brutality almost beyond belief—revelations of sickening and revolting cruelty—he goes on :

" They had adopted a child, and John was very fond of the babe, and his wife became very much attached to it.

" He left home one morning early, came back about eleven o'clock; he was drunk, and he then said that it was time the child had gone after its mother—that he was not going to be troubled with other people's brats. However, he soon went out again, and did not return home until just about dusk. When he staggered up-stairs, the windows in the room were raised, as the weather was quite warm. His wife was just in the act of lighting the lamp as John went over to the settee, upon which she had just laid the child. Without a single word, he picked up the child and threw it out the window. The woman flew down the stairs to the street, and there she found the babe—it was dead; the head was smashed. She fainted at the sight. Oh, it was horrible! A crowd soon collected. She was, with the child, taken into the house. And now she was in a dilemma; her husband was a murderer, and yet she loved him still ; for she knew, or felt then, that it was not his nature to commit a violent wrong, save when his action was controlled by rum. She therefore sought by stratagem to release him from any charge, and battled a little while with her conscience, and then, with grief and sorrow depicted on her countenance, she told these persons around her that she had been sitting at the window with the child in her arms, where she had fallen asleep, and that the child rolled out of her arms and fell to the pavement. Unfortunately for her, she

was believed. The child was buried, and there was nothing
afterward said about it. John sometimes spoke of it, but never
without bringing tears in his eyes. She believed that he never
forgave himself for having committed the murder."

The man's habits grew worse. At last, after suffering the torments of the damned, his wife left him.
He could not discover her whereabouts. The writer
goes on :

"One Sunday he came to my house, and, as he appeared to
be sober, I invited him in. He apologized for calling on
Sunday, but wished to know if his wife still worked for me, or
if I had seen her lately. I told him she had done no work for
me for many months, and that the last time I saw her she told
me she was living in New Jersey. He then said that he met
her in the street the night before (Saturday); that she would
not speak to him; and that if he could find her he would kill
her. He appeared much irritated. I then talked with him,
and tried to convince him that he alone was in fault; that if
he would abandon rum there was no doubt happiness in store
for him; that I would give him employment; and that if he
would keep sober and industrious his wife would find it out
and return to him. I suppose he staid an hour; and before
he left he became softened, and promised to reform.

"On the following Sunday, about noon, as I was walking in
the neighborhood of the Exchange, I saw a crowd around a
bulletin board. I crossed over, and judge of my surprise when I
read as follows : ' *Horrid Murder !* Last evening, at nine o'clock,
a man named John C——, a tailor by trade, followed his wife
into a house in Front street, below South street. She had been
out in the street for a bucket of water; he saw and followed
her up into the third story, when he stabbed her in forty different places. The screams attracted persons to the spot; and
when they attempted to take hold of him, he cut himself across
the stomach, and died in a few moments, having committed a

double murder. At the inquest, it was proved that he was under the influence of rum.'"

These incidents suggest a third "damnable result" of this appetite—crime. The chaplain of a prison once told Mr. Gough that seven-ninths of the commitments there were due to drink. Statistics show that three-fourths of the crimes would be uncommitted, and that three-fourths of the prisons would be empty and useless, were it not for liquor. The Bench and the Bar corroborate the statisticians. The courts, the police, the whole repressive machinery of government, from the arrest up to the gallows,—are the bubbles that float on a glass of rum. Mr. Gough quotes an ex-convict as writing:

" During my stay in prison, the question kept rising in my mind, what brings all these men here ? Day after day I asked those with whom I came in contact, what brought them to prison ? I got as an answer the same dull, dismal old story, over and over again—rum did it."

In a letter to Mr. Gough, Canon Farrar refers to an English temperance newspaper which habitually publishes a ghastly column called, " Fruits of the Traffic," made up of clippings from the daily press, and adds: " This column records calamity after calamity, crime after crime, shipwrecks, conflagrations, kickings and tramplings of women, maimings and murders of children,—all of which are directly attributed to the effects of drink, by the declarations of judges, by the reiterated testimony of witnesses, and by the constant, remorseful confessions of the criminals themselves."

Experts, like Judge Noah Davis, of New York, and

Mr. Fred H. Wines, together with a host of experienced and impartial observers, confirm Mr. Gough's
"exaggerations," because they have seen where the
shots strike.

A fourth "damnable result " is the cost. Mr. Gough
figured it out in three columns. In the first column,
he set down the effects of liquor upon the individual,
the family, and the State, as outlined in this chapter:
this he called the moral cost. In the second column,
he placed the direct amounts expended for liquor
per annum; in the 'seventies, $750,000,000: this he
called the money cost to the consumers. In the third
column, he put the resultant pauperism, insanity,
sickness, and crime. Three-fourths of the pauperism,
three-fourths of the insanity, three-fourths of the
sickness, and three-fourths of the crime are the spawn
of drinking habits.[1] Ciphering out the expenses thus
entailed, and adding it, the advocate of temperance
set down the stupendous total of $1,350,000,000! This
he called the indirect cost. Combining the totals of
the second and third columns (for 'tis impossible to
estimate the groans and tears and sorrows of the
first), Mr. Gough showed the aggregate annual cost
of the traffic in intoxicants in the United States, to
be $2,000,000,000.

The only possible offset to this sum, is the revenue
paid by liquor to the Federal, State, and local authorities—$135,000,000. So that the yearly cost to the
American people of this trade is TWO THOUSAND MIL-
LIONS of hard dollars (less the $135,000,000 returned

---

[1] *Vide* " Cyclopædia of Temperance," Article on " Cost of the
Drink Traffic."

in taxes and licences)—without going into the impossible mathematics of the degradation and misery produced by it! [1] Nor did John B. Gough leave the matter here. Having traced the footprints of rum, he proceeded to ask:

> Are we to pass from chamber to chamber of this great temple of abominations, and look at what we see, as though it were a cabinet of curiosities, and gaze coldly on all these scenes of shame and horror that are painted on its walls ; or are we to be aroused by these facts merely to talk the vague language of philanthropy, and to sigh over wretchedness, while we do not so much as lift a single finger to help the wretched ? "[2]

In the footprints of rum Mr. Gough recognized the cloven foot of the devil. And he believed it to be the coequal duty of Church and State to arrest and chain this devil for two thousand million years—a year for every dollar he cost the country in a twelve-month.

---

[1] This cost annually increases at the rate of from $40,000,000 to $50,000,000.

[2] The facts and statements in this chapter are taken from " Sunlight and Shadow," chaps. xviii and xix. See also " Cyclopædia of Temperance," *in loco.*

PART X.

The Third English Visit

"Ah, how good it feels!
The hand of an old friend."
—LONGFELLOW, *Christus*, Part III.

I

AFTER EIGHTEEN YEARS.

On the 10th of July, 1878, Mr. Gough accompanied by his wife and two nieces, sailed for Britain once more, to be gone for an indefinite time. His object was rest, and not campaigning. But, in compliance with urgent requests, he consented to make thirty public addresses at strategic points.

The voyage was pleasant. Liverpool was safely and duly reached. There it seemed as though all temperance England had turned out to welcome the world-famous native of Sandgate. "The National Temperance League," the "United Kingdom Alliance" (former rivals, now, happily, in harmony), bands of hope, cold-water armies, local organizations, large numbers of reformed men, many of them rescued by Mr. Gough's eloquence or personal efforts, all with banners flying, the rub-a-dub-dub of drums, the blare of music, and hearty British cheers—extended a national greeting, and made the scene an epoch. The address of welcome contained the names of one hundred thousand teetotalers !

By-the-by, Mr. Gough gives the origin of the term *teetotal.* "At a meeting in Preston, England, he says, at which Joseph Livesey (one of the founders of the temperance movement in England) presided, a

man named Dickey Turner said : 'Mr. Chairman, I
finds as how the lads gets drunk on ale an' cider, an'
we can't keep 'em sober unless we have the pledge
total ; yes, Mr. Chairman, tee-tee-total.'   The man
was a stammerer, and the term was born of his
stammer.   For Mr. Livesey instantly replied : 'Well
done, Dickey—we will have it teetotal !"[1]   Then
and there the first English total abstinence society
was formed.

From Liverpool, with his right hand aching and
his ears ringing, the tourist went to London—magnificent and splendid ; rich, and poverty-stricken ; sober
and drunken ; Christian, and pagan — to change
Dryden a little—

> " A *town* so various that it seemed to be
> Not one, but all mankind's epitome."

Here there was another hurricane of hospitable
enthusiasm.   A garden-party was given in his honor
in the grounds of Westminster Abbey.   Mr. Gough
remarks :

" If it is true that there are ' sermons in stones,' where shall
we go for a better sermon than to Westminster Abbey ?
It stands gray and hoary and majestic, rich with the memories
of the past, and consecrated with the bones and ashes and
reputations of the great !   All that Britain contained or con-
tains of the illustrious or good, of genius or culture, have
trodden its aisles, have come hither to worship, to admire, to
mourn, or, it may be, after life's fitful fever, to sleep.   Here
majesty, amidst pomp and splendor, has assumed the crown,
and amid equal pomp and circumstance has laid it down ; here
the nation has mourned the bard whose verse is as immortal

---

[1] " Platform Echoes," p. 550.

as her tongue; and here she has wept the greatest of her statesmen—dead." [1]

For the benefit of untraveled readers, and to locate the scene, Mr. Gough adds: " In the neighborhood of the Abbey we are in the center of English civilization, and near the brain of government—that Downing street from which England, Scotland, Wales, Ireland, aye, and lands remote, peopled by alien races, professing alien creeds, speaking alien tongues, are ruled; Royalty resides in close proximity; and in ermined gown and solemn wig and official pomp, the proud Peers of Britain assemble to legislate, not a stone's-throw from this sacred shrine." [2]

Here, then, under the walls of historic Westminster, within sight of St. Stephen's, the teetotaler was *fêted*. Around him thronged friends new and old—among the former, the American minister, and Dr. Arthur P. Stanley, Dean of the Abbey, already an historic figure in life, who spoke words of welcome, and personally played the *cicerone* to his guest; among the latter such of the " old guard " as survived—for eighteen years form a Niagara of fate into which friends as well as enemies pour, and are lost in the ghastly spray! Cruikshank, Dr. Guthrie, William Arnot, and many more, were missing; and the thought of them, and the heartache, brought a mist of tears into the visitor's eyes while smiles were on his face—a rainbow athwart a storm-cloud.

After two or three weeks in the metropolis, during which Mr. Gough and the ladies with him were the recipients of marked social honors, the party crossed

---

[1] " Sunlight and Shadow," p. 34.   [2] " Sunlight and Shadow," p. 34.

to the Continent. We will not follow them thither. They revisited the old haunts, snuggled into some new ones, but upon the whole had a wet time, as the weather was persistently unpropitious. Tourist life on the Continent is absolutely dependent on sunshine —a butterfly existence while it lasts. Hence the Goughs, discouraged by the patter, patter, patter of the rain, scudded back to London, and took lodgings at No. 185 Piccadilly. They were gone a month.

We suspect, if the truth were told, that the busy American, like most Yankees, natural or naturalized, took his pleasures sadly, and rather hurried the ladies on this trip. He was so used to work that he made work of play. To do nothing but gape, and eat, and sleep, and wake to gape again, made the restless lecturer more fidgety than ever. He had no time for this—he had just arrived; and no time for that—he was just departing. Perhaps it was just as well for all concerned, that he should perspire back to smoky London, where he would surely find plenty to do, and vary his idleness. What a second nature habit is ! Those easy-going saunterers on the Parisian boulevards might have taught the rushing American how to moderate his pace and enjoy himself. He could certainly have taught them how to quicken their saunter into usefulness, and find enjoyment in the service of men. 'Tis pity they could not have swopped habits for awhile.

Mr. Gough's initial speech was made in Mr. Spurgeon's Metropolitan Tabernacle, on Tuesday evening September 22d, to an audience of over seven thousand people, with Sir Charles Reed, Member of Parliament, a prominent man " in the city," and a total

abstainer in the chair. The speaker repeated his
earlier oratorical and moral triumphs. Although now
past sixty years of age, rotund in form, with Rip Van
Winkle beard and half-gray hair, his hearers of
eighteen years before marked no diminution in his
fire on the platform or his zeal off of it; while the
new generation acquainted with his name as a doubtful tradition, heard and saw for themselves, and were
convinced that their elders had not exaggerated, and
could not overstate the happy fact.

The scene in Mr. Spurgeon's vast church, was repeated at each of the lecturer's thirty appearances in
various parts of Britain. But what amazed and delighted Mr. Gough was the discovery that the cause,
of old denounced as fanaticism or weak sentimental-
ity, was now established upon a sure basis of recognized common sense, and had won to its advocacy and
practise very many of the most able and prominent
of Englishmen—and in all walks of life. A quarter
of a century earlier, ay, even eighteen years before, it
had been difficult to get anybody who *was* anybody
to preside at a teetotal meeting. Now it was a mere
question of selection—the available celebrities were
countless. The New England teetotaler recites with
justifiable pride the names and titles of some of the
chairmen at his meetings in 1878. As he enumerates
them, there flit before us the men who made and
marked Great Britain in the middle of the nineteenth century: Samuel Morley, one of the merchant
princes and philanthropists of London, "a tall, well-
made man, with serious, but intelligent and attractive
face "—Canon Farrar, as well known abroad as at
home, and author of the most popular of all recent

lives of Christ—William Lawson, M.P., with an income of $500,000 a year, a "jolly good fellow," but not in the bacchanalian sense, one of the wittiest men then in public life—the two leading physicians of the day, Dr. Richardson and Sir Henry Thompson, equally eminent as authors in their profession—the Lord High Chancellor, Earl Cairns, standing next to the throne in official circles, and chairman of the House of Lords, "a stately man, of chastened eloquence, who did not need his gown and wig, or a seat on the woolsack, to impress the beholder"—the Duke of Westminster, "a small, thin, dark-complexioned man, not celebrated as an orator," nor needing such celebrity since he had enough as the wealthiest man in England—Samuel Bowly, a "city" magnate, tall, erect, and manly, who showed at seventy how well teetotalers can bear "the heat and burden of the day"—Sir Fitzroy Kelly, Lord Chief Baron of England, "with a fine, expressive countenance, and a wonderful power in his delivery, standing perfectly still, no gesture, the thumb of his right hand in his waistcoat pocket, simply talking"—John Bright, an old friend, new-met, greatest of England's orators in our day, and the friend of America when she needed friends in England;—these, and many others, were pronounced abstainers, and lent Mr. Gough the luster of their presence when he spoke.

Quite as remarkable was the change in the attitude of the Established Church towards temperance reform and reformers. Previously, a teetotal clergyman of the Church of England was as rare as a white blackbird. Now, most of the blackbirds had turned white ! Ecclesiastical dignitaries crowded one another in their willingness to be identified with the "Hillside" teetotaler while on his third circuit, and jostled against civil officials, also "willin'," like *Barkis*. Canon Farrar presided twice when Mr. Gough spoke in Exeter Hall. Dr. Temple, the Bishop of Exeter—the successor, before he entered the episcopate, of Dr. Arnold, as master of the famous school at Rugby—was in the chair when Mr. Gough lectured at Plymouth. At Croydon, the Bishop of Rochester presided; at Owestry, the Bishop of Bedford; at Oxford, Canon Ellison; at Southampton, Bishop (then Canon) Wilberforce; at York, the Dean of the famous cathedral there; at Swansea, the Honorable Wm. Henry Fox Talbot, a *savant*, with medals enough to furnish a museum, the Lord Lieutenant, and "father of the House of Commons"; in Dublin, the Lord-Mayor; and in Glasgow the Lord-Provost, who also entertained the Goughs at his palatial residence. At Rochdale three Mayors were on the platform ('tis to be hoped the speaker was quieter than usual that night!)—his Honor of Rochdale in the chair, and their Honors of Bury and of Oldham, on either hand, in the full insignia of their office.

Really, temperance had become fashionable in the very realm of Bass's ale. Nor did the unwonted presence of these grandees abash the orator or dull the edge of his incisiveness. In one of his London speeches he said:

"Last Sunday, between twelve and one o'clock, I went down to the locality known as 'Seven Dials.' I went to see what could be seen there. There were crowds of people in the street. Many persons were surrounding an earnest temperance reformer, who was telling them some wholesome truths. I

16

looked at the people. There was one woman who seemed to me to have but one garment on her. It was a cold day. She stood shivering in the cold, but she had three pence in her hand, and stood watching the door of 'The Grapes.' I saw men hanging about, licking their white lips,—waiting for those doors to open at one o'clock.[1] I saw boys and girls of fifteen years of age, in the most wretched state of poverty. My heart ached as I saw those crowds waiting for the public-houses to open, all having their few pence clenched in their hands. The temperance reformer who spoke to them, said: ' Why, some of you haven't got any shirts on, and yet you are going to pay the money that should go to buy some into the brewery. What is the consequence? The consequence is that you are shirtless, and that the people who ought to be engaged in supplying what you need, are without employment, because the ware-houses are overstocked. Why don't you buy, and make a market for linen, shirting, and leather, instead of making a market for beer, when you get nothing but misery by it ?'

"I stood and looked at the crowd, and then looked all over the front of that public-house; and (I speak my own senti-ments) as I looked at the names on the sign—

"'Trueman, Hanbury, and Buxton,'

I thought—so help me God !—I would not have my name on such a place for all the money spent in drink, and that is £160 - 000,000 sterling a year. It is to me astounding that in Eng-land men should get their living and make money, and grow rich *out of the pennies of the poor*." [2]

Great as the growth of temperance sentiment had been, Mr. Gough realized, as he moved about, that it must be even greater if England would witness the abolition of her most appalling curse.

But it was encouraging to find the attention of

---

[1] In London, public-houses were closed until that hour on Sunday.
[2] "Platform Echoes," pp. 608, 609.

Church and State directed to it, and the public conscience wide awake.

Among those with whom Mr. Gough became intimate at this time were Joseph Parker and the late
Charles H. Spurgeon. He made pen-sketches of both
of them. With regard to the former he writes :

"Dr. Parker is a remarkable man. I often walked twice on
the Sabbath from Piccadilly to Holborn Viaduct, a distance of
two miles each way, and felt amply repaid for my eight miles'
walk. . . . Let me give my impressions on hearing him
for the first time. His first words revealed a magnificent
voice. The reading of the hymn convinced one that he had
studied elocution. The impressive manner in which he uttered
the sentence, 'Let us worship God,' showed his perfect control
over every intonation ; and the reading of the Scriptures manifested his knowledge of the power of appropriate emphasis.
The prayer was beyond and above criticism. In the beginning
of his discourse I was disturbed and annoyed by his manner,
entirely new to me—thoroughly different from anything I had
ever seen ; but I soon forgot his manner in the intense interest
awakened by the sermon. . . . His utterance of words and
sentences was occasionally startling. Once, in speaking of the
bulwarks that were being broken down in these days of lax
living and lax doctrine in the church, he said of one doctrine
after another, *gone!* the Devil, *gone!* and God—*going!* No
one can imagine the force and power of the intonation." [1]

The American was a frequent visitor at Dr. Parker's
house, where he found the great preacher "childlike
—not childish." Their interchange of thought and
feeling was free and stimulating. Referring to the
charge of egotism made against Dr. Parker, he says :

"What man, conscious of great power, with an influence

---

[1] "Sunlight and Shadow," pp. 397 and 399.

sufficient to establish and maintain a church so complete in all its appointments, and with the ability to keep an audience week after week and year after year, filling the spacious edifice, with no diminution but rather an increase, till the place is becoming too strait; sustaining a Thursday-noon lecture attended by thoughtful men who crave and can only be satisfied with strong meat, and being able to meet all the demands of the intellectual throngs who attend his ministry; I ask, what man, conscious of all this, must not necessarily be self-confident, or rather self-reliant, and that not offensively? There are some men so painfully conscious of their defects, shortcomings, and failings, as not to realize and be thankful for the gifts God has given them—so excessively humble that their superfluity of humility is as painful to witness as the egotism of another." [1]

Mr. Gough heard Mr. Spurgeon away back at the time when both made their London *entrée*. With a limited education (four years at a common school in Colchester, and a few months in an agricultural college at Maidstone), the inspired boy preached his first metropolitan sermon to a congregation of two hundred people in a church (Park Chapel) that seated twelve hundred. "Before three months," says Mr. Gough, "the question in London was – I remember it well in 1853—'Who is this Spurgeon?'"

He appreciatively notes the successive upward steps in the career of his friend:

"In one year Park Chapel was enlarged, during which time Spurgeon preached in Exeter Hall. It was in that hall that I first heard him, as a young man drawing immense audiences. He had secured the ear of the people. In 1856 Park Chapel was inadequate to receive the crowds who flocked to hear him,

---

[1] "Sunlight and Shadow," p. 394.

and the Royal Surrey Gardens Music Hall was engaged. Here he preached to twelve thousand people every Sunday until the present Tabernacle was finished—in 1861. This seats five thousand and five hundred persons, with standing-room for one thousand more. When the Church removed from Park Chapel it had eleven hundred and seventy-eight members. In 1877 the membership was five-thousand one hundred and fifty-two. The immense amount of work performed by this one man is astonishing. He has published fifteen hundred sermons in volumes, and more than one hundred singly. He has published a commentary on the Psalms in five volumes called the 'Treasury of David.' He has issued sixteen other works, beside compiling a hymn-book, conducting a monthly magazine, and writing prefaces and introductions to other men's works."[1]

Mr. Gough, like every one else who heard him, was instantly attracted by Spurgeon's voice — "rich, melodious, under perfect control. Twelve thousand people could hear him distinctly in the open air, twenty thousand in the Crystal Palace."

He drove Mr. Gough out to see his "Orphanage," at Stockwell, where there was then two hundred and forty orphans; and the visitor speaks enthusiastically of what he saw—especially of a scene at the bedside of a little dying pauper waif, whom the great preacher's beneficence had rescued, and with whom he engaged in prayer and conversation in the last dread hour—greater and grander, then, Gough thought, than when swaying the mighty multitude at his will.

Of Spurgeon's pithy and quaint style, his friend gives several specimens. A contentious man, he calls "a stoker for Satan's fires." One who speaks well

---

[1] "Sunlight and Shadow," p. 402.

and means ill, he says, "hangs out the sign of the angel, while the devil keeps the house."

The companionship of Parker and Spurgeon was a well-spring of refreshment to Gough through all the months of this third English visit. It was in the latter's Tabernacle that he uttered his celebrated witticism on the hornet: "We are assured that alcohol is nutritious—it makes men lively! (a pause) well, if a man should sit down on a hornet's nest it would make him lively—but I question how much nutrition there would be in it!"

THE STREETS OF LONDON.

BEING in London for recreation, with plenty of time at his disposal, the New-England observer and exponent of the poor and miserable, spent a great many hours in the streets. They were to him theater, circus, panorama, church—something of each and a good deal of all. He was as fond of them as Dr. Johnson was, as Charles Lamb was, as Dickens was, and as Phillips was of the cow-path thoroughfares of his native Boston. "The people in the London streets, by day or night," he confesses, "fascinated me, and I never wearied of strolling about and watching them."

With regard to its demarcations, Mr. Gough remarks:

"London is several cities rolled into one. If you walk along Regent street, it is a city of gorgeous shops; if you turn to the West End, of parks and palaces; if you travel to St. Giles, of gin and dirt; in Belgravia, it is grand and rich; in Pimlico, it is poor and pretentious; in Russell Square, it is well-to-do. . . . Fashion migrates to the west; actors and musicians live about Brompton; the medical students take possession of whole streets in the vicinity of their respective hospitals; the inns of court are chiefly inhabited by barristers; France, Italy, Hungary, Poland, you will find represented by the cafés and cigar-shops, billiard-rooms, and restaurants of Leicester Square; Wapping, Rotherhithe, and the Commercial Road abound with

sailors of every nation under the sun ; Quakers live about Ed-
monton and Stoke-Newington ; Jews congregate in Houndsditch.   In short, the swells in the parks, the millers in Mark
Lane, the graziers in the new Cattle Market, the prim, pale
lads in ' the city,' the silk-weavers in Spitalfields, and the sugar-
bakers of Whitechapel, really form distinct communities, and
seem absolutely localized in their ideas."

As in all great cities, a crowd easily gathered.

"One evening," says Mr. Gough, "I started in a
cab from the Midland Railway station for Piccadilly,
accompanied by a lady. We had passed the 'Seven
Dials' and were in Gerard street, when the horse
staggered and fell. At once a crowd of men, women,
boys, girls, started out of the very ground.

"' Vot's hup, cabby ? '

"' Vy, don't yer see vot's hup? My 'orse is down ;
that's vot's hup.'

"' He's got the staggers,' said one, ' blest if he
'asn't.'

"'Vun of ye sit on 'is 'e'd, and vee'l git 'im out of
the shafts in a jiffy,' said another.

"Such a din ! boys laughing, girls screaming at
every fresh struggle of the wretched horse, or pitying
him, with ' Poor thing ! Vot a shame !' The beer-
soaked cabman was perfectly bewildered. Some one
shouted — ''Eres the bobbies' (police). By their
direction, we transferred our luggage to another cab;
and, paying half a crown in fees, beside the cabby's
fare, we got away, leaving the poor horse on the
ground and the crowd undiminished." '

Our stroller comments upon the street boys and

---

¹ " Sunlight and Shadow," pp. 60–61.

girls: "I found them, after twenty years, just the same—keen, sharp, impudent. Coming through the Strand, a flake of soot fell on my mustache. I began to run my fingers through the hair, when a ragged bit of a boy looked up at me, and said, with a perfectly sober face, 'It looks werry nice, sir!'"[1]

Mr. Gough was amused yet saddened by these children of the pave—their home, a cellar—their father, a drunkard—their mother, a shameless beggar —their sisters, with livid, withered, sad faces, plying their dreadful trade—the brothers, trained to crime, and scientifically wicked.

"At one of the ragged schools, on a Sunday night," he says, "as the clock struck eight, several of the boys rose to go. 'The lesson is not over,' said the teacher, 'stay.' The reply was, 'We must go to business.' 'What business?' 'Why, we must catch the people as they come from the churches and chapels.' They were pickpockets!"

Dickens's picture of *Fagin* and his pupils was not fiction, but fact. One of these boy thieves said to Mr. Gough: "There ain't no genius in pickin' a pocket; that's only slight o' 'and—anybody could do that. I'll tell yer vere the genius is. Ven you've got a gent's vipe (handkerchief) out of his pocket, and he turns round and says, 'Somebody's picked my pocket!' and you looks 'im right in the face, and says, ''As there, sir? that's werry 'ard on you sir,—that's cheek, that's genius.'"

Some of the explorer's experiences were far from pleasant.

---

[1] "Sunlight and Shadow," p. 61.

"On a certain occasion," he writes:

"I was strolling on a tour of observation up Holborn Hill— it was before the splendid Holborn Viaduct was engineered— and I turned into Gray's Inn Lane. On the opposite side of the street, around the entrance to a court, in a very bad local- ity, I saw a group of tatterdemalions, men, women, and chil- dren, some fluttering in rags, the very refuse of the slums, evidently in a state of great excitement; something out of the common order had occurred.

" As I was curious to know, for I often learn some lessons from the street folk, and get some ideas of strange phases of human nature in a crowd, I crossed over. Expecting to hear some foul language, somewhat in characater with the appearance of the crowd I was approaching, I soon heard expressions like these: ' Ah, God bless me, deary, deary me, poor thing: well, well, ah well, poor thing.' These were words of sympathy from human hearts for human sorrow. A man had fallen from a scaffold in a neighboring street, and was being brought home dead; and all this commotion was sympathy for the newly-made widow and her children. On the outskirts stood a very bad-looking man, with the closely cropped bullet-head. The bull-neck, the tiger-jaw, the small light-blue eye, made a sinister-looking animal, one you would not care to meet alone in a dark street at night. He had a cat-skin cap, a belcher handkerchief tied round his neck, and he evidently belonged to what are termed loosely the criminal classes. I said to him:

"' What's the matter here, sir?'

" He turned his eye full on me for a moment, and then said to the crowd:

"' Stand out of the vay, vill ye! 'ere's a swell vants to know vat's the matter.'

" I was not much of a swell, but I did want to know what the matter was.

" A woman told me the facts of the case, and pointing to a miserably faded creature, with three or four ragged children clinging to her skirts, said:

"'That's the woman that's lost her husband.'

" I was startled by this time to find that the crowd had closed in upon me, and I must confess I was frightened ; my knees grew weak, and I felt a dryness of my lips and throat from apprehension. Quickly it flashed through my mind—quicker than I can write it,—' Here I am in the midst of a crowd of the worst characters in London. I am shut out from all help ; no policeman near should they see fit to assault me. I have a gold watch in my pocket, gold and silver in my purse. Some of these men and boys are thieves by profession ; I do not like it. They might strike me a blow, drag me down this court, and no one would be the wiser. I should be missing,' etc., etc. All this was very foolish, perhaps. The bullet-headed man was close to me, and I did not like that ; my sensations were not agreeable.

" Summoning up courage, I turned to this man, and pointing to the woman, I said :

"' Is this woman very poor, sir ? '

" He replied, savagely :

"' Vat do you mean by that, hey ? Poor ? God Almighty help the woman ! Look at her, vill ye ? '

" I did look : all the womanhood apparently crushed out of her. So I boldly pulled out my purse, as I said :

"' Well, she looks as if she needed help ; poor thing, I am willing to help her. I'll give her a half sovereign, if it will do her any good. Shall I give it to you, sir, or to some of these women, or shall I give it to the poor woman herself ? '

"' God bless you, sir,' said one of the women ; ' give it to 'er ; she needs it bad.'

"' Thank you, sir,' said another.

" One with a blackened eye, said, holding up a child :

"' 'Ere's one of the children, sir.' I turned to go away. A passage was opened for me ; and though I am convinced there were men there who would have garrotted me for a shilling, or brained me for half a crown, yet every man as I passed out of the crowd, touched his rag of a cap, and said, ' thank ye, sir !' even my friend with the belcher and the cat-skin cap fitting close to his cropped head, looked more like a human being than an animal."[1]

The London costermongers[2] (strolling retailers of vegetables) greatly interested Mr. Gough. They form a numerous class, numbering over sixty thousand. He says of them:

"The working life of a coster is spent in the streets, and his leisure is very much devoted to the beer-shop, the dancing-room, and the theater; yet there are exceptions, some of them being very sober, orderly, God-fearing people. Home has few attractions to a man whose life is a street-life. They have their own beer-shops, theaters, and other places of amusement, They are rather exclusive, and like to be let alone. They are true to each other. If a coster falls ill, and gets into the hospital, he is visited by scores of his fellows.

"Religion is rather a puzzle to the costermongers. They see people coming out of church, and, as they are mostly well-dressed, they somehow mix up being religious with being respectable, and have a queer sort of a feeling about it. They will listen to the street-preacher; but I think the most unimpressible of all with whom I have been brought into contact, on purely moral and religious subjects, are the London costermongers. They do not understand how it is possible that you can feel any interest in their spiritual welfare; but if you relieve the necessities of any one in distress, you are at once popular.

"Once near Houndsditch I saw some poor, pinched little creatures playing in the gutter. I said to one, 'Do you want an orange?' The child looked up, half timid, half scared, and said nothing. I stepped up to the stand and took an orange, and offered it to the child; it was at once taken; and then

---

[1] "Sunlight and Shadow," pp. 139–144.

[2] They got their name from a peculiar kind of apple, called "costard," which they used to sell.

they flocked around me, and I must have given twenty or thirty oranges away, when I saw a group of costers looking on. As I left the crowd, the men gave a hurrah, and said, 'That's a gentleman'; whereas if I had offered them a tract, I might have had some chaffing.

"The life of a coster-boy is a hard one from morning till night : at first hallooing for his father, then in business for himself with a barrow; next he looks out for a girl to keep house for him. Very many are not married to the women with whom they live, yet they are very jealous, and sometimes behave very badly to the girl. One fellow, about sixteen, said, ' If I seed my gal a-talking to another chap, I'd fetch her sich a punch of the 'ed as 'ud precious soon settle that matter.'

"These boys are very keen ; as an old coster said, ' These yung 'uns are as sharp as terriers, and learns the business in half no time. I know vun, hate years hold, that'll chaff a peeler monstrous sewere.'

"As I said, they have strange ideas about religion. In the ' London Labor and London Poor' there are very many interesting details in reference to this class. One of them said, ' I 'ave heerd about Christianity: but if a cove vos to fetch me a lick of the 'ed, I'd give to 'im again, vether he was a little vun or a big 'un.' The idea of forgiving injuries and loving enemies seems to them absurd. One said, ' I'd precious soon see a henemy of mine shot afore I'd forgive 'im.' Said another, ' I've heerd of this 'ere creation you speaks about. In coorse God Almighty made the world, but the bricklayers made the 'ouses, that's *my* opinion. I heerd a little about the Saviour: they seem to say He vos a goodish sort of a man; but if He says that a cove is to forgive a feller as 'its 'im, I should say that he knows nothing about it.'" [1]

It would be endless to follow Mr. Gough in all his investigations up in the garrets of poverty, down in

---

[1] "Sunlight and Shadow," pp. 94–96.

the cellars of misery, among reeling sailors; in the midst of prostitution, in front of gaudy "gin-palaces "—"blazing lighthouses of hell," enticing and damning on every side. He paints them all as with Hogarth's brush, or the pencil of his old friend, Cruikshank. He likens himself, in these peregrinations among the unsewered classes, to a farm-hand who was constantly astonishing the old farmer for whom he worked by doing unexpected things, and who one day went into the barn and hung himself. Looking at the dangling form, the farmer said: "What on earth will that fellow do next?"

What is English philanthropy doing to better this badness? Much. City missionaries are everywhere afoot, devoting themselves chiefly to house-to-house visitation. And these are reinforced by street preach-ers—a rough and ready, but devoted and effective, body of Christian workers, many of them mechanics and working men, who give their spare hours to this service of humanity, and disclose great shrewdness and ingenuity in their methods of approach and address.

Moreover, there are abounding benevolent institu-tions and reformatory refuges set down in the midst of the greatest need, as centers of physical and moral help. And they go about their work in the most practical way—giving a clean shirt before speaking of a clean heart; feeding hunger before exhort-ing it; nursing sickness before bidding it prepare for death. This is the method of Christ, who incor-porated His word of salvation in an act of salva-tion, and reached and renewed the heart through a renovated body. Mr. Gough was in hearty accord with such humanitarianism in religion—believed in and practised it.

As intemperance was the main cause of the profligacy and squalor of the London streets, he was glad to find that the temperance people were actively engaged in the advocacy of their panacea along the sidewalks. He met a noble lady, the Honorable Maude Stanley, and frequently accompanied her in walks of philanthropy. Under her guidance, he remarks :

"I spoke in the vicinity of 'Five Dials' to an audience of four hundred, gathered from the garrets and cellars of the neighborhood, and after the address a temperance society was formed. It was a motley crowd, presenting vivid contrasts. There were the right honorable and the costermonger; the countess and the harlot ; the gentleman and the thief ; the refined and the degraded ; the rich and the poor—and the Lord, the Maker of them all." [1]

The result of that meeting was the opening of a "coffee-palace," called the "Stanley Arms," on the very spot, with Dean Stanley and other prominent persons for its sponsors. Miss Stanley has written often and admirably upon her work among the lowly, and the American found in her a kindred spirit.

Among the philanthropic agencies in London streets, he mentions Hoxton Hall. This had been a "music hall"—a vile place, and the ruin of many persons of both sexes,—a temple of abominations. In 1878 it was converted into a Gospel station, similar to Jerry McAuley's "Cremorne Mission," in New York, which, indeed, suggested the idea. Mr. Gough

---

[1] "Sunlight and Shadow," p. 160.

was profoundly interested in this venture, and spoke there repeatedly. One of these addresses, given under the auspices of the Blue Ribbon Army (a temperance organization connected with the hall), is thus outlined by the London *Times :*[1]

"On Saturday Mr. Gough, the temperance lecturer, addressed an audience at the Hoxton Temperance Music Hall, Hoxton street, composed mainly of 'reformed men and women.' The hall was thronged an hour before the time announced for the lecture. The audience was composed, with very few exceptions, of working men and women, and when the Rev. J. Johnstone, in the prayer prefacing the address, begged for the Divine guidance on those who had fled from the temptations of drink, a fervid 'Amen' was murmured from many lips. Sacred songs, under the leadership of Mr. William Noble, the honorary director of the Gospel temperance movement, were sung very heartily by the people, and Mr. Noble then asked all those who had signed the pledge in that hall to stand up. Nearly the whole of the audience rose, and he proceeded to say that among those were many reformed drunkards, as well as reformed men and women who had been moderate drinkers. He asked them to repeat their vow, and they, upstanding, solemnly said, 'I promise, by God's help, to abstain from all intoxicating liquors, and to discountenance their use in others. The Lord help me to keep this vow for Christ's sake. Amen.' Mr. Noble went on to say that Mr. Gough had given upwards of thirty addresses to the working classes of London without fee or reward, and in these the Hoxton people had largely shared.

"Mr. Gough had told the committee of the Blue Ribbon Army, that if they cared to take a large hall and make a charge for admission, his address should be in aid of the fund to carry on that mission, and if they had done so there would have been ten thousand people to hear him; but the committee had de-

---

[1] October 6, 1879.

cided to have a meeting whereat the people who had been ben-
efited by Mr. Gough's labors could assemble to bid him farewell. Mr. James Rae, late of the Royal Artillery, Mr. Morgan,
and Mr. Robert Rae, the secretary of the National Temperance
League, then spoke, and acknowledged the services of Mr.
Gough to the temperance cause.

"On behalf of the mission, Mr. John Smith, a French-polisher,
presented Mr. Gough with an album containing portraits of
those who had firmly enlisted themselves in the Blue Ribbon
Army. When Mr. Gough stood forward to receive the gift, a
poor woman pressed to the front, and presented Mrs. Gough
with a bouquet of autumnal flowers. Mr. Gough, who was received with repeated cheers, said he was unequal to the task of
making a speech that night, for he was quite exhausted. Touching, however, upon the fact of finding devoted gentlemen acting as door-keepers to that hall, he said he would rather be in
that position himself than have all the profits of the largest Bur-
ton ale brewery for fifty years. He would rather have the
lowest menial position in a work like that of the Blue Ribbon
Army, than hold the highest position in a work coupled with
any action which would do harm to a single soul. He proceeded to address his audience upon the pledge which they had
repeated, and after remarking that it was thirty-seven years
since he had signed a similar pledge, he added that though he
could not excuse drunkenness, yet it must be allowed that the
circumstances under which drunkards were made were different. The appetite for drink, once obtained, never wholly for-
sook men. They must pray to be kept from this appetite."

Yes, if there was sorrow in the streets of London,
there was also pity there. If Womanhood walked
discrowned and attended by demon shadows, Purity
also trod the pavements with her feet sandaled in
love. If Manhood hiccoughed and staggered along,
the angel of Sobriety steadied the bewildered feet and
guided them in ways of pleasantness and paths of

peace. If children were trained to be professionally wicked, they were also eagerly sought and taught to be divinely good. Where peril lurked, like a bloody leaper, ready to kill and craunch, safety was also ambushed to deliver and restore.

"Why do you not come any more for cold victuals?" asked a lady of one of these street Arabs, whom she had been in the habit of supplying.

"'Cos, ma'am," said he, "dad's signed the pledge, and we git hot victuals at home!"

III.

A SILVER TROWEL.

THERE is no form of human appreciation quite so grateful to a prominent man as that which comes from the scenes and associates of childhood. A man's birthplace is apt to resent a success of which it had no premonition, and in which it played no part. The estimate it formed in "the day of small things," it does not like to find mistaken. 'Tis an impeachment of the local judgment. It prefers to believe the outside world in error. Consequently, when his birthplace is won to revise its first opinion and echo a fellow townsman's honorable fame, he feels the compliment, and gives it a value far beyond its actual worth.

On the 5th of June, 1879, a recognition of this kind made John B. Gough very happy. Sandgate indorsed his standing in the world, and adopted him as a kind of patron saint.

It had long been a desire of his to set in the center of his native town a visible monument to temperance. This desire ripened into a purpose. The practical cast of his mind led him to prefer utility to ornamentation—both, if possible, but the first anyhow. "I have it!" he cried, "I will build a Coffee Tavern."

Friends were consulted. Funds were quietly but quickly collected. Mr. Gough, accompanied by a throng of temperance co-workers, went down to lay the corner-stone, on a date which marked, almost to a day, the fiftieth anniversary of his departure to play the part of Columbus and discover a name and reputation in the world.

Sandgate was in gala-dress. The citizens lined the sidewalks along the straggling street. A procession composed of the local clergy, the military of the neighborhood, the temperance societies, and the visitors, with the orator in their midst, marched, with banners flying and bands playing, toward the site of the new hostelry. And now, see! amid the cheers of the throng, the people unharness the horses, and themselves drag the carriage in which the grizzled Sandgate boy sits blushing and embarrassed—making a scene quite like the triumphal march of Trajan when he came back to Rome leading in the retinue of his conquest the races and customs depicted on his famous column, and encircling it from base to capital; only *this* is a retinue of peace and good will.

The center of the village is reached. The orator alights and delivers a characteristic address. He is in his happiest mood. The people laugh and cry by turns. The skies are in sympathy with temperance, and baptize the occasion with copious showers of cold water. No one cares; no one moves. He takes a silver trowel and with this lays the corner-stone of "The Gough Coffee Tavern." The darkness falls. The crowds disperse. And "God bless John Gough!" is the slogan of the hour.

Ever after, among all the trophies of love that decorate the home at "Hillside," this silver trowel holds first place. Lift it, and read the inscription:

"PRESENTED TO

J. B. GOUGH, ESQ.,

ON HIS LAYING THE

CORNER-STONE

OF

COFFEE TAVERN,

IN

SANDGATE, KENT,

JUNE 2D, 1879."

In looking about his birthplace, Mr. Gough was glad to see marks of improvement. As the waters of the channel rolled in upon the sands, erasing old impressions and smoothing them for new ones; so had the tides of time washed in and out of Sandgate, obliterating something of the past and preparing for the present. Certain landmarks were still visible —"the street," the older houses, the castle. But since "the days of auld lang syne" the population had multiplied three and a half fold, and now numbered 2,400; the outlying villas were more numerous; the summer saunterers on the sands looked smarter; the *morale* was higher, and smuggling had faded into tradition.

Not long after the laying of the corner-stone the "Gough Coffee Tavern" was completed and thrown open, advertising its namesake in a significant manner, and exemplifying his hospitable spirit towards man and beast.

PART XI.

The Hoary Head

" The hoary head is a crown of glory, if it be
found in the way of righteousness.'
                                        —PROV. xvi. : 31.

I.

OLD ACTIVITIES IN NEW RELATIONSHIPS.

THE preparation and publication of "Sunlight and Shadow," in 1880, signalized Mr. Gough's return to Yankeeland, in October, 1879. The book gave recent British experiences, supplemented by incidents, anecdotes, and *Goughiana*, covering the decade since the appearance of the revised and enlarged "Autobiography," in 1871, and was itself richly autobiographical, and therefore athrob with vitality. Being marked by all the peculiarities of its author, it met with quick success.

There was a continuous demand for printed copies of Mr. Gough's lectures. These were extant on both sides of the Atlantic, in words snatched from his lips, often incorrect (for he was the most impossible of speakers to report) and full of absurd mistakes. Thirty-six distinct lectures he had revised and allowed to go out, in England, in a penny edition, one lecture in each number, which sold to the extent of 1,000,000 copies. While in Great Britain three reporters from London followed him from place to place. Four metropolitan journals printed his speeches in full; many others abbreviated them; and the provincial press was equally enterprising. Moreover, letters from the four quarters of the globe came to "Hillside" assuring the orator that the reading of these speeches had been the means of leading many to reform.

Influenced by these considerations, and encouraged by judicious advisers, Mr. Gough issued " Platform Echoes," in 1884, a book composed of temperance and miscellaneous records of the platform, and profusely illustrated. It makes an interesting and worthy memorial. But we regret the form of it. The division into chapters is a poor substitute for a division into speeches. The addresses are thus mutilated and disguised. Moreover, since Mr. Gough so consistently disclaimed authorship, and since he was an acknowledged king of the platform, he might more wisely have collected his lectures, and given them to the world in an authentic edition. " Platform Echoes," instead of being a book of scrappy chapters, ought to have been a volume of connected public addresses. However, like its predecessors, it circulated readily and rapidly—and continues so to do.

Although never a partisan, the reformer was a party man. He recognized the truth that in a free country, government must be administered by party. Since its organization at Philadelphia, in 1856, he had acted with the Republican party. Its leaders had been his personal friends. Its history he read in the grandest achievements of the nineteenth century. In later years, however, its course had been marked by moral vacillation. From the temperance standpoint, the "party of moral ideas" was immoral. It had made promises before election to hold Prohibition voters, and broken them after election as easily and jauntily as dicers break their oaths. Temperance

men, like Clinton B. Fisk and Governor St. John ;
moral reformers, like Frances E. Willard and Mary A.
Livermore, were disgusted out of Republicanism.

Mr. Gough staid longer ; but at last he, too,
became a come-outer. Quoting the epigram of
Wendell Phillips, he said : "The men who made the
Republican party are in the grave ; the men whom
the Republican party made are in Congress." And,
being in Congress, they refused to do anything for
temperance. The prestige of government was perpetually with the foes of government, and the affairs
of society were administered by the outcasts of
society. Liquor was in office, and temperance was
out,—and was, therefore, naturally *put out*.

In early days, the liquor traffic was not organized. The manufacturers and venders were numerous, but they were not affiliated. Ardent spirits
were bought and sold side by side with legitimate foods and drinks over the counter of the grocery
or in the tavern. In the lapse of time all this has
changed. The liquor traffic has consolidated itself
into a vast, centralized oligarchy, as compact and
insolent as the slave-power used to be. With an
enormous capital, directly invested in the business ;
with an even greater wealth, indirectly but conse-
quentially concerned ; with tens of thousands of
saloons, each absolutely controlling from eight to ten
voters ; with appetite and social custom as active
allies; it dictates to political parties, writes the death-
warrants of politicians, or secures their promotion,
according as they serve or oppose its cause, buys up
or browbeats legislatures, terrorizes the community
by assaulting or assassinating unpurchasable or

undaunted opponents, and flares a legalized right to be in the faces of the husbands and fathers and sons it ruins, the wives and mothers and daughters it bows in want and mortification and sorrow to the earth, the children it pawns to ignorance and poverty and vice, and the public it seeks to damn.

"When bad men combine," remarks Edmund Burke, "the good must associate, else they will fall one by one, an unpitied sacrifice in a contemptible struggle." In obedience to this precept of the great master of political philosophy, the friends of temperance had met in Chicago in 1869 (September 1st), and formed a Prohibition party, whose avowed object was the legal destruction of the liquor traffic. Like most third parties, it made slow progress. In the Presidential election of '72 it threw 5,607 votes in six States; in '76, 9,737, in eighteen States; in '80, 9,678, in sixteen States; in '84 (the period of which we write), 150,626, in thirty-four States—an encouraging gain.[1]

Governor St. John, of Kansas, was the candidate of the Prohibition party in '84. He was a man who had Mr. Gough's entire confidence, and the veteran was more than glad to vote for him. In explanation of his course, he wrote:

"For forty-two years I have been fighting the liquor trade —the trade which robbed me of seven of the best years of my life. I have long voted the Republican ticket, hoping always for help in my contest from the Republican party. But we have been expecting something from that party in vain; and

---

[1] In 1888 the Prohibition vote was 249,945. In 1892 it was 270,710.

now, when they have treated the most respectful appeal, from the most respectable men in the country, with silent contempt, I say it is time for us to leave off trusting, and to express our opinion of that party."[1]

In the same year, only a few days before the election, he wrote a letter to *The Voice*, in New York, the Prohibition organ, in which he said:

" I have one vote to be responsible for that has always been given to the Republican party from the beginning of its existence to this present year. . . . I hoped to find in the Republican party, as a party of high moral ideas, protection against the liquor traffic, instead of protection for it, and have been unwilling to aid in making this grand cause a football to be kicked between political parties. . . . This year, however, has seen strange things. Surprising disintegrations have been going on in the two old parties. Both have either open affiliations with, or a cowardly and shameful servility to, the arrogant set of rings and lobbies of this drink trade, which lifts its monstrous front of $750,000,000 of money spent directly in it, with an equal sum in addition taxed upon the people to take care of its miserable results."[2]

Such was the choice and action of John B. Gough, in 1884. At the same time, in a passage illustrative of his catholicity of spirit and feeling as a reformer, he wrote:

" While I stand unflinchingly on the platform of total abstinence and absolute prohibition, combining their forces for the entire abondonment of the drinking customs and the annihilation of the manufacture and sale of alcoholic beverages,— I hold out my hand to every worker as far as he can go with me, if it is but a step."[3]

---

[1] " Cyclopædia of Temperance," Art. " Gough," p. 194.
[2] *The Voice*, October, 1884.   [3] " Sunlight and Shadow," p. 482.

Through these years, in the midst of these readjust-ments, the lecturer who " hailed " from " Hillside," but was seldom there,

> " The round of his simple duties walked,
> And strove to live what he always talked."

Wherever he went, there was a generous rivalry among the most charming homes, for the honor of his entertainment. In an affecting page of the " Au-tobiography " he refers to this fact:

" Among the results of my public life, most valuable and ap-preciated, are the pleasant homes I have found in this country and Great Britain ; the association with some of the best and noblest ; and the familiar intercourse with so many of the wise and good ;—this, next to the fact that I may have been able, by God's blessing, to accomplish something toward the amelioration of the condition of the poor and degraded, and the upbuilding of the cause of the Master—has been to me a source of the highest gratification. I could fill page after page with the record of kindness received in the homes where I have found a welcome. The recollection of them crowds upon me." [1]

None of his friends were closer than two whose eminence almost equaled his own, — the Rev. Dr. Wm. M. Taylor, of New York, and the Rev. Dr. Theodore L. Cuyler, of Brooklyn. It was during his second British tour that he made Dr. Taylor's ac-quaintance, at Liverpool, where he was then settled. When Dr. Taylor came to fill the pastorate of the Broadway Tabernacle, New York, in 1872, this ac-quaintance matured into intimacy. Whenever he could do so, Mr. Gough so timed his visits to New

---

[1] " Autobiography," p. 549.

York as to spend the Sunday there, and listen to this prince of preachers. "No man ever opened up the Scriptures to me as he did," says the visitor; "whenever I go to the Tabernacle I am helped and comforted." [1]

Mr. Gough met Dr. Cuyler when the latter was in the Theological Seminary at Princeton, away back in 1844, on the occasion of his first speech at that venerable seat of learning. On both sides, it was a case of love at first sight—a love never afterwards cooled or clouded through evil or through good report. "I visited him in his first manse, at Burlington, N. J.," writes Mr. Gough; "then many times in Trenton, afterwards in New York, when he was at the Market Street Church, and since his settlement over the Lafayette Street Church, Brooklyn." It was a source of regret that the exigencies of his calling forbade the lecturer from hearing this preacher often. But as a correspondent he got into the heart of his friend. "I have read many of Horace Walpole's letters," he says, "all of Cowper's that are published, a large proportion of Charles Lamb's, but, in my opinion, Dr. Cuyler's letters, of which I have a large package, are superior to them all. If selections from his correspondence with different individuals for the last thirty-five years were published, they would constitute one of the most readable of books." [2]

Mr. Gough valued his opportunities on the platform and his friendships off of it, chiefly as ways and means for waging his moral warfare. As time passed and

---

[1] "Sunlight and Shadow," p. 417.
[2] "Sunlight and Shadow," p. 419.

his youth receded, instead of hating liquor less he hated it more. Thought, feeling, observation, inflamed his advocacy.

" While I can talk against the drink," he exclaimed, " I'll talk; and when I can only whisper, I'll do that; and when I can't whisper, I'll make motions. They say I'm good at that! "

Like all earnest men, Mr. Gough found his patience severely taxed by palterers. Honest opponents he could reason with. Liquor-dealers he knew where to find—there was something admirable in their fixedness. But on the road to the celestial city, " Mr. Timid " and " Mr. Expediency," and " Mr. Facing-bo h-ways," were characters at once common and detestable. On this point he would have agreed with a recent spicy writer's estimate:

" The saloon-keeper is ' a man of quality '—of one quality, especially—stay-putness. Wherever you left him, you will find him, if you go back.

" Morally and religiously he varies like other people. Politically he is absolutely genuine, admirable. In Iowa or Illinois he is the same, the soul of political faithfulness to his dominant issue. In a winning race he wears his honors lightly ; in a hopeless minority he fairly shines. Tell him ' It is no use,' ' You will throw your vote away,' ' Stick to educational methods,' and such irrefragable reasoning—to Christian men—and he will ' smile, and smile, and be a villain still.' He has an idea and believes in it. He can neither be flattered, ' fixed,' frightened, nor fooled.

" He not only stands for ' personal liberty '; he is ready to fall with it. The American eagle, winged, beaked, taloned, and roosting on a streak of lightning, is an ordinary barn-fowl as an emblem of liberty compared to him, alert, aproned, with the law's lightning in his license skewered to his wall, the national colors under his feet, and his head towering amidst clouds of public sentiment colossally innocuous to him—serene as Jupiter he is 'there,' like the distilleries round about Peoria; and he wins, not only the election—that could be borne —but he wins by the votes of men that abhor him. For in contrast that would be very funny if it were less mysterious and humiliating is the average man of what is called the 'better class' politically. With him principles are things of topography; convictions are held with a certain sense of proportion, and relative to the world, the flesh, and the party. He is Prohibitionist in Kansas, prohibitionish in Massachusetts, prohibition-oid in South Carolina, a 'sentiment-maker' in Auburndale, a sentimental fakir in Boston. Yet, if you should meet him in Kansas, he would say that he was a Prohibitionist, not because it was Kansas, but because he was he. He will tell you that he wore out his chaise hauling Prohibition voters in Sioux City, but is now filling the pulpit of St. Demijohn, in Omaha, and suits; that he stumped Iowa for the amendment, and has not changed his mind, but would not read a notice of a W. C. T. U. meeting in his present charge. Call on him in Omaha, and he will tell you that he is in favor of the best law that the average local sentiment will approve; by which process of reasoning he would be, if he lived in Sheol, a contented devil. He believes in 'final perseverance' of the liquor traffic, and in justification by bargain and sale at the best obtainable figure." [1]

---

[1] John G. Woolley, "The Golden Rule," August 10th, 1893, p. 921.

II.

As a veteran of temperance, whose life synchro-
nized with its organization into a social and political
movement, Mr. Gough's philosophy of the cause
deserves careful study. He was not a scholar, in
the academic sense, but he was a close and accurate
observer. And he knew his own limitations. If he
was unable to discuss certain phases of the subject at
first hand, he knew just where to go for the required
information, so that he could speak with authority
at second hand. Thus, either through personal experience, or because of access to supreme authorities, he
was master of the encyclopædia of the reform he
advocated.

Mr. Gough contended that alcohol is an alien principle, not included in the scheme of life. One-fourth
of life, and that the most exposed portion, viz.,
infancy and childhood, is spent without any use of it
—as the remaining stages are by most Orientals, and
by ever-enlarging numbers of abstainers in Europe
and America, to their immense physical and moral
gain.

He quotes the celebrated B. W. Richardson, M.D.,
on the physiology of alcohol, to show that it is not a
natural food:

" If you ask science for a comparison of alcohol and of man, in respect to the structure of both, her evidence is as the sun at noon in its clearness. She has taken the body of man to pieces; she has learned the composition of its structure—skin, muscle, bone, viscera, brain, nervous cord, organs of sense. She knows of what these parts are formed, and she knows whence the components came. She finds in the muscles fibrine; it came from the fibrine of flesh, or from the gluten or albumen of the plants on which the man has fed. She finds tendon and cartilage and earthy matter of the skeleton; they were from the vegetable kingdom. She finds water in the body in such abundance that it makes up seven parts out of eight of the whole; and that she knows the source of readily enough. She finds iron; that she traces from the earth. She finds fat; and that she traces to sugar and starch. In short, she discovers, in whatever structure she searches, the origin of the structure. But, as a natural presence, she finds no ardent spirit there in any part or fluid. Nothing made from spirit. Did she find either, she would say the body is diseased, and, it may be, was killed by that which is found.

" Sometimes in the bodies of men she discovers the evidences of some conditions that are not natural. She compares these bodies with the bodies of other men, or with the bodies of inferior animals, as sheep and oxen, and finds that the unnatural appearances are peculiar to persons who have taken alcohol, and are indications of new structural changes which are not proper, and which she calls disease. Thus, by two tests, science tries the comparison between alcohol and man. She finds in the body no structure made from alcohol; she finds in the healthy body no alcohol; she finds in those who have taken alcohol changes of the structure, and those are changes of disease. By all these proofs she declares alcohol to be entirely alien to the structure of man. It does not build up the body; it undermines and destroys the building.

" One step more. If you question science on the comparison which exists between foods and alcohol, she gives you facts on every hand. She shows you a natural and all-sufficient and standard food. She calls it milk. She takes it to pieces; she

says it is made up of casein, for the construction of muscular
and other active tissues; of sugar and fat, for supplying fuel to
the body for the animal warmth; of salts for the earthy, and
of water for the liquid parts. This is a perfect standard.
Holds it any comparison with alcohol? Not a jot. The comparison is the same with all other natural foods."

Wilson's "Pathology of Drunkenness," is referred
to as "a most vivid and fearful revelation of the
progress from conviviality to casual and habitual
intoxication, and the constitutional and mental results.
Wilson traces the disturbance of the circulation, the
disorder of the functions of digestion, the disease of
the liver, of the kidneys, of the lungs, the tubercular
degeneration, the brain disease, the apoplexy, which
are some of the constitutional results; while loss or
confusion of memory, mental aberration, delirium,
lunacy, and suicide are some of the mental results.
The springs of life are tainted at their source,
and their currents diffusing themselves everywhere
throughout the system, the one as the basis of
vitality, the other as the origin of its leading
phenomena, have the traces of their altered qualities
everywhere apparent." [1]

With reference to the alcoholic stages, he further
quotes Dr. Richardson:

"A man or woman sitting down or standing up
to drink wine, or other stimulant, always starts on
the way that leads through four stages towards an
easily realizable destination : Stage one, is that gentle
stimulation called moderate excitement, or 'support.'
Stage two is elevation—whatever that may mean. It

---

[1] "Sunlight and Shadow," p. 447.

is not elevation of character, of that I am satisfied. Stage three is confusion of mind, action, and deed, with sad want of elevation. Stage four is complete concatenation of circumstances—all the stages perfectly matured, the journey completed, the traveler lying down, absolutely prostrated in mind and in body. The destination is reached, and is found to be a human being dead drunk."

In this connection, he relates an Arabian fable of the vine :

"The devil matured the vine with the blood of four animals: First, with that of the peacock ; and when the vine began to put forth leaves, with the blood of the ape ; when the grapes began to appear, with the blood of a lion; and, lastly, when they were quite ripe, with the blood of a hog : which is the reason, the Arab says, that the wine-bibber at first struts about like a peacock, then begins to dance or sing, and make grimaces like an ape, then rages like a lion, and finally lies down in a ditch, like a hog."[1]

It is while in the third stage of drunkenness, the stage in which Dr. Richardson in the above extract asserts that the victim is "confused in mind, action, and deed," or the "lion state," according to the Arabian fable,—that the drunkard is usually moved to become a criminal. "I have read somewhere," says Mr. Gough, "an old legend, in which a man was offered his choice of three voluntary acts: to murder his father, burn down his house, or get drunk. Laughingly, he chose the latter as the least objectionable of the three. He got drunk. While in that state he became furious. Enraged at his father's attempt to control him, he

---

[1] "Sunlight and Shadow," p. 474.

struck him a blow with a hammer which lay near, and killed him; then, filled with horror at the deed, he set fire to the house, hoping to destroy the body and hide his crime." [1]

The apostle of temperance maintained that knowingly and willing to drink what will thus paralyze the reason and inflame the passions, is sinful:

" I believe that when a man knows that the use of intoxicating liquors is detrimental to his health, injurious to him in body and mind, hinders his useful labor, and will solely for his sensuous gratification use it, then he commits sin. . . .

" Drunkenness is a sin unlike others, in that it carries its penalty with it in the suffering and enslavement of its victim. It is but the penalty for violated law ; the sin is not in the penalty, but in the violation of law. Now, is there no wrong in drinking, unless it produces what we call drunkenness or intoxication ? If you mean by drunkenness a persistent use of alcoholic beverages, knowing all the consequences, then it is always and ever sin against the body, the mind, the soul, and society, and a grievous sin against God. But is there no sin in the intoxication that consists in mere exhilaration, elevation, or excitement ; or even the slight confusion of thought, without staggering or stammering ? If the brain is disturbed in its action and the power of the will weakened, or if the self-control is affected, the perception stimulated while its accuracy is destroyed : if the judgment is perverted, if the drinker will go where he would not go without it, say what he would not say without it, think as he would not think, and do as he would not do without it; though his utterance may not be thick, his eye may be clear, his gait steady, and no outward appearance giving evidence— is he not in some degree tipsy, inebriated, drunk ?

" Can a man steal a little, lie a little, swear a little, and be innocent ? Are there any degrees by which you may measure

---

[1] " Sunlight and Shadow," pp. 448, 449.

the enormity or the veniality of these practices? I would fasten the sin on the *cause*, not on the *effect*, be it greater or less."[1]

In answering the assertion that wine has been the concomitant and promoter of civilization, the lecturer quotes an eminent writer as saying:

" It is said that the use of wine and its allies has been the source of the power of the most powerful nations. It is said that the wine-cup has been the fountain of that wit and poetry and artistic wisdom, if I may use the term, which has made the illustrious men of the world so illustrious and so generally useful as they have been to the world. Take away the wine-cup, it is argued, and the whole intellectual life must needs become ' flat, stale, and unprofitable.' It were indeed a pity if this were the lookout of total abstinence, a second deluge of water, with not so much as a graceful dove and an olive-branch to cheer the trackless waste. It were indeed a pity of pities if this were the final lookout of total abstinence in the intellectual sphere. Can it be that all intellectual energy and hilarity must die out with the abolition of the wine-cup? . . .

' Science, ever fair, says that some nations and wonderful peoples that have lived have been wine-drinkers at certain periods of their history. But she draws also this most important historical lesson, that the great nations were, as a rule, water-drinkers purely, until they became great; then they took to wine and other luxuries, and soon became little. Up to the time of Cyrus, the Persians were water-drinkers; they became all-powerful, and then also became such confirmed wine-drinkers that, if they had some great duty to perform, they discussed the details of it when inflamed with wine, and rejected the judgment or revised it when they had become sober, and *vice versâ*. Surely this was the acme of perfection as a test of wine. Curiously, it didn't answer. With its luxury Persia succumbed, fell into hands of less luxurious conquerors, and, like a modern rake, found its ' progress' anything but progressive in the end.

[1] " Sunlight and Shadow," pp. 449-450.

"The Greeks in their first and simple days were clothed in victory over men and over nature. They grew powerful; they sang and danced, and all but worshiped wine; but it did not sustain them in their grandeur, as it ought to have done if the theory of such sustainment be correct. The Roman rule became overwhelming out of the simplicity of its first life. It rose into luxury, and made wine almost a god. But Rome fell. Wine did not sustain it. It is all through history the same. There is not an instance, when we come to the analysis of fact and circumstance, in which wine has not been to nations, as to man individually, a mocker. It has been the death of nations. It has swept down nations, as it sweeps down men, in the prime of their life, and in the midst of their glory."

So much for the evil of intemperance, and the nature of it, as it lay in the perception and philosophy of Mr. Gough.

Let us turn, now, to his scheme of reform.

He pleaded first and last and all the time for total abstinence, as "a certain, effectual cure. It never fails, it cannot fail. It stops the supplies, and the evil must cease; it dries up the spring, and there can be no stream. Prevention is better than cure. It is worth a life-effort to save a drunkard, to lift a man from degradation, but to prevent his fall is far better."[1]

As it concerns a reformed man, total abstinence he esteemed the only possible course. His own experience, and the experience of tens of thousands of others, spoke on this point in trumpet tones. The appetite for liquor is created by indulgence. This is a physiological effect which remains after reform. When the desire is gone, appetite lies couchant—like the pet tiger that licks its master's hand till blood is

---

[1] "Sunlight and Shadow," Chap. xxxii, *passim*.

tasted—then hold him who can! One glass will rouse this appetite, and unmake the new-made. The only safety for the reformed drunkard is total abstinence.

In pleading with the moderate drinker, Mr. Gough says:

" I appeal to him on a higher ground than mere self-preservation. I ask him to abstain for the sake of others. . . . In view of the terrible nature of this evil, and of the fact that the *drunkards are all drawn from the ranks of moderation;* that, when death makes gaps in their ranks, they are filled by recruits from the army of moderate drinkers,—we must speak out, and implore the moderate drinker to give up his gratification for the sake of others. I do not accuse such an one of willfully doing harm. I ask him to investigate, and to test his position." [1]

Mr. Gough sought to reinforce total abstinence by basing it upon religious principle. He knew men could abstain who had never drank, that men could abstain who had been moderate drinkers, and that men could abstain who had been drunkards, by an act of the will. But he was convinced that such abstainers, whichever of these classes they belonged to, were in chronic peril. He believed the grace of God to be more reliable than the grace of the will. Personally, when he first signed the pledge, he kept it by the grace of the will, five months,—then broke it. When he re-signed it, under the grace of God, he never broke it. Temperance he regarded as a Christian virtue—one of many; and he put it, where Peter did, between manliness and knowledge; and where Paul did, between righteousness and judgment to come. The development of an harmonious Christian charac-

---

[1] " Sunlight and Shadows," pp. 476–477.

ter would embrace and fortify temperance.   Hence
his desire to bring the pledge under the grace of God.
"I tell men," he says, "to abstain by the power of
their will; but every day they abstain in their own
strength, in the midst of temptation, they do it at a
risk.   When they put forth all their energies, and
then trust in God's grace, they are safe." [1]

He did not believe that the grace of God takes away
the appetite for liquor in the case of a reformed man.
On this point he remarks :

" Does any one believe that the inflamed state of the stomach,
as shown in Sewall's plates,—the congestion, the complete
disorder of the whole nervous system—and all the irritation
that causes the desire, can be removed with no inconvenience
and no effort ; and that the whole constitution can be as free
as when the first glass was taken ?   I do not believe it, except
by a miracle. . . .   Remember when Paul prayed that the
thorn in his flesh might be removed, the answer was, ' My
grace shall be sufficient for thee '—though the thorn was not
removed ; and remember, also, that God will not permit any
who trust in Him to be confounded or put to shame." [2]

Mr. Gough strongly condemned the use of alcoholic
wine at the communion table, as unsafe for those who
had come into the Church through the door of reform,
and urged the adoption of the unfermented juice of
the grape—now largely, we wish we could say generally, used at the Lord's Supper :

"When I first began a Christian life I partook of the
the Communion when intoxicating wine was used.   I once told
the minister that the church smelt like a grog-shop after the

---

[1] " Sunlight and Shadow," pp. 459, 460.
[2] " Sunlight and Shadow," pp. 464, 465.

ordinance, and that the odor of alcohol was on every com-
municant's breath. . . . What was its effect on me? The
small draught warmed my stomach. It brought back vividly
the old sensations, though it did not mount to my head and
affect my brain; yet it was a reminder of the old, bad times,
and called up associations connected with the use of this very
article in another way than as a religious ordinance. . . .
I was startled by the pleasant sensations produced by the
alcohol even in that small quantity. I could not help that if I
took it, and I determined to use it no more." [1]

Touching the warrant for drinking which some men
pretend to discover in the Bible, and the long con-
troversy over *tirosh*, *yayin*, *oinos*, *gleukos*, and other
terms, he says:

"There has been much discussion—many volumes written,
some strong feelings expressed, and, I think, bitterness engen-
dered—over the wines of Scripture. I pay very little attention
to this agitation, as the subject is of no particular moment to
me. I am not learned, and know nothing of Hebrew or Greek;
and if learned men say that the Bible sanctions the use of alcoholic wine, that the Saviour made and drank intoxicating wine,
I can only reply that I do not believe it. But there is no
necessity for argument with me, as I do not understand the
question, and it is perfectly immaterial to me what wine the
Saviour made and drank, as it is what clothes He wore, or
what food He ate; for I am no more bound to drink what He
drank than I am to eat what He ate, or to wear the kind of
clothing in which He was appareled." [2]

Furthermore, he adds:

"I do not go to the Bible for a command, 'Thou shalt abstain from intoxicating liquors.' I do not seek for a command

---

[1] "Sunlight and Shadow," pp. 462-463.
[2] "Sunlight and Shadow," p. 484.

in the Bible to abstain from gambling, horse-racing, prize-fighting, dog-fighting, cock-fighting, and all that sort of thing. As a Christian man I abstain from these things, believing them to be detrimental to the best interest of society; and because I am a Christian it is not only lawful for me to do so, but a bounden duty. . . . With my views of Christianity and its claims upon me, by my allegiance to God, by my faith in Christ, by the vows I took upon myself in His presence and before His people, I am bound to give up a lawful indulgence, if, by so doing, my example will save a weaker brother from falling into sin. That is my position; can you take that away from me? I will hold it, and take my stand upon it in the day of judgment." [1]

Out of his wide experience in meeting objections of all kinds, he gives several instances of amusing exegesis:

"I was told of a Cameronian in Scotland who declared he had a command to drink spirits, 'for,' said he, 'are we not told to try the spirits?' And so he would sample every whiskey-bottle that was presented to him, quoting Scripture at the same time. I heard a man defend gambling from the passage, 'The lot is cast into the lap, but the whole disposing thereof is of the Lord.' It is told of another that he refused to believe the Bible because it was opposed to personal cleanliness; and when asked for evidence, he quoted the passage, 'He that is filthy, let him be filthy still.'" [2]

Mr. Gough brought prohibitory law to the aid of total abstinence and religious conviction. This was the third essential principle in his conception of the trinity of temperance. It was the objective point of his agitation.

---

[1] "Platform Echoes," pp. 257–258.
[2] "Sunlight and Shadow," p. 488.

The right to prohibit seemed to him as clear as sunshine. The public safety is the highest law. Whatever menaces that, may and should be prohibited. All Governments act upon this principle. France and Germany prohibited the importation of American pork—why ? To protect the stomachs of their people against trichinæ. The United States suspended immigration in 1892. On what ground ? Because there was cholera in Europe and Asia, and immigration threatened infection.

By the right of eminent domain, the sovereign power seizes private property, appraises it, and appropriates it to public use.

By parity of reasoning prohibition is avouched. If the State adjudges the manufacture and sale of liquors as a beverage to be inimical to the welfare of the community, its right to prohibit is self-evident—like the truths Jefferson catalogues in the commencement of the Declaration of Independence.

But in a free community, while the abstract right is beyond successful question, the power to exercise it is dependent upon public opinion. Any law, however wholesome, which has not a friendly public opinion to operate it is worse than no law—is a dead letter, and tends to bring all other laws into contempt. In the present state of the popular conscience, a prohibitory law could not be enforced in America. "Grand juries would not indict ; district attorneys would not prosecute ; petit juries would not convict ; judges would not sentence ; and governors would pardon."

Mr. Gough, with characteristic good sense, rejoiced that there was not now a prohibitory clause in the

Constitution of the United States. At the same time, he worked early and late to secure such an amendment! Why? Because he knew that the agitation necessary in order to carry the measure would be a "campaign of education." It would be impossible to win a constitutional prohibitory amendment, without first enlightening public opinion and vitalizing the conscience of the community. With this done, a national law prohibiting the liquor traffic would be as easily enforced as is the national law against slavery or against polygamy. "I believe," said Mr. Gough, "that a prohibitory law based on the public sentiment of antagonism to drink, will be successfully enforced ; and just in proportion as it is upheld by a spasmodic effort, without sufficient sentiment to back it, it will be a failure, and in my opinion worse than nothing." [1]

Thus believing, he devoted himself to the manufacture of public opinion, and made himself a doctor of the public conscience. "I cry out for assistance from every quarter," he said. "Small help is better than no help, and I will not refuse any aid given from any source to pull down the stronghold of intemperance." [2]

Toward those agents and agencies that were directly coöperative with him in his purpose, the temperance apostle turned with loving heart and smiling face. "The National Temperance Society and Publication House," in New York, "The Voice," "The Good Templars," "The Sons of Temperance," "The

[1] "Sunlight and Shadow," p. 481.
[2] "Sunlight and Shadow," p. 482.

Templars of Honor," and all similar associations, he encouraged in their efforts to circulate the literature of cold water, to educate the public mind, and to secure legislative enactments against the drink.

Above all, he welcomed and valued and cheered the presence and counsel and labor of women in the good cause. Referring to the formation of the "Woman's Christian Temperance Union," in 1874, as the outgrowth of the women's crusade against liquor in certain Western States—"a most wonderful movement, which roused the whole people to a consideration of the evils of drunkenness, creating an interest such as this country has not seen since the days of Washingtonianism "—he did not hesitate to say that he considered this "the most efficient organization in the United States to-day." [1]

Mr. Gough thought well of "Refuges" and "Homes," where a reformed man finds shelter and sympathy during his first few days of conflict with appetite—"where appeals are made to his conscience, representing his drunkenness not as a mere peccadillo, but as a sin against his body and soul, and as a sin against God." [2] He also approved of the coffee-palace movement in England, and of such coffee-houses as the "Model" and the "Central" in Philadelphia. But for many so-called temperance hotels and restaurants he had a profound contempt—places, he affirms, "where they charge as much for dirt and discomfort as you are required to pay in any other place for cleanliness and comfort." He adds:

"I once went into one of these, decoyed by the signboard,

---

[1] "Sunlight and Shadow," p. 495.   [2] "Sunlight and Shadow," p. 503.

and sat down at a table where the cloth looked like a map of the United States, stained with mustard, coffee, and grease, and with crumbs scattered all over it; the place reminding you of Coleridge's description of Cologne, in which he counted seventy-five distinct smells. I called for a steak, and can hardly describe the sights that met my eyes while that steak was in preparation. First the bread was put on the table—not a very attractive loaf; then some butter that had been cut with a dirty knife. The steak, how can that be described! It reminded you of the man who refused to partake of a similar steak on the ground that it was an infringement of Goodyear's patent for india-rubber. I asked for a cup of tea. It came, reminding you again of the customer who said, 'If this is tea, I want coffee; if it is coffee, I want tea.' In the sugar a wet spoon had been so often dipped that it had caked into little drops of discolored sweetness. The spoon itself was sticky; and the whole affair was so utterly destructive to all healthy appetite, that I left as hungry as I entered." [1]

Mr. Gough, like all men with clear brains, healthy livers, and knowledge of the facts, was an optimist. While facing and fighting existing evils, he saw and rejoiced in the law of progress, and sang, with Tennyson:

" Yet I doubt not through the ages one increasing purpose runs,
And the thoughts of men are widened with the process of the suns."

He mentions the surprising improvements in locomotion (a topic on which he was *au fait*), in communication, in personal comfort, brought about by steam, electricity, sewing-machines, chloroform, photography, and a multitude of strange and curious inven-

---

[1] " Sunlight and Shadow," p. 504.

tions, which have done more for human advancement
in the last few decades than had been done in all the
previous lifetime of our race ; and remarks :

" As I contemplate the past, how much there is to fill the
thought and stir the pulses in view of the wonderful progress
in all directions, and the great changes that have taken place
since my remembrance, and even since my first entry on public
life.

" In 1842, Louis Philippe was King of the French. In 1848
came the Republic, growing into the Empire. Again, in 1871,
after the Commune, came the Republic, routing the Empire.
Four great wars have agitated Europe: the Crimean, the
Italian, the Franco-German, and the war of Russia with
Turkey. In 1857 the great East Indian mutiny startled the
world. In 1847 occurred the war of the United States with
Mexico, and in 1861 commenced the war for the Union.

" What great reforms have been inaugurated in the past forty
years! In nearly all the civilized portions of the globe, from
Japan to Christianized Madagascar, from India to our own free
country, the battle is going on, and the fight becomes more
earnest. Glance rapidly over the world and see. The United
States has given freedom to her slaves; Russia has emanci-
pated her millions of serfs. Germany is fighting the double
battle in sight of the world, with a keen, relentless, moral des-
potism on the one hand, and on the other the struggle between
the license of materialism and the freedom that walks in stead-
fast obedience to Divine law. Italy, instead of being a nest
of petty States, united only in dense ignorance and abject
slavery, now walks among the nations, free to drain her
stagnant moral marshes ; free to say to all her people, ' Rise,
for thy light has come.' France has made leap after leap
for civil and political freedom and equal rights: and though
not yet landed on the safe side, still her dissatisfactions
are noble, and inspire the world with sympathy toward her
struggles. England is bravely grappling with internal problems, and burden after burden is being lifted from the shoulders

19

of her people. Turkey is being pierced with loopholes for light. Egypt tolerates Christian schools. Spain has seen the Inquisition crumble. China's Emperor is moving to prevent opium from paralyzing his millions of subjects. Japan asks of the United States teachers of schools after the method of to-day, and takes the Christian Sabbath for her Sabbath ;—all this when her ports, with one exception, were barred against the commerce of the world at the opening of this century. Hear the proclamation of the Queen of Madagascar, where till recently heathenism reigned supreme, with savage cruelties and perse-cutions to the death of all who dared avow the Christian name :

"' I, Ranovalomajaka, by the grace of God, and the will of my people, Queen of Madagascar, defender of the laws of my kingdom, this is what I say to you, my subjects : God has given me this land and kingdom ; and concerning the rum, you and I have agreed it shall not be sold, because it does harm to your persons, to your wives, and children ; makes foolish the wise, makes more foolish the foolish, and causes people not to fear the laws of the kingdom, and especially makes them guilty before God.'" [1]

Such was John B. Gough's philosophy of temper-ance. Those who have been wont to regard him as a mere minstrel of the cause, telling stories of re-form, as the troubadours in the Middle Ages sang of love and war from castle gate to castle gate, with no grasp of information, nor any power of origination—have been wofully mistaken in their estimate of the man. This survey of his views should suffice, in it-self, to indicate and vindicate the depth of his pene-tration, the reach of his knowledge, the kindliness of his charity, and the weight of his brain. We ques-tion whether any other man of his generation was as

---

[1] " Sunlight and Shadow," pp. 512–513.

thoroughly master of the encyclopædia of temperance as John B. Gough. Certainly, none other could equal him in the ability to handle ·the subject before the people.   Here, by common consent, like Burns's "Pink o' Womanhood," he

" .   .   .   blooms without a peer."

III.

BEGGARS, BORROWERS, AND BORES.

MR. GOUGH devotes three amusing chapters of "Sunlight and Shadow"[1] to the beggars, borrowers, and bores with whom he had enjoyed (?) a long and expensive acquaintance. All men in public life have similar experiences. Those whose lives are more retired may get from the recital a new reason to be grateful for privacy. Hence, we extract from the lecturer's big budget a few specimen cases. They serve to "point a moral," if they fail to "adorn a tale":

"When in England, twenty-five years ago, I boasted that I knew nothing in America of the system of writing begging letters, so prominent there; but I really think we can now fairly challenge competition in that line with any country in the world. I rather think it is an imported nuisance and not indigenous to the soil of America. . . . Every mail brings me such letters. One says:

"'Having heard that you were a very benevolent man, and knowing you were not a poor man, for I saw it stated in the paper the other day the amount of your income, I make bold to ask you a favor. My folks are respectable though not very well off, and I wish to go to a music-school for three years. My father has a rich uncle, whom I wrote to help me, but he

---

[1] XXI., XXII., XXIII., pp. 304-40. *Vide* his "Autobiography," pp. 531-534, for further instances.

thought himself too poor. The cost will be $500 a year. I wish you would send me a check for $500 for three years, or a check at once for $1,500.   Pardon my boldness, but I do so much wish to go, etc., etc.

"'P. S.—A check payable to bearer.'

"Another:

"'You talk of serving the Lord.   You will serve Him by helping me.   I want $1,000 to get a home.'

"Another:

"'I asked the Lord where I should get $100, and He whispered your name.   Now if you go to the Lord, perhaps He'll tell you to send it to me.'

"Another:

"'If you only knew how happy $100 would make me, you would send it, for you are abundantly able.'

"Again:

"'I want $1,000 to educate two nieces, and I write to you.'

"The most annoying class among the so-called respectable beggars are those who apply to you personally, and by appeals to your sympathy obtain money they never mean to repay.

"A young American in England begged me to lend him £10 for a passage home.   He could be sent home by steerage, but he could not endure a steerage passage ; spoke of his relatives, and said, 'I can give you an order on my mother.'   The money was lent and two pounds additional for some comforts for the voyage.   The order on his mother was given.   I have it now. When the gentleman reached this country he had the coolness to write me not to present the order to his mother, as it would be of no use, for she had no money—and that is the last of that transaction.   .   .   .   These people, many of them, never intend to repay.   I write as a sufferer; for from 1845, when they began on me, till now, the game has been going on—a losing one to me, for I have notes and promises to pay to an amount that would hardly be believed of one in my circumstances.   All I can say is, that the amount might be put down in five figures, with the figure five at the head of the sum. Over and over again have I declared that I will lend no more money to persons unknown to me, but they make such fair promises that I think, ' This must be a real case '; and like *Mr. Harlop,* ' I am taken in.' "

He goes on:

" A very curious plan adopted by some of these professionals is to take advantage of the credulity of their intended victims. I give portions of a letter received, purporting to come from my mother, who has been dead forty years.

Poor, dead woman ! she has forgotten how to spell, for she writes that this letter is to be attended to ' immegertely ':

" ' John, I, your mother, can speak to you through a medium in Bath, Maine.' (She seems to have learned something of geography; for when she was a denizen of this earth, I doubt if she knew there was such a place as the above.) ' You and this medium are strangers; but if you will come to her, my dear boy, I can convince you that I still live to enjoy my son's prosperity.' (No necessity to go to Maine to know that the dear mother lives.) ' Do not think or believe your mother does not help you and bear you up,' etc., etc. ' John, my son, fear not ; God has given you great gifts, and He has given great gifts to the one I am controlling to-day. I wish you would help her to come out of her poor condition she is in. If you knew what a gem she is, I know you would help her. Come and see me. I, your mother, send this. Come and talk to me through this medium. If you feel disposed to help her, do. From your mother to John.' "

One of his mails brought the following request from an aspirant:

" Being in need of a moddle lecture, I send to you for assist-ance. My request is that you will please compose a moddle lecture from the *extracts* of your old lectures and give it a sub-ject—a lecture that will take about an hour to repeat. I have heard of no man that can tie a lecture together with choice anecdotes such as you can, and indeed, sir, eloquence has dis-tilled her choicest nectar upon your lips. I have spoken several times on temperance," etc., etc.

Always willing to accommodate, Mr. Gough gives the following hints for a "Moddle" lecture, to aid any who may be fired with ambition:

"Your subject might be 'Reminders.' You can introduce it by stating briefly or at length, according to the time you have, that for a conversation it is necessary to start a theme, and then all is easy. Describe a company of people sitting dull and silent, with nothing to say; no subject to interest them. How shall they engage in a stirring game of conversation? Let some one tell a story, no matter what it is, and it will be sure to remind some one of the company of something else. There you are—'that reminds me' of a man who had but one story, and that was about a gun. He would impatiently watch, when in company, for a chance to repeat his story. When all was still, he would let fall a book, or stamp with his feet, then start and say: 'Oh, dear, how it startled me! It reminded me of a gun. Talking of guns, 'reminds me,'—and then came the story.

"This story of a gun reminds me of a famous hunter who had shot tigers in Africa. Conversing with a German about sport, he said, 'I care nothing for sport unless there is an element of danger in it.' The German replies, 'Ah! you vant danger? Vell, you go shoot mit me, dere vill be de danger. Vy, I shoot my brother in his stomich, toder day!' Talking of shooting reminds me of the man who had a heavy charge in his gun, and taking aim at a squirrel, fired. Over went he, and the squirrel ran twittering up the tree. 'Oh!' said he, as he picked himself up, 'if you had been at this end of the gun, you would not have run so fast.' That reminds me of two negroes, who were out shooting, and coming to a wolf's hole, one said, 'Dar's a wolf's hole.' 'I reckon dar is,' said Jem. 'I wonder wedder de ole un's in dat hole.' 'Dar ain't no wolf in dat hole, it don't look like dar was a wolf dar. I reckon dar's young uns.' 'Reckon dar may be young uns: s'pose

you go in dar, Cuff, and see wedder dar is or not.' 'Go in
yourself, Jem. I'll stand at de hole and watch for de wolf. If
I see him coming, I'll let you know.' 'All right'; and Jem
crept into the hole. Soon the wolf came up with a swinging
trot, and made straight for the hole. Cuff was too late, and
could only seize the wolf's tail, and then it was, pull wolf and
pull Cuff, the wolf's body completely filling the hole. Jem said,
'Cuff, what makes the hole so dark?' 'Is de hole dark?'
'It's all darkened up, what makes it?' 'Well, I reckon, if dis
wolf's tail comes loose, you'll know what makes de hole so dark.'
Talking of negroes reminds me of a colored man who, when
asked whether he knew the way to a certain place, said, 'I
wish I had as many dollars as I know where dat place
is.' This mistake of the negro reminds me of a Dutchman,
who wanted a man to go out of his store, and said, 'Go out of
my store. If you don't go out of my store, I'll get a policeman
vot vill.' Talking of Dutchmen, reminds me of two who went
into Delmonico's and got lunch. The price was higher than
they expected, and one of them was very angry, and began to
swear. 'Vot's de matter?' 'Matter enough; noine tollars
for lunch,—I vill swear!' 'Ah, nefer mind,' said the other,
'nefer mind. The Lord has punished dat Delmonico already,
very bad.' 'How has he punished him?' 'Vy, I've got my
pocket full of his spoons.' Talking of spoons, reminds me of a
politician,—and so you get into politics, and finish your lecture
ad lib."

Mr. Gough had many adventures with bores :

" I was quietly reading one summer day under the tree, when
a servant announced that a gentleman wished to see me.
   "' Who is he?'
   "' I don't know.'
   "' Did he give his name?'
   "' No, sir.'
   "' Where is he?'
   "' At the front door, in a buggy.'

"So, hoping that he would not keep me long, I went to the front door ; there sat a young gentleman in an open buggy

"'How do ye do, Gough ?'

"'How do you do, sir ?'

"'Don't know me ?'

"'No, sir.'

"'Don't know me ?   Look at me.'

"I looked at him.

"'Now don't you know me ?'

"'No, sir; I do not recollect you.'

"'Why, you stopped at my father's house once, when I was a boy. Know my father ?'

"'No.'

"'Don't know my father?   Well, I do.   Ha, ha! that's a joke.   Well, how do you do ?   I got a buggy in Worcester, and drove out here on purpose to see you.'

"'Will you walk in ?   I will see that your horse is hitched.'

"He walked with me into the parlor.

"I have a framed picture near the door, entitled 'The Return from the Deer-Stalking': a woman is rowing a boat across the loch, while a gentleman in a hunting cap and dress is in the stern.   When he saw it, he said :

"'Ah, a picture!' holding his half-closed hand to his eyes to get a good sight.   'That's a good picture.   Queen Victoria and Prince Albert, I suppose ?'

"I said, 'Hardly ! Queen Victoria would not be likely to row a boat across the loch.'

"'Ah, I dare say ; but you've been to England, and it struck me that it was the Queen.'

"Turning to another picture called 'Langdale Pikes,' he said —going through the same motions with his hands—'Ah, a very pretty farm scene.'

"I said, 'That is not a farm scene ; that is a view of Langdale Pikes, in Cumberland.'

"'Yes.   Well, I see some cows there, and didn't know but what it was an English farm scene.   Been to England, you know.   By the way, I want to see your library.'

"I took him into the room. As he looked around, he said :

"What a lot of books! Here's where you cook up your lectures, eh ?   Read 'em all ? '

"And so he went around the room talking nonsense, till he came to the two volumes of the 'History of British Guiana.'

"'Oh! there, I knew you were a practical man ! I like practical men. You're a farmer, and here's the book. I see you're practical.'

"I said ; 'What has that book to do with farming ? '

"'Why, don't you see, the History of British Guano ? That's practical—learn its history before you use it ! '

"'And so for three mortal hours did that man drive one wild."

But the bored in this case got even with the bore —or at least turned the *rencontre* to account:

"A circumstance occurred some years after, in connection with this visit, and I give it as a sequel. It is so ridiculously absurd that one can scarcely believe it to be possible, but I record the simple fact. I give no names ; and if the individual should happen to read this, he would not probably recognize the picture as any representation of himself. I was stopping in the hotel of the town where I was to lecture that evening, when this gentleman called, who said he had come to town to hear my lecture. We chatted awhile, and he left me. While I was speaking, I saw him in the audience. Soon I came to a point where I needed an illustration of the stolidity or stupidity of a regular bore, when the idea seized me—'Why not use this gentleman's visit at my house ? Ah, it would be too barefaced.' The temptation grew on me, and as I was speaking I argued the point. 'I do not believe he will take, yet it will hardly do.' Still I seemed to be seized with an almost irresistible desire to use the circumstance of his visit. Perhaps it was impudent, but I did it. As I looked on his face, and remembered him at my house, the risk of his taking it grew less, and I told the whole story through. He seemed to enjoy it, for he laughed when

others laughed.   After the lecture was over, he called on me at
the hotel.   Now, I thought, I shall catch it; but to my utter
surprise, he said:

"'Well, Gough, I enjoyed your lecture first-rate; but the best
part of the whole was about that man who called on you; for
don't you remember I called at your house once, and I remember your library and pictures.   It was first-rate.'

"'It is almost past belief that any man should be so obtuse,
but so it was.'"

One afternoon, in Roxbury, Mass., the lecturer was
resting preparatory to an address which he was to
deliver that evening.   Two ladies called, and asked
to see him.

His wife replied: "Mr. Gough is resting."

"We will keep him but a minute, we came from the
next town, and wish very much to see him."

"So I was called," he says, "and came into the
room half asleep in not very good humor.   There
were two strange ladies seated on the sofa, who
looked at me and then complacently smiled at each
other.

"'Ladies, did you wish to see me?'

"'Yes, we called for that purpose.'

"'What did you want?'

"'Oh, we do not want anything.   We live in
Hingham, and we've heard you lecture, and, we were
in Roxbury, and we found out where you lived, and
we don't want anything, but we thought we would
like to see how you looked in the daytime, for we've
never seen you except in the evening.'

"'Is that all?'

"'Yes, that's all we wanted.'

"'Good afternoon, ladies.'

"And I went back to my room with my rest completely broken by the curiosity that desired to see how I looked in the daytime."

As the disturbed sleeper returns to his sofa, we may all of us cry as he did:

> "O, wad some Pow'r the giftie gie us,
>   To see oursels as ithers see us!
> It wad frae monie a blunder free us,
>   And foolish notion."

IV.

THE platform adventures of platform monarchs are of perennial interest. Those who are themselves public speakers study them for instructive hints and suggestions—and sometimes in search of the secret of Dickens's " Circumlocution Office,"—" how not to do it." To others they give a peep into a strange world, as fascinating as a glance behind the scenes is to the play-goer.

In some phases of his career, Mr. Gough has (unconsciously and modestly) borrowed the pen of Boswell, and described himself in the *rôle* of Dr. Johnson. Nowhere is he more satisfactorily confiding than upon this theme.

As to his methods of preparation, he tells us that at the start he " only told a story." " I had no literature," he says, " no scientific knowledge, no beautiful thoughts clothed in beautiful language. I had a story to tell, and I told it. It was a story of privation, of suffering; a story of struggle and final victory; a story of hope and despair; a story of God's mercy; a story of life—every word of which I felt in the deepest depths of my own soul. . . . I knew nothing of grammar or rhetoric. ·Logic was a term that I could not define. I had occasionally an idea,

when I went before an audience, that I should relate
some story, or use some illustration; but when,
where, or how, I could not tell. . . . For seventeen years I was constantly on the lookout—in traveling, conversation, reading, strolling the streets, in
society—for illustrations, incidents, facts that I could
use in temperance lectures; not exactly storing them
in my mind, but letting them float on the surface,
ready at the moment when required." [1]

As an instance of the readiness with which he
turned daily happenings to account, take this occurrence:

"At Rhinebeck, many years ago, I was entertained by Mr.
Freeborn Garretson, who then resided on a beautiful estate near
the Hudson River.

"We were walking through the grounds one morning, when
he said to me: 'I am sorry you do not see us in the summer-
time; we now look very barren and desolate; the trees are so
utterly without foliage, they might be dead trees for all the evidence they give of life. It is winter time with us now; but
come to us in the summer, and under the shade of these grand
trees you may enjoy a cool and exquisite refreshment.'

"I went in the evening to the lecture, and as I was passing
into the church, a gentleman said to me: 'I am glad you are
come to help us, for the temperance cause is dead in Rhinebeck.'

"During my speech, I said, 'A gentleman said to me on the
threshold of this house this evening, 'the temperance cause is
dead in Rhinebeck.' No, it is not dead; it was born in the
Church of Christ, and can never die."

"Then Mr. Garretson's remarks in the morning flashed into
my mind, and I said: 'If I should say to you, as I passed
through the streets of your village, 'Cut down these dead trees,'

---

[1] "Sunlight and Shadow," p. 349.

you would say, 'They are not dead.' If I tell you there is no
evidence of life, there is no bud, no blossom, no leaf, and ask
you to cut them down, and plant living trees, you might tell me:
'It is winter-time with us now. There is neither bud, blossom,
nor leaf, but the sap is in these trees; and by-and-by the warm
spring rain will water the roots, the sun will shine on the
branches, and they will bud, blossom, and leaf out, and as

> "'The tree-tops stir not,
> But stand and peer on Heaven's bright face, as though
> It slept, and they were loving it,'

'you may stand under their deep shade, and enjoy the cool
refreshment thereof.' So with our temperance-tree. There
may be but few, if any, signs of life. It may be winter-time
with us; but the sap is in the tree, and by-and-by the refreshing
rain of public sentiment will water the roots, and the warm sun
of woman's influence will shine upon the branches, and it will
bud, and blossom, and leaf out; and the branches, hanging
heavy with foliage, shall touch the earth, and spring up again,
like the banyan-tree, and cover the land, and under its shade
every poor victim of this vice shall find a refuge.'

"' Now, when I commenced my speech I had no idea I should
use Mr. Garretson's remarks, and the line of poetry I had read
a few days before in *Festus*." [1]

Mr. Gough assures his readers that he never wrote
or studied his illustrations. These were all worked
out on the platform and before the audience—" an
awful risk," as he confesses. As for the anecdotes
which he told in such numbers and with such effect,
he says: " When I find a good story, I appropriate it,
and use it. Some stories I make by putting a funny
thought into a narrative or dialogue, some I find in
the newspapers, some are related to me by others, and

---

[1] " Sunlight and Shadow," pp. 350, 351.

some occur in my own experience. . . . I think
the public will not charge me with introducing a
funny story except to illustrate a point, and, besides,
I find that a good story, well told, relieves an audience
wonderfully." [1]

In his use of stories, and in his manufacture of them,
Mr. Gough resembles two other geniuses, one of the
past, the other of the present, viz., Daniel O'Connell
and Chauncey M. Depew, both of whom have made a
similar confession.

In his earlier years on the platform, Mr. Gough was
so incessantly occupied that he had little time for intellectual culture. Whatever reading he did was
desultory and useless because of ill-direction or bad
choice. It may be said of him, as perhaps of no other
man, that he got a liberal education on the platform.
Feeling more and more, as draughts were made upon
his mind, the need of knowledge, he went in search
of it,—taught himself to think,—learned how to read,
—mastered the subjects on which he spoke,—and
graduated from one of the best universities in the
world—the University of Adversity, with experience
for the faculty, men and women for fellow students,
life for a text-book, and character for his diploma.

After the second return from Great Britain, Mr.
Gough, as we have seen,[2] pursued a different method
of preparation, and began to write his lectures. All
of those on miscellaneous topics were thus produced.
In the enjoyment of leisure, throned in an ample
library, with an intellect self-trained, and aided by
the habits of the platform, he prepared, as any scholar

---

[1] " Sunlight and Shadow," pp. 354–355.   [2] *Ante*, p. 212, *sq.*

might and would, with painstaking diligence, and pen in hand.

The later, like the earlier, efforts, however, lacked a logical form. Mr. Gough was sensitive on the subject of logic.

"I am not logical, he says with gentle irony, I cannot possibly be logical, when so many wiser men than I am, declare that I am not. I never pretended to logic; I hardly know what it means. I have an idea that logic may be used to prove strange things. When I was a boy I heard that a young student visiting his home during his vacation, was asked by his father to give him a specimen of logic. 'Well,' said he, 'I can prove that this eel pie is a pigeon.' 'How so?' asked the father. 'Why an eel pie is a Jack pie, a Jack pie is a John pie, and a John pie is a pie-John (pigeon).' 'Good!' exclaimed the father, ' now for that I'll make you a present of a chestnut horse to-morrow.' On the morrow, with a bridle on his arm, the young logician accompanied his father to the field, when they stopped under the shade of a tree.

"'There's your horse, bridle him.'

"'But I see no horse.'

"'Certainly, there is a horse—a chestnut horse.' And the old gentleman touched a horse chestnut with his foot, adding: 'If a John pie is a pie-John, a horse chestnut must be a chestnut horse; its a poor rule that will not work both ways.'"[1]

There is a good deal of reason in Mr. Gough's suspicions of logic. 'Tis an open question whether it

---

[1] "Autobiography," pp. 323, 324.

does not conclude erroneously as often as it does rightly. The two most consummate logicians in American public life were Jonathan Edwards and John C. Calhoun. Edwards's logic carried him into hyper-Calvinism ; Calhoun's logic led him into the bog of Nullification, out of which Andrew Jackson (who knew no more about logic than Gough did) dug him with the spade of common sense !

Without logic, Mr. Gough produced all the best effects of logic. He convinced, he converted, he inspired. He *had* logic; not, indeed, in the form of the schools, but in that *best* form—the spirit and truth of it.

He set a just value on vocal training:

" I would advise every aspirant to eloquence to carefully cultivate the voice, to acquire a perfect command of that organ if possible. By careful, earnest, and frequent training, a defective voice may not only be improved, but an astonishing mastery be gained over it. A naturally harsh voice, which, without cultivation would grate upon the ear of others, may be so brought into subjection as to become musical in its modulations. A power may be gained of uttering loud, clear, prolonged, trumpet tones, or sounds as sweet and penetrating as the echoes lingering about the soul long after it has ceased haunting it—as some voices will for ever.

" No man with an incurable defect in his voice should seek to become an orator. Think of a speaker attempting pathos or sublimity, if he pronounces *m* like *b*, and *n* like *d*. ' O by bother, by bother ! " ' My dabe is Dorval ! ' ' Freds, Robads, cudtrybed ! ' The power and beauty of language are utterly destroyed.

" I once heard a man who preached occasionally, and who invariably pronounced *n* like *l*. For instance : ' My brethrel, pass roul the coltributiol box, but dolt put rusty lails or buttols ill, but mully. If you put ill buttols, put 'em ill with holes ill 'em, lot with all the holes jalled ilto wull!'

"But, seriously, a cultivated or a naturally good voice is one great essential. It is said that when William Pitt uttered his torrents of indignant censure, or withering sarcasm, his voice assumed an almost terrific sound." [1]

Notwithstanding his lifelong practice, this veteran of the platform acknowledges that his dread of an audience grew instead of decreasing:

"Often my fear has amounted to positive suffering, and seldom am I called upon to face an audience when I would not rather by far run the other way. A very large audience depresses me at first sight. I have often begged the chairman to make an address, and give me time to recover. When I begin, trembling seizes upon every limb; my throat and tongue are dry and feverish; my voice hoarse or husky. . . . I think in my whole experience I never volunteered a speech, nor asked for an invitation to address an audience. After the first nervousness has passed, I have but little sensation except the desire to make my audience feel as I feel, see as I see, and gain dominion for the time being over their wills and affections. If I succeed in this or think I have their sympathy, and especially should they be responsive, the fever is all gone: then comes a consciousness of power that exhilarates, excites, and produces a strange thrilling sensation of delight." [2]

The truth is that this timidity goes with the oratorical temperament. He who would make others sensitive to him must be sensitive to them. Sympathy is the subtle nexus which binds speaker and hearers for the time being in one mutually responsive

---

[1] "Sunlight and Shadow," p. 377.
[2] "Sunlight and Shadow," pp. 341-342.

whole. Magnetism is generated by this feeling—magnetism, which is the secret of the orator's irresistible attractiveness. All great speakers are afflicted as Gough was. A beginner once complained to Wendell Phillips of stage-fright. "Ah," replied the Agitator, "if you ever make a speaker you'll carry that 'stage-fright' with you throughout your life. I never began a speech which I wouldn't have given $500 to be safely through!" Yet Mr. Phillips was the most entirely composed of speakers—apparently. The elder Pitt, whose courageous genius "conquered for his country one great Empire on the frozen shores of Ontario, and another under the tropical sun at the mouths of the Ganges," shook with fear whenever he faced the House of Commons—the throne of this Jupiter of the tongue; and (foolishly) drank incredible draughts of port to quiet his nerves. Daniel Webster, when a boy, broke down as often as he tried to declaim a piece in school; and, when a man, assured Mr. Everett that his heart beat like a trip-hammer when he even thought of rising to speak.

When this timidity has been "talked through," there comes to all "masters of assemblies," a self-possession which enables them to ride upon the wildest storm.

"Like all other speakers," remarks Mr. Gough, "I have been placed in embarrassing circumstances, and a certain amount of self-possession has been necessary to overcome an unexpected difficulty or opposition, especially such an interruption as often occurred in the earlier days of temperance work. On such an occasion I lost all fear and became self-possessed, watching for an opportunity to retaliate. The secre-

tary of the National League in London once told me
that he was tempted to induce some one to hiss me,
as the sound of a hiss seemed to stir me up to a more
vigorous speech.

"I was never utterly put down by an opposition in
public addresses. I have been sorely tried. On more
than one occasion I found it was of no use to employ
arguments with those who were determined to annoy
me, but if possible would think of some apt story to
get the laugh on them; and then I always succeeded
in maintaining my ground." [1]

Mr. Gough was quick at repartee—an invaluable
gift in a public speaker. At one of his meetings a
man attempted to make a disturbance. "Put him
out !" shouted the audience. "Do not put him out,"
cried Gough; "let him remain: he reminds me of the
woman who was taking her squalling child out of a
church, when the minister said—'Do not take the
baby out; it does not disturb me.' 'No,' retorted the
woman; 'but you disturb the baby.' This baby
doesn't disturb me, but I probably disturb him."

He knew how to rebuke sharply yet kindly.

"Once," he says, "a couple of young ladies had
taken a seat directly in front of me, and I had hardly
commenced when they began to whisper and giggle,
and became so excited in their conversation that they
were evidently annoying others. I did not like to tell
them to stop talking, so I said: 'A minister told me
that he regretted very much rebuking two young
ladies who were disturbing him and others by talking
during his discourse, for he was told that one of these

---

[1] " Sunlight and Shadow," p. 372.

young ladies had just secured a beau, and that she was so exceedingly tickled about it, she could not refrain on all occasions when she could get a listener from expatiating on the dear young man's perfections; there seemed to be so many of them she could never exhaust the enumeration; and when she began to talk about her beau, she went on interminably. Just so whenever I see two young ladies talking together in a church, or at a lecture, I imagine one or the other, or both, have got a beau, and it would be hardly fair to disturb them, so I let them talk.' The whisperers troubled me no more."[1]

With all his self-possession he was once nearly upset. He thus tells the story:

" I was engaged to address a large number of children in the afternoon, the meeting to be held on the lawn back of a Baptist church in Providence, R. I. In the forenoon a friend met me and said:

"'I have some first-rate cigars, will you take a few?'

"'No, I thank you.'

"'Do take a half a dozen.'

"'I have nowhere to put them.'

"'You can put half a dozen in your cap.'

" I wore a cap in those days, and I put the cigars into it, and at the appointed time I went to the meeting. I ascended the platform, and faced an audience of more than two thousand children. As it was out of doors I kept my cap on, for fear of taking cold, and I forgot all about the cigars.

" Towards the close of my speech I became much in earnest, and after warning the boys against bad company, bad habits, and the saloons, I said:

"'Now, boys, let us give three rousing cheers for temperance and for cold water. Now, then, three cheers. Hurrah!'

---

[1] " Sunlight and Shadow," p. 376.

"And taking off my cap, I waved it most vigorously, when away went the cigars right into the midst of the audience.

"The remaining cheers were very faint, and were nearly drowned in the laughter of the crowd.

"I was mortified and ashamed, and should have been relieved could I have sunk through the platform out of sight. My feelings were still more aggravated by a boy coming up the steps of the platform with one of those dreadful cigars, saying:

"'Here's one of your cigars, Mr. Gough.'

"Though I never afterwards put cigars in my hat when going to a meeting, I am ashamed to say it was some time after that before I gave up cigars altogether."[1]

Mr. Gough justly affirms that the reaction of an audience upon the speaker is immense.

"Sit cold, critical, determined not to be moved," he says, "and let the speaker see a slight sneer on your face; look at him as who should say, 'What are you going to do next?' and you will destroy his elasticity; and unless he has the ability to turn from you, he will be seriously embarrassed. But take your place with the desire to be interested, look at the speaker, as if you would say, 'We have come expecting and desiring to be pleased; now do your best, and we will show our approval,'—and you encourage him to do his best."[2]

In illustration of this affirmation, he describes a couple who came to hear him, and who sat in the front seat:

"They were a middle-aged pair, and attracted my attention

[1] "Sunlight and Shadow," pp. 380, 381.
[2] "Sunlight and Shadow," pp. 374, 375.

at once. As I arose they greeted me with a smile, and evidently settled themselves to listen and enjoy. As I proceeded, I found them growing more and more interested, and at every point I made, one would nod at the other. At a funny story they laughed heartily. By-and-bye I related a pathetic incident. Then the smiling face was changed to a sober, then to a sad expression. Soon the man began to sniff a little, feeling for his handkerchief, which he did not find—having probably forgotten it, and left it at home. He felt in each of his pockets, then wiped his eyes with his hand. Seeing his wife's handkerchief in her lap, he took it and began using it. The wife next began to sniff, and felt for the handkerchief. Missing it, she found her husband using it; and so, with a loving, wifely motion, she leaned towards him, and taking an end of the handkerchief, she wiped her eyes with it. One handkerchief for two."[1]"

Apropos, speakers are frequently asked whether they individualize when they face an audience, or talk to them *en masse*. Mr. Gough crumbled the aggregate up into detail :

" When I rise there is an involuntary selection of the persons to whom I shall speak; my will has nothing to do with it. Glancing over an assembly, my eye rests on certain individuals in different parts of the house, and to them my speech is largely addressed. I seem compelled to speak to them and to no others. The rest of the people are in the aggregate. If I move these, I move the rest; if these are sympathetic I feel it; if they are unmoved I am distressed. I have more than once talked for some minutes exclusively to one person who seemed stolid or indifferent, trying all methods to move him."[2]

Like some other great speakers—Henry Clay, for

---

[1] " Sunlight and Shadow," p. 375.
[2] " Sunlight and Shadow," p. 345. ·

one—he had no verbal memory. Hence he could never rely upon reaching the end of an attempted quotation :

" I tried once to quote the sentence, ' Locke says we are born with powers and faculties capable of almost anything.'

" I began very confidently with my quotation. ' Locke says, we are born.'

" There I stuck fast, and could not remember another word.

" So I said, ' We are born ; I suppose we *are* born ; but what we are born *for* in this connection, I am sure I do not know.' " [1]

Mr. Gough had a good many laughable introductions.   In Lockerbie, Scotland, the chairman said:

"I wish to introduce Mr. Gough, who is to speak to us on the subject of temperance, and I hope he'll prove far better than he looks." [2]

Another of his chairmen said:

"I rise to introduce Mr. Gough, famous in both hemispheres for his sublime, as well as for his ridiculous." [3]

But an English presiding officer capped the climax. Mr. Gough says: " He aspirated his H's, and put them hon when they hought to 'ave been hoff and took them hoff when they hought to 'ave been hon.   Wishing to compliment me, and remembering that Samson slew a thousand with a jaw-bone, and some time after, being thirsty, obtained, by miracle, water from the dry bone,—he said: " Ladies and Gentlemen, hi wish to hintroduce the horator of the hevening; 'e comes from the hother side of the Hatlantic; 'e is to speak

---

[1] " Sunlight and Shadow," p. 345.
[2] " Sunlight and Shadow," p. 382.   [3] " Autobiography," p. 334.

on the subject of temperance—a very dry subject—but when we 'ear hour transhatlantic horator
discourse hon the subject of temperance, we
may imagine the miracle again performed by which
the prophet was refreshed with water proceeding
from the jaw-bone of a hass!'

"Oh, dear!" exclaimed the "horator," "if he had
only stopped at jaw-bone I should not have minded
it; but that awful 'H' almost extinguished me."[1]

He gives an exquisite illustration of address shown
by one chairman in complying with custom without
sacrificing his own views:

"'Friends' often presided at my lectures, and on one occasion, a gentleman belonging to that Society, was invited to
take the chair. He was one of the most refined and cultivated
men I ever met. We were often his guests, and were charmed
with him. He was in the committee-room, when the chairman
of the committee asked him if he would be kind enough, before
he introduced me to call on the Rev. W. R——, rector of
C—— Church, Chelsea, to offer prayer. Now, it was quite
contrary to his ideas to give any man a title, or to ask any man
to pray. He smiled, and bowed assent. I wondered how he
would manage—when he rose, and said in his sweet clear
voice:

"'If W. R. feels moved to pray, this audience will be
silent.'

"It was admirably done. The audience *was* silent, the
prayer *was* offered, for the reverend gentleman *did* feel moved
to pray; and afterwards I was introduced."[1]

In the course of his professional career, Mr. Gough

---

[1] "Autobiography," p. 334.
[1] "Autobiography," pp. 334, 335.

traveled 450,000 miles and delivered 8,606 addresses before more than 9,000,000 hearers. This record is without a parallel in ancient or modern times. Even for this wiry itinerant it would have been impossible if he had not gone into early partnership with steam.

V.

THE professional season of 1885–6, opened auspi-
ciously. Mr. Gough had never been in greater demand. Applications lay on his desk in the "Hillside"
library thick and white as snowflakes. He made
selections, mapped down his route, and began work.
His health was good, and had been through the preceding summer.

On Monday, the 15th of February, 1886, his itinerary
brought him to Frankford, a section of Philadelphia.
That evening he faced an immense audience, and
commenced his lecture in usual form. He had spoken
about twenty minutes, when he stepped forward, and,
with thrilling intensity of tone and an appealing gesture, said: "Young man, keep your record clean."
At this moment his hand was lifted to his head and
pressed against the place wounded in Sandgate in
his childhood,[1] then the arm dropped and hung
limp,—he tottered, fell, and lay helpless. Amid great
confusion, he was lifted from the floor, carried to the
residence of his friends Dr. and Mrs. R. Bruce Burns,
in Frankford, and tenderly nursed through the night.
A telegram summoned Mrs. Gough to her husband's

---

[1] *Ante,* p. 26.

side. Apoplexy! as plain a case, said the physicians, as was ever seen. "Will the patient live?" was the anxious inquiry. "He may," was the answer, "but his activity is over." That would have been death in life to John B. Gough. He was spared the trial of chronic invalidism. Lapsing into unconsciousness, he passed away on the 18th inst., in the sixty-ninth year of his age. It was the form of departure he would have selected had the choice been given him—death in the harness.

The tireless humanitarian hated ostentation. He had often expressed a dislike for public funerals. His well-known wishes were respected in the last sad rites. A quiet, informal gathering of more immediate friends and neighbors united with the family in paying a final tribute of respect and affection at "Hillside," on the 24th of February. The Boylston pastor, the Rev. Israel Ainsworth, and the Rev. Drs. D. E. Means and George H. Gould, of Worcester, and Wm. M. Taylor, of New York, conducted the simple services. The coffin lay in the library, among the books he loved so much—dear, unconscious intimates. Near it, across a chair, hung a faded handkerchief. This handkerchief had a history. Years before, in England, it had been brought to Mrs. Gough by a woman, who said:

"I am very poor. I would give your husband a thousand pounds, if I had it—I can only give him this (presenting the handkerchief). I married with the fairest prospects before me, but my husband took to drinking, and everything went, until, at last, I found myself in one miserable room. My husband lay drunk in the corner, and my sick child lay moaning on my knee. I wet this handkerchief with my tears. My husband met yours. He spoke a few words and gave a grasp of the hand; and now for six years my husband has been all to me that a husband can be to a wife. I have brought your husband the very handkerchief I wet that night with my tears, and I want him to remember that he has wiped away those tears from my eyes, I trust in God for ever."

This was among the most prized of all Mr. Gough's mementoes. Often, in showing it, he would say:

"You do not think it worth three cents, but you have not money enough to buy it from me."

The most eloquent lips were cold and tame that day compared with this fluttering rag! If all the tears he had wiped away, and all the lives he had been instrumental in rehabilitating, could have spoken, what a testimony they would have given!

On the following Sunday, memorial services were held in many places, from Maine to California, of which, perhaps, the most representative one was that in the Mechanics' Hall, at Worcester—the scene of some of the orator's most notable experiences. Here, Protestants and Catholics, clergymen and laymen, twined upon his brow a garland of everlasting.

A man's life is his fittest epitaph. The foregoing pages recite the experiences, reveal the emotions, and repeat the words of John B. Gough. They have been written in vain if the reader feels any need of elaborate characterization in this closing chapter. Yet a few words of broad and final estimate may be adventured.

John B. Gough's gifts have overshadowed his graces. He has never received credit for the sterling moral and mental faculties which fed his surpassing oratory. Manhood is better, and rarer, than genius. Those who knew the great advocate of temperance found the man off the platform even more admirable than the orator on it. He had in complete development those moral and religious elements of character upon which Mr. Webster lays such stress in his sketch of that great lawyer, Jeremiah Mason. In his career, morality was the bud and religion the flower. He had the Puritan conscience. Without this, his sensitiveness and natural inclination to yield would have incapacitated him for the warfare he felt called to wage. Steadied by this, he "bore right up and steered right on," undeterred by the assaults of foes or by the more insidious entreaties of mistaken friends.

True, in his unsheltered youth he sinned grievously—so did Augustine. But as Monica planted deep in Augustine's heart the leaven which by-and-by leavened the whole lump, so did Jane Gongh imbue her son with principles which eventually brought him to himself and dominated his after life. In his dissipated days, Gough made debts, as many as his different residences, and as large as his opportunities. Almost as soon as he reformed, he went back over that long, wide track and paid those debts, principal and interest. As a reformer, his sympathy for the drunkard did not blind him to the sin of drunkenness, which he never failed to condemn *as* sin.

No sooner did he discover his peculiar talent than he consecrated it. He held life and opportunity to be synonyms of duty. Ability, in his view, was a sacred trust, to be used for the glory of God and the relief of man's estate. "Pythagoras," says Lord

Bacon, "being asked what he was, answered, 'That if Hiero was ever at the Olympian games, he knew the manner, that some came as merchants, to utter their commodities, and some came to make good cheer and meet their friends, and some came to look on; and that he was one of them that came to look on.'" Upon which the great Englishman remarks: "But men must know that in this theater of men's life, it is reserved only for God and angels to be lookers-on." Moral and religious principle lay at the bottom of Gough's character, and inspired him with a lofty purpose. In moral earnestness he has had few peers among public men.

Intellectually, Mr. Gough was far above the average. His mind was at once deep and broad. His generalization and his analysis were alike admirable. Order and proportion characterized his mental constitution. The reflective and perceptive faculties were in harmonious adjustment. Zeal was tempered by prudence, justice by mercy, and self-confidence by modesty, — which latter quality was, however, in excess. Who ever exceeded him in humor? and who ever subdued humor to more serious uses? His mind was preëminently fair. Judgment held the scales even, so that he was seldom betrayed either in private or in public, into an intemperate utterance.

Indeed, the basis of Mr. Gough's mental operations was robust common sense,—"so called," according to an eminent publicist, "not because it is so very common a trait of character of public men, but because it is the final judgment on great practical questions to which the mind of the community is pretty sure eventually to arrive." Common sense held Gough aloof from the excesses into which his ardent temperament might otherwise have hurried him, and poised his singularly long and successful apostleship at an equal remove from the *isms*, on the one hand, and the " doubtful disputations," on the other hand, of an era of " sane giants, and giants gone mad."

Greatness is like money; it is easier won than held. The greatness which Gough achieved he retained— further proof of the fine balance of his powers His intellectual resources are indicated and vindicated by the surprising fact that he was able to argue substantially one question before two hemispheres, through all the changes of thought and feeling on the subject of half a century, without any abatement of popular interest either in the theme or in the orator. Nor was this due to his oratory alone. For oratorical fashions, like other fashions, have their day. Mere tricks of speech and taking mannerisms tire when the novelty wears off. It was the good sense behind the utterance, and winging it, that sustained the *orator* by compelling respect for the *man*.

Speaking, as he did, with abandon, and enacting a drama, half farce and half tragedy, there was constant danger of saying or doing something objectionable. Yet Mr. Gough never did a vulgar thing, nor ever said a word that would bring a blush to the cheek of modesty. A remarkable fact, when his origin is remembered. "Without early training," says one of his biographers, " or early culture, he took on both with wonderful facility ; was welcomed, not merely tolerated, in the best society, and moved in it the acknowledged peer of gentlemen, scholars, and statesmen. He never forgot the bitter and

degrading experiences of his early years ; but no vul-
garity in word, and no discourtesy or rudeness in act
ever reminded others of it."

Of his generosity the rogues who plundered him
for forty years could speak, if they would.   The poor
and needy, too, fed on it, and were grateful.   As for
his sympathy, it was as wide as human necessity.   He
kindled a fire on the hearthstone of his heart, at which
friend or foe, tramp or gentleman was free to warm
his hands.

Mr. Gough's social disposition próved a snare at
first ; but, later, it became a source of delight to himself and to others.   Throughout America he was
the most welcome of guests.   Children (of whom he
was passionately fond) greeted him as a playmate,
while their parents found in him a fascinating companion.   He romped with the youngsters and talked
with the elders with impartial facility.   When he
went away it was hard to say whether nursery or
drawing-room missed him the most.

But it was in his own home that this great-hearted
man was at his best.   He loved to have the family
around him, and entertained them endlessly.   He
had two domestic passions—music and reading.   In
the twilight, he would seat himself at the melodeon
and improvise, without knowing a note, counting the
time by a self-invented system; sometimes (especially
before his voice was broken by wear and tear) burst-
ing forth into song, comic or pathetic as the whim
seized him—*Gough* at the melodeon, as on the platform!   Oftenest, perhaps, he read aloud, in which
charming art he was an adept.   When alone in the
library, if any passage in a book particularly pleased

him, he would rise, find some one, and share the enjoyment by reading it aloud.

One bad habit he had—he disliked to go to bed. If he could get any one to sit up and be read or talked to, he would read or talk on until morning. Some of his most inimitable stories and recitations were given to these midnight audiences of the fireside. When thus belated he did retire, he hated to get up, and would sleep long after the other members of the household were hard at work.

The relations between Mr. and Mrs. Gough were ideal. She had a strong character of the best New England type, and supplied any defects which existed in him with feminine tact and self-outpouring. The comfort of his home, and his easy circumstances, were largely due to her.[1]

Mr. Gough's powers as a speaker have been analyzed in previous chapters. He was preëminent as an orator in two nations of orators. Yet he had one singular defect. Although he wrote voluminously and spoke oftener and more acceptably than almost any other man, he could not coin striking phrases. He never photographed an epoch, or put the whole duty of the hour in an inspired sentence. Talleyrand crowded a great truth for all time in a *môt*—"Everybody is cleverer than anybody." The younger Pitt, in moving for a committee to examine into the state of English representation, in the days of close boroughs, asserted that these were the strongholds of that corruption to which he attributed all the calamities of

---

[1] Mrs. Gough died at " Hillside," after a long illness, April 19, 1891. Upon her decease, " Hillside " passed out of the family.

the nation, and condensed the evil in a phrase which was soon on all lips: "This corruption has grown with the growth of England, and strengthened with her strength, but has not diminished with her diminution, nor decayed with her decay." Carlyle summed up the history of a hundred wretched years in a thrilling climax; "The eighteenth century committed suicide by blowing its brains out in the French Revolution." Wm. H. Seward focused the philosophy of the civil war in the phrase "irrepressible conflict." Charles Sumner indicated the public policy of the war for the Union, when, in pleading for the arming of the blacks, he cried: "The question is not whether we shall carry the war into Africa, but whether we shall carry Africa into the war." Gladstone declared that "the European struggle in one of the masses against the classes." Macaulay's prose is as epigrammatic, as Pope's verse. Cervantes, in *Don Quixote*, supplied the whole Spanish nation with proverbial philosophy.

Gough's speeches and books are searched in vain for such happy inspirations. He has left few memorable sayings. This was not due to his lack of education. The defect was constitutional. Richard Brinsley Sheridan owed no more to schools than Gough did. Nevertheless, Sheridan's speeches are full of *môts*, while his plays sparkle with epigrams. Bunyan was not a learned man, yet the immortal tinker gave the world its finest allegory. Shakespeare was not a scholar; but his plays are handbooks of familiar quotations. The truth is, that Gough did not possess the literary faculty. He could not balance dainty periods, nor utter brilliant phrases. He was clumsy with the pen, and, in speaking, vitalized his matter by his manner. His style was discursive—made so partly by the habits of the platform, but more by the bent of his genius.

We are confident that an academic education would have hurt more than it could have helped him. Samson was probably a better-looking man after Delilah had shaved off his hair—but his strength was gone! A fastidious culture would have refined away much of Gough's popular power. What he might have gained in routine knowledge would have poorly compensated us for what he must have lost in spontaneity. One day on a journey he met Wendell Phillips. In the course of their chat he lamented his lack of education. "Why," replied the great master of classic speech, "any scholar who hears you perceives at once your lack of educational training, so-called; but"—added he, with a smile—"perhaps in your case the world is all the better for that."

One memorable sentence Mr. Gough did utter—not because of any sparkle in it, but because of its practical turn and accurate self-photography. All the events of his career,—the tragic mournfulness and failure of its opening, the moral jubilancy and triumph of its close, those five hundred thousand miles of wearisome travel, the nine thousand fervid lectures, the nine millions of eager hearers on both sides of the Atlantic, —are condensed and voiced in his last and dying words: "*Keep your record clean!*"

INDEX.